# Hardly Knew Her

# Hardly Knew Her

*Stories*

# Laura Lippman

HARPER LUXE

*An Imprint of HarperCollinsPublishers*

LP
M
LIPP

"The Crack Cocaine Diet," first published in *The Cocaine Chronicles;* copyright © 2005 by Laura Lippman.

"What He Needed," first published in *Tart Noir;* copyright © 2002 by Laura Lippman.

"Dear Penthouse Forum (A First Draft)," first published in *Dangerous Women;* copyright © 2005 by Laura Lippman.

"The Babysitter's Code," first published in *Plots with Guns;* copyright © 2005 by Laura Lippman.

"Hardly Knew Her," first published in *Dead Man's Hand;* copyright © 2007 by Laura Lippman.

"Femme Fatale," first published in *Geezer Noir;* copyright © 2006 by Laura Lippman.

"One True Love," first published in *Death Do Us Part;* copyright © 2006 by Laura Lippman.

"Pony Girl," first published in *New Orleans Noir;* copyright © 2007 by Laura Lippman.

"ARM and the Woman," first published in *D.C. Noir;* copyright © by Laura Lippman.

"Honor Bar," first published in *Dublin Noir;* copyright © 2006 by Laura Lippman.

"A Good Fuck Spoiled," first published in *Murder in the Rough;* copyright © 2006 by Laura Lippman.

"Easy as A-B-C," first published in *Baltimore Noir;* copyright © 2006 by Laura Lippman.

"Black-Eyed Susan," first published in *Bloodlines;* copyright © 2006 by Laura Lippman.

"Ropa Vieja," first published in *Murderers Row;* copyright © 2001 by Laura Lippman.

"The Shoeshine Man's Regrets," first published in *Murder and All That Jazz;* copyright © 2004 by Laura Lippman.

"The Accidental Detective" © 2007 by Laura Lippman.

"Scratch a Woman" © 2008 by Laura Lippman.

HarperCollins books may be purchased for educational, business, or sales promotional use. For information please write: Special Markets Department, HarperCollins Publishers, 10 East 53rd Street, New York, NY 10022.

FIRST HARPERLUXE EDITION

HarperLuxe™ is a trademark of HarperCollins Publishers

Library of Congress Cataloging-in-Publication Data is available upon request.

ISBN: 978-0-06-173487-8

08 09 10 11 12 ID/RRD 10 9 8 7 6 5 4 3 2 1

# Contents

## Part 3: My Baby Walks the Streets of Baltimore

## Part 4: Scratch a Woman

# Introduction

By anyone's estimation, Laura Lippman is doing all right. She's a *New York Times* bestselling author, is highly respected by her peers and the critical establishment, and has carved out a nice life for herself in Baltimore, a city she loves and represents. Which begs the question: why a short story collection?

It's not like she needs to feed the pipeline with product. This isn't a stopgap measure to appease the public while she struggles with her next book. She's certainly not delinquent in the delivery of a novel to her publisher. Shoot, Laura has consistently published quality, challenging novels every year since she's been at this. Plus, she's found a large audience.

So now, time to cash in. Right?

That's what you'd assume. Readers should be wary, having been burned in the past by writers who have exploited their success by publishing tossed-off collections of odds and ends and never-should-have-been short stories. But once you begin to read this anthology, you'll find that Laura's stories stand apart from her novels in revelatory and satisfying ways. Plus, they're beautifully written and contain the kind of offbeat observations and insights that someday, no doubt, will come to be known as "Lippman moments." Finally, these stories tell actual stories. Laura, thankfully, is not afraid of plot. (Can you hear me, writing school graduates? Lord, have mercy.)

Do not expect the obvious. There are two Tess Monaghan stories included here, for the Monaghan faithful. One is the crowd-pleasing "The Shoeshine Man's Regrets," in which Tess gets an old shoeshine man off (not like that, and you ought to wash your mind out with soap for thinking it). As a bonus, there is a clever, revealing "interview" with Tess, "The Accidental Detective" (all respect to Baltimore's own Anne Tyler), as well.

The centerpiece of this book is a novella, "Scratch a Woman," that was written for this collection. To say that it is about a suburban prostitute and her twisted sister does not do it justice. It has so much going on in it, in terms of ideas, that it could easily be expanded into a novel (and a very interesting film). It is one of the finest pieces of writing that Laura has done.

The rest of the collection includes tales told from a variety of viewpoints. I count five first-person stories, and many others from the perspective of women ranging from teens to aged, two from men who have been less than faithful to their wives (spousal betrayal being somewhat of a recurring theme in these stories, and if you're thinking of pulling the trigger yourself, rest uneasy that, in Laura's world, cheating never ends well), and two from the POV of young black men. In all of them, I was completely convinced of the voices. And, in case anyone got the impression that Laura only knows Baltimore, there is an entire section devoted to stories set in places like Dublin ("Honor Bar"), Washington, D.C. ("ARM and the Woman"), and New Orleans (the harrowing "Pony Girl," a mythic ode to the dark side of the party).

There are many high moments, points when you stop reading and say, "Damn, she's good," but let me mention just a few. "Easy as A-B-C," concerning a working-class contractor and his psychosexual relationship with one of the new breed of moneyed Locust Point residents, says more about the changing modern city, in its economical way, than most novelists manage in their latest door-stopper. "The Crack Cocaine Diet" hits like a bat to the temple, a "wacky" tour de force from Laura that is as funny as it is surprising. "Hardly Knew Her," describing a Beth Steel family in 1975 Dundalk—a girl, Sofia, and her degenerate gambler father is stunning in its emotional nuance and period detail. In "Femme Fatale," a woman of sixty-eight gets involved in senior citizen porn, with unexpected results. "Dear Penthouse Forum (A First Draft)," whose plot I will not describe, is inventive and somewhat twisted. Actually, it's kinda sick (get help, Laura, but don't stop writing).

With each year, and each book, Laura Lippman's work has gotten deeper, more intricate, and more ambitious. This collection makes a strong case for her range and talent. She got both, in spades.

*George Pelecanos*
SILVER SPRING, MARYLAND

# PART ONE

# Girls Gone Wild

# The Crack Cocaine Diet

I had just broken up with Brandon and Molly had just broken up with Keith, so we needed new dresses to go to this party where we knew they were both going to be. But before we could buy the dresses, we needed to lose weight because we had to look fabulous, kiss-my-ass-fuck-you fabulous. Kiss-my-ass-fuck-you-and-your-dick-is-really-tiny fabulous. Because, after all, Brandon and Keith were going to be at this party, and if we couldn't get new boyfriends in less than eight days, we could at least go down a dress size and look so good that Brandon and Keith and everybody else in the immediate vicinity would wonder how they ever let us go. I mean, yes, technically, they broke up with us, but we had been thinking about it, weighing the pros and cons. (Pro: they spent money on us. Con: they were childish. Pro: we had them. Con: tiny dicks, see above.) See, we were being methodical and they were just all impulsive, the way guys are. That would be another con—poor impulse control. Me, I never do anything without thinking it through very carefully. Anyway, I'm not sure what went down with Molly and Keith, but Brandon said if he wanted to be nagged all the time, he'd move back in with his mother, and I said, "Well, given that she still does your laundry and makes you food, it's not as if you really moved out," and that was that. No big loss.

Still, we had to look so great that other guys would be punching our exes in the arms and saying, "What, are you crazy?" Everything is about spin, even dating. It's always better to be the dumper instead of the dumpee, and if you have to be the loser, then you need to find a way of being superior. And that was going to take about seven pounds for me, as many as ten for Molly, who doesn't have my discipline and had been doing some serious breakup eating for the past three weeks. She went facedown in the Ding Dongs, danced with the Devil Dogs, became a Ho Ho ho. As for myself, I'm a salty girl, and I admit I had the Pringles Light can upended in my mouth for a couple of days.

So, anyway, Molly said Atkins, and I said not fast enough, and then I said a fast-fast, and Molly said she saw little lights in front of her eyes the last time she tried to go no food, and she said cabbage soup and I said it gives me gas, and then she said pills, and I said all the doctors we knew were too tight with their scrips, even her dentist boss since she stopped blowing him. And, finally, Molly had a good idea and said: "Cocaine!"

This merited consideration. Molly and I had never done more than a little recreational coke, always provided by boyfriends who were trying to impress us, but even my short-term experience indicated it would probably do the trick. The tiniest bit revved you up for hours and you raced around and around, and it wasn't that you weren't hungry, more like you had never even heard of food, it was just some quaint custom from the olden days, like square dancing. I mean, you could do it in theory, but why would you?

"Okay," I said. "Only where do we get it?" After all, we're girls, girly girls. I had been drinking and smoking pot since I was sixteen, but I certainly didn't buy it. That's what boyfriends were for. Pro: Brandon bought my drinks, and if you don't have to lay out cash for alcohol, you can buy a lot more shoes.

Molly thought hard, and Molly thinking was like a fat guy running—there was a lot of visible effort.

"Well, like, the city."

"But where in the city?"

"On, like, a corner."

"Right, Molly. I watch HBO, too. But I mean, what corner? It's not like they list them in that crap Weekender Guide in the paper—movies, music, clubs, where to buy drugs."

So Molly asked a guy who asked a guy who talked to a guy, and it turned out there was a place just inside the city line, not too far from the interstate. Easy on, easy off, then easy off again. Get it? After a quick consultation on what to wear—jeans and T-shirts and sandals, although I changed into running shoes after I saw the condition of my pedicure—we were off. Very hush-hush because, as I explained to Molly, that was part of the adventure. I phoned my mom and said I was going for a run. Molly told her mom she was going into the city to shop for a dress, and we were off.

The friend of Molly's friend's friend had given us directions to what turned out to be an apartment complex, which was kind of disappointing. I mean, we were expecting rowhouses, slumping picturesquely next to each other, but this was just a dirtier, more run-down version of where we lived, little clusters of two-story townhouses built around a courtyard. We drove around and around and around, trying to seem very savvy and willing, and it looked like any apartment complex on a hot July afternoon. Finally, on our third turn around the complex, a guy ambled over to the car.

"What you want?"

"What you got?" I asked, which I thought was pretty good. I mean, I sounded casual but kind of hip, and if he turned out to be a cop, I hadn't implicated myself. See, I was always thinking, unlike some people I could name.

"Got American Idol and Survivor. The first one will make you sing so pretty that Simon will be speechless. The second one will make you feel as if you've got immunity for life."

"O-kay." Molly reached over me with a fistful of bills, but the guy backed away from the car.

"Pay the guy up there. Then someone will bring you your package."

"Shouldn't you give us the, um, stuff first and then get paid?"

The guy gave Molly the kind of look that a schoolteacher gives you when you say something exceptionally stupid. We drove up to the next guy, gave him $40, then drove to a spot he pointed outto wait.

"It's like McDonald's!" Molly said. "Drive-through!"

"Shit, don't say McDonald's. I haven't eaten all day. I would kill for a Big Mac."

"Have you ever had the Big N' Tasty? It totally rocks."

"What is it?"

"It's a cheeseburger, but with like a special sauce."

"Like a Big Mac."

"Only the sauce is different."

"I liked the fries better when they made them in beef fat."

A third boy—it's okay to say "boy," because he was, like, thirteen, so I'm not being racist or anything—handed us a package and we drove away. But Molly immediately pulled into a convenience store parking lot. It wasn't a real convenience store, though, not a 7-Eleven or a Royal Farms.

"What are you doing?"

"Pre-diet binge," Molly said. "If I'm not going to eat for the next week, I want to enjoy myself now."

I had planned to be pure starting that morning, but it sounded like a good idea. I did a little math. An ounce of Pringles has, like, 120 calories, so I could eat an entire can and not gain even half a pound, and a half pound doesn't even register on a scale, so it wouldn't count. Molly bought a pound of Peanut M&M's, and let me tell you, the girl was not overachieving. I'd seen her eat that much on many an occasion. Molly has big appetites. We had a picnic, right there in the parking lot, washing down our food with diet cream soda. Then Molly began to open our "package."

"Not here!" I warned her, looking around.

"What if it's no good? What if they cut it with, like, something, so it's weak?"

Molly was beginning to piss me off a little, but maybe it was just all the salt, which was making my fingers swell and my head pound a little. "So how are you going to know if it's any good?"

"You put it on your gums." She opened up the package. It didn't look quite right. It was more off-white than I remembered, not as finely cut. But Molly dove right in, licking her finger, sticking it in, and then spreading it around her gum line.

"Shit," she said. "I don't feel a thing."

"Well, you don't feel it right away."

"No, they like totally robbed us. It's bullshit. I'm going back."

"Molly, I don't think they do exchanges. It's not like Nordstrom, where you can con them into taking the shoes back even after you wore them once. You stuck your wet finger in it."

"We were ripped off. They think just because we're white suburban girls they can sell us this weak-ass shit." She was beginning to sound more and more like someone on HBO, although I'd have to say the effect was closer to *Ali G* than *Sopranos.* "I'm going to demand a refund."

This was my first inkling that things might go a little wrong.

So Molly went storming back to the parking lot and finds our guy, and she began bitching and moaning, but he didn't seem that upset. He seemed kind of, I don't know, amused by her. He let her rant and rave, just nodding his head, and when she finally ran out of steam, he says:

"Honey, darling, you bought heroin. Not cocaine. That's why you didn't get a jolt. It's not supposed to jolt you. It's supposed to slow you down, not that it seems to be doing that, either."

Molly had worked up so much outrage that she still saw herself as the wronged party. "Well how was I supposed to know that?"

"Because we sell cocaine by vial color. Red tops, blue tops, yellow tops. I just had you figured for heroin girls. You looked like you knew your way around, got tired of OxyContin, wanted the real thing."

Molly preened a little, as if she had been complimented. It's interesting about Molly. Objectively, I'm prettier, but she has always done better with guys.

I think it's because she has this kind of sexy vibe, by which I mean she manages to communicate that she'll pretty much do anyone.

"Two pretty girls like you, just this once, I'll make an exception. You go hand that package back to my man Gordy, and he'll give you some nice blue tops."

We did, and he did, but this time Molly made a big show of driving only a few feet away and inspecting our purchase, holding the blue-capped vial up to the light.

"It's, like, rock candy."

It did look like a piece of rock candy, which made me think of the divinity my grandmother used to make, which made me think of all the other treats from childhood that I couldn't imagine eating now—Pixy Stix and Now and Laters and Mary Janes and Dots and Black Crows and Necco Wafers and those pastel buttons that came on sheets of wax paper. Chocolate never did it for me, but I loved sugary treats when I was young.

And now Molly was out of the car and on her feet, steaming toward our guy, who looked around, very nervous, as if this five-foot-five, size 10 dental hygienist—size 8 when she's being good—could do some serious damage. And I wanted to say, "Dude, don't worry! All she can do is scrape your gums until they bleed." (I go to Molly's dentist and Molly cleans my teeth and she is seriously rough. I think she gets a little kick out of it, truthfully.)

"What the fuck is this?" she yelled, getting all gangster on his ass—I think I'm saying that right—holding the vial up to the guy's face, while he looked around nervously. Finally he grabbed her wrist and said: "Look, just shut up or you're going to bring some serious trouble to bear. You smoke it, I'll show you how, don't you know anything? Trust me, you'll like it."

Molly motioned to me and I got out of the car, although a little reluctantly. It was, like, you know that scene in *Star Wars* where the little red eyes are watching from the caves and suddenly those weird sand people just up and attack? I'm not being racist, just saying we were outsiders and I definitely had a feeling all sorts of eyes were on us, taking note.

"We'll go to my place," the guy said, all super suave, like he was some international man of mystery inviting us to see his etchings.

"A shooting gallery?" Molly squealed, all excited. "Ohmigod!"

He seemed a little offended. "I don't let dope fiends in my house."

He led us to one of the townhouses and I don't know what I expected, but it certainly wasn't someplace with doilies and old overstuffed furniture and pictures of Jesus and some black guy on the wall. (Dr. Martin Luther King Jr., I figured out later, but I was really distracted at the time and thought it was the guy's dad or something.) But the most surprising thing was this little old lady sitting in the middle of the sofa, hands folded in her lap. She had a short, all-white Afro and wore a pink T-shirt and flowery ski pants, which bagged on her stick-thin legs. Ski pants. I hadn't seen them in, like, forever.

"Antone?" she said. "Did you come to fix my lunch?"

"In a minute, Grandma. I have guests."

"Are they nice people, Antone?"

"Very nice people," he said, winking at us, and it was only then that I realized the old lady was blind. You see, her eyes weren't milky or odd in any way, they were brown and clear, as if she was staring right at us. You had to look closely to realize that she couldn't really see, that the gaze, steady as it was, didn't focus on anything.

Antone went to the kitchen, an alcove off the dining room, and fixed a tray with a sandwich, some potato chips, a glass of soda, and an array of medications. How could you not like a guy like that? So sweet, with broad shoulders and close-cropped hair like his granny's, only dark. Then, very quietly, with another wink, he showed us how to smoke.

"Antone, are you smoking in here? You know I don't approve of tobacco."

"Just clove cigarettes, Grandma. Clove never hurt anybody."

He helped each of us with the pipe, getting closer than was strictly necessary. He smelled like clove, like clove and ginger and cinnamon. Antone the spice cookie. I couldn't help noticing that when he took the pipe from Molly's mouth, he replaced it with his lips. I didn't really want him to kiss me, but I'm so much prettier than Molly. Not to mention thinner. But then, I hear black guys like girls with big behinds, and Molly certainly qualified. You could put a can of beer on her ass and have her walk around the room and it wouldn't fall off. Not being catty, just telling the literal truth. I did it once, at a party, when I was bored, and Molly swished around with a can of Bud Light on her ass, showing off, like she was proud to have so much baggage.

Weird, but I was hungrier than ever after smoking, which was so not the point. I mean, I wasn't hungry in my stomach, I was hungry in my mouth. And what I wanted, more than anything in the world, were those potato chips on the blind lady's tray. They were Utz salt 'n' vinegar, I had seen Antone take them out of the green-and-yellow bag. I looooooooooooooooooooooove

Utz salt 'n' vinegar, but they don't come in a light version, so I almost never let myself have any. So I snagged one, just one, quiet as a cat. But, like they say, you can't eat just one. Okay, so they say that about Lay's, but it's even more true about Utz, in my personal opinion. I kept stealing them, one at a time.

"Antone? Are you taking food off my tray?"

I looked to Antone for backup, but Molly's tongue was so far in his mouth that she might have been flossing him. When he finally managed to detach himself, he said: "Um, Grandma? I'm going to take a little lie-down."

"What about your guests?"

"They're going," he said, walking over to the door with a heavy tread and closing it.

"It's time for *Judge Judy!*" his granny said, which made me wonder, because how does a blind person know what time it is? Antone used the remote control to turn on the television. It was a black-and-white, total Smithsonian. After all, she was blind, so I guess it didn't matter.

Next thing I know, I'm alone in the room with the blind woman, who's fixated on Judge Judy as if she's going to be tested on the outcome, and I'm eyeing her potato chips, while Antone and Molly start making the kind of noises that you make when you're trying so hard not to make noise that you can't help making noise.

"Antone?" the old lady called out. "Is the dishwasher running? Because I think a piece of cutlery might have gotten caught in the machinery."

I was so knocked out that she knew the word "cutlery." How cool is that?

But I couldn't answer, of course. I wasn't supposed to be there.

"It's—okay—Granny," Antone grunted from the other room. "It's—all—going—to—be—Jesus Christ—okay."

The noises started up again. Granny was right. It did sound like a piece of cutlery caught in the dishwasher. But then it stopped—Antone's breathing, the mattress springs, Molly's little muffled grunts—they just stopped, and they didn't stop naturally, if you know what I mean. I don't mean to be cruel, but Molly's a bit of a slut, and I've listened to her have sex more times than I could count, and I know how it ends, even when she's faking it, even when she has to be quiet, and it just didn't sound like the usual Molly finish at all. Antone yelped, but she was silent as the grave.

"Antone, what are you doing?" his granny asked. Antone didn't answer. Several minutes went by, and then there was a hoarse whisper from the bedroom.

"Um, Kelley? Could you come here a minute?"

"What was that?" his granny asked.

I used the remote to turn up the volume on Judge Judy. "DO I LOOK STUPID TO YOU?" the judge was yelling. "REMEMBER THAT PRETTY FADES BUT STUPID IS FOREVER. I ASKED IF YOU HAD IT IN WRITING, I DON'T WANT TO HEAR ALL THIS FOLDEROL ABOUT ORAL AGREEMENTS."

When I went into the bedroom, Molly was under Antone and I remember thinking—I was a little high, remember—that he made her look really thin, because he covered up her torso, and Molly does have good legs and decent arms. He had a handsome back, too, broad and muscled, and a great ass. Brandon had no ass (con), but he had nice legs (pro).

It took me a moment to notice that he had a pair of scissors stuck in the middle of his beautiful back.

"I told him no," Molly whispered, although the volume on the television was so loud that the entire apartment was practically reverberating. "No means no."

There was a lot of blood, I noticed. A lot.

"I didn't hear you," I said. "I mean, I didn't hear you say any words."

"I mouthed it. He told me to keep silent because his grandmother is here. Still, I mouthed it. 'No.' 'No.'"

She made this incredibly unattractive fish mouth to show me.

"Is he dead?"

"I mean, I was totally up for giving him a blow job, especially after he said he'd give me a little extra, but he was, like, uncircumcised. I just couldn't, Kelley, I couldn't. I've never been with a guy like that. I offered him a hand job instead, but he got totally peeved and tried to force me."

The story wasn't tracking. High as I was, I could see there were some holes. How did you get naked? I wanted to ask. Why didn't you shout? If Grandma knew you were here, Antone wouldn't have dared misbehave. He was clearly more scared of Granny than he was into Molly.

"This is the stash house," Molly said. "Antone showed me."

"What?"

"The drugs. They're here. All of it. We could just help ourselves. I mean, he's a rapist, Kelley. He's a criminal. He sells drugs to people. Help me, Kelley. Get him off me."

But when I rolled him off, I saw there was a condom. Molly saw it, too.

"We should, like, so get rid of that. It would only complicate things. When I saw he was going to rape me, I told him he should at least be courteous."

I nodded, as if agreeing. I flushed the condom down the toilet, helped Molly clean the blood off her, and then used my purse to pack up what we could find, as she was carrying this little bitty Kate Spade knock-off that wasn't much good for anything. We found some cash, too, about $2,000, and helped ourselves to that, on the rationale that it would be more suspicious if we didn't. On the way out, I shook a few more potato chips on Granny's plate.

"Antone?" she said. "Are you going out again?"

Molly grunted low, and that seemed to appease Granny. We walked out slowly, as if we had all the time in the world, but again I had that feeling of a thousand pairs of eyes upon us. We were in some serious trouble. There would have to be some sort of retribution for what we had done. What Molly had done. All I did was steal a few potato chips.

"Take the Quarry Road home instead of the inter-state," I told Molly.

"Why?" she asked. "It takes so much longer."

"But we know it, know all the ins and outs. If someone follows us, we can give them the slip."

About two miles from home, I told her I had to pee so bad that I couldn't wait and asked her to stand watch for me, a practice of long standing with us. We were at that point, high above the old limestone quarry, where we had parked a thousand times as teenagers. A place where Molly had never said no, to my knowledge.

"Finished?" she asked when I emerged from behind the screen of trees.

"Almost," I said, pushing her hard, sending her tumbling over the precipice. She wouldn't be the first kid in our class to break her neck at the highest point on Quarry Road. My high school boyfriend did, in fact, right after we broke up. It was a horrible accident. I didn't eat for weeks and got down to a size 4. Everyone felt bad for me, breaking up with Eddie only to have him commit suicide that way. There didn't seem to be any reason to explain that Eddie was the one who wanted to break up. Unnecessary information.

I crossed the hillside to the highway, a distance of about a mile, then jogged the rest of the way. After all, as my mother would be the first to tell you, I went for a run that afternoon, while Molly was off shopping, according to her mom. I assumed the police would tie Antone's dead body to Molly's murder and figure it for a revenge killing, but I was giving the cops too much credit. Antone rated a paragraph in the morning paper. Molly, who turned out to be pregnant, although not even she knew it—probably didn't even know who the father was, for sure—is still on the front page all these weeks later. (The fact that they didn't find her for three days heightened the interest, I guess. I mean, she was just an overweight dental hygienist from the suburbs— and a bit of a slut, as I told you. But the media got all excited about it.) The general consensus seems to be that Keith did it, and I don't see any reason to let him off the hook, not yet. He's an asshole. Plus, almost no one in this state gets the death penalty.

Meanwhile, he's telling people just how many men Molly had sex with in the past month, including Brandon, and police are still trying to figure out who had sex with her right before she died. (That's why you're supposed to get the condom on as early as possible, girls. Penises drip. Just FYI.) I pretended to be shocked, but I already knew about Brandon, having seen Molly's car outside his apartment when I cruised his place at 2 A.M. a few nights after Brandon told me he wanted to see other people. My ex-boyfriend and my best friend, running around behind my back. Everyone feels so bad for me, but I'm being brave, although I eat so little that I'm down to a size 2. I just bought a Versace dress and Manolos for a date this weekend with my new boyfriend, Robert. I've never spent so much money on an outfit before, but then, I've never had $2,000 in cash to spend as I please.

# What He Needed

My husband's first wife almost spent him into bankruptcy. Twice. I am a little hazy about the details, as was he. I don't think it was a real bankruptcy, with court filings and ominous codes on his credit history. Credit was almost too easy for us to get. The experience may have depleted his savings, for he didn't have much in the bank when we married. But whatever happened, it scared him badly, and he was determined it would never happen again.

To that end, he was strict about the way we spent money in our household, second-guessing my purchases, making up rules about what we could buy. Books, for example. The rule was that I must read ten of the unread books in the house—and there were, I confess, many unread books in the house—before

I could bring a new one home. We had similar rules about compact discs ("Sing a song from the last one you bought," he bellowed at me once) and shoes ("How many pairs of black shoes does one woman need?"). It was not, however, a two-way street. The things he wanted proved to be necessities—defensible, sensible purchases. A treadmill, a digital camera, a DVD player and, of course, the DVDs to go with it. Lots of Westerns and wars.

But now I sound like him, sour and grudging. The irony was, we both made good money. More correctly, he made decent money, as a freelance technical writer, and I made great money, editing a loathsome city magazine, the kind that tells you where to get the best food/doctors/lawyers/private schools/flowers/chocolates/real estate. It wasn't journalism, it was marketing. That's why they had to pay so well.

Because I spent my days instructing others how to dispose of their income, I seldom shopped recreationally. I didn't even live in the city whose wares I touted, but in a strange little suburb just outside the limits. Marion was an unexpectedly pretty place, hidden in the triangle created by three major highways. It should have been loud. It wasn't. It was quiet, almost eerily so, except when the train came through. Our house was a Victorian, pale green, restored by the previous owners.

It needed nothing, which seemed like a blessing at first but gradually became unsettling. Houses were supposed to swallow up time and money and effort, but ours never required anything. We were childless, although we had a dog. When my husband found the house and insisted we move from the city, I had consoled myself by thinking the new place would absorb the energy I never got to put into raising a family. But its only demand came on the first of the month, when I wrote the mortgage check.

One day last January, I came home and tossed a bag on the kitchen table. White, with a black-blue logo, it was from the local bookstore. Christmas was past, no one's birthday was on the calendar. I had no excuse for buying a book. I hadn't read anything in weeks, much less the required ten. Which is not to say I always obeyed the rules. I broke them all the time but was careful to conceal this fact, smuggling in purchases in the folds of my leather tote, letting them blend with what we already owned until they took on a protective coloring. "This sweater? I've had it forever." "That book? Oh, it was a freebie, came to the office by mistake."

But on this particular January day, I came through the kitchen door after dark, let the dog leave footprints over my winter white wool coat, and threw the bag down so it landed with a noticeable smacking sound. My husband, who was preparing dinner, walked over to the table and opened the bag. It contained a first novel, plump and mushy with feeling. I steeled myself for his response, which could range anywhere from snide to volcanic. I was prepared to tell him it was collectible, that this first edition would be worth quite a bit if the writer lived up to the ridiculous amounts of praise heaped on him.

But all my husband said was, "That looks good," and went back to his sauce.

Over the next few weeks, I brought more things home. CDs, which I didn't even bother to remove from their silky plastic wrapping. More books. A new winter coat, a red one with a black velvet collar and suede gloves to match. Moss green high heels, a silk scarf. He approved of everything, challenged nothing. He began to think of other things we could buy, things we could share. Season tickets to the opera? Sure. A new rug for the dining room? Why not. Built-in bookshelves? Of course.

One night in bed he asked: "Are you happy?"

"I'm not unhappy."

"That's what you always say."

True.

"Why can't you talk to me?"

"Because when I tell you what I feel or what I'm thinking, you tell me I'm wrong. You tell me I don't know my own mind. I'd rather not talk at all than hear that."

"You don't know what you want."

This was true.

"You were a mess when I met you."

This was not.

"Everything you've accomplished is because of me."

"But," I pointed out, "I haven't actually accomplished anything."

"Are you going to leave me?"

I gave the most honest answer I dared. "I don't know yet."

He threw himself out of bed and ran downstairs. I went after him, found him in the kitchen, pouring bourbon into a stout glass of smoky amber. He had not approved of those glasses when I bought them, but he used them all the time. He finished his drink in two gulps, poured another. I got a bottle of white wine from the refrigerator and sat with him.

"Do whatever you have to do," he said at last. "But understand, there will be consequences."

"Consequences?" I assumed he meant financial ones, perhaps even a blow to my reputation. In my circle of friends and business associates, I was famous for being happily married, if only because that was the version I insisted on. His absence made it an easy illusion to sustain. Although I had to socialize a lot, because of my job, my husband never came along. He liked to say I was the only person whose company he craved. He thought this was romantic.

"You will come home one day, and there will be blood all over the walls," he continued, not unpleasantly. "I'll kill myself if you leave. I can't live without you."

"Don't say that."

"Why not? It's just the truth. If you don't want to live with me, then I don't want to live."

"You're threatening me."

"I'm threatening myself."

"A person who would kill himself has no respect for life. It's not a big leap, from killing yourself to killing someone else."

"I'd never hurt you. You know that."

We stayed up all night, talking and drinking, debating. We had done this in happier times, taking the opposite sides on less loaded topics. He demanded to know how he had disappointed me. I couldn't find any real answers. A few minutes ago, I had been not unhappy, but I had assumed my condition was my fault.

Now, all I could think was that I was a prisoner. A thug was threatening the life of someone I loved, had taken him hostage. That thug was my husband, my husband was his hostage. I was trapped.

But then, I had always been trapped. By my job, which I hated, and by this house, whose only require-ment was that we make as much next year as we did last year. I could give up books and CDs and coats with velvet collars, but those economies of scale would make no difference. Like everyone else we knew, we were addicts. We were hooked on our income. He was hooked on my income. My servitude made his freedom possible. I wanted to be a freelancer, too, to leave the world of bosses and benefits. One day, he promised, one day. And then we bought the house.

I couldn't talk about this, for some reason. Pressed for the concrete reasons of my discontent, I couldn't say anything, except to complain about the train, the drag of commuting. We had only one car, so I took the local train to work, which jounced and jolted, making five stops in eleven miles. It was wonderful in the morning, the paper in my lap, a travel mug of my own coffee in hand. But the last train on this line left the city at 7:30. At day's end, I always felt as if I was on the run, a white-collar criminal returning to my half-way house. I talked about the train until three or four in the morning, until my eyes dropped with sleep, his with boredom and bourbon.

When I came home the next day, there was a new Volvo waiting for me in the driveway. Green, with a beige leather interior and a CD player.

"Now you don't have to take the train anymore," he said.

The car was just the beginning, of course. We responded to our marital crisis in the acceptable modern way: we threw fistfuls of money at various people in what is known as the mental health profession. I found them in my magazine's "Best Doctors" issue. His psychiatrist. My psychiatrist. A licensed clinical social worker who specialized in couples therapy and who believed in astrology and suggested bowling as a way to release aggression. A specialist in social anxiety disorders, who prescribed various tranquilizers for my husband. Another licensed social worker, whose beliefs seemed more sound, but whose work yielded no better results. He gave us homework, we did it dutifully, but neither one of us could see how it was helping. I wanted to talk about the suicide threat, which I considered vile. My husband disavowed it, downplayed it. He wanted to talk about my secret plan to "stabilize" him so I could leave with a clear conscience. The social worker said we both had to give up our insistence on these topics and move on.

"Are you scared?" my shrink asked me in February.

"Very," I said. He told me to search the house for a gun the next time I was left alone, but I was almost never left alone. Finally my husband went to the grocery store, but I didn't find a gun. I was almost disappointed. I wanted hard evidence of the fear I felt, I wanted to be rational. I did discover that my husband was stockpiling the tranquilizers from his doctor. He had claimed to have trouble sleeping since I admitted I thought about leaving. Why? I wanted to ask. Are you watching me all night? Do you think I'd slip out then? How little he knew me if he thought I'd leave that way. I imagined him killing me as I slept, then killing himself. I began to have trouble sleeping, too, and it was my turn to get a prescription, my turn to stockpile.

But how would he do it, my skeptical sister asked. "He can barely summon up the energy to change a lightbulb, he's not organized enough to buy a gun. I hate to say it, but he would be lost without you."

Her words hung there, making us both glum.

"I'm not saying you should stay," she added. "Only that you shouldn't be scared of him."

"But you're saying what he said, more or less. If I leave, I have to be prepared to face the consequences."

"Are you?"

"Almost."

I had no reason to stay, but I had no reason to leave. Until, it seemed to me, he said what he said, revealed how far he would go to keep me. I believed in my marriage vows, if not in the God to which I had made them. My husband didn't hit me, he didn't cheat on me. I knew no other reason to leave a spouse. Oh, yes, he was lazy, and he liked to tie one on now and then, upending the bourbon bottle in his mouth to celebrate this or that. Or, more frequently now, to brood. But I couldn't fault him for that. I couldn't really fault him for anything, except for the fact that he was willing to ignore my misery as long as I stayed. He was prepared to make that deal, to do whatever he could to keep me there.

I thought there were rules for leaving, a protocol. I thought there would be a good time or a right time. I realized there would never be a good time.

"What can you get out of the house without him being suspicious?" my shrink asked me in early March.

"Myself," I said. "Maybe a laptop."

"You can't take a few things out, over several days?"

"No," I said. "He'd notice." And it was only when I said it that I realized it was true: he was keeping an inventory. He was going through my closet while I was at work, checking my underwear drawer, looking under my side of the bed. He was spying on me as surely as I had spied on him when I went looking for the gun he never bought. All those things—the CDs, the books, the shoes, the clothes, the Volvo—were meant to weigh me down, to keep me in place. That's why he had allowed me to have them. He was piling bricks, one by one, in front of the exit, burying me alive.

"Then it will have to be just you and your tooth-brush," my shrink said. "Call from your sister's house after work and tell him you're not coming back."

I came home from that session planning to do just that. But my husband knew me too well. He could see it in my face, in my eyes. He backed me into a corner in our bedroom that night, demanding to know why I was unhappy, how I could turn on him. Forever and ever, I had said, I who valued words and vows above all else. How could I think of leaving? He did not touch me. He didn't have to touch me to scare me. He demanded every secret, every fear, every moment of doubt I had ever experienced—about us, about myself. I sat in the corner, knees to my chest, shaking with sobs. I began to think I would have to make up confessions to satsify him, that I would have to pretend to sins and lapses I had never experienced. He stood above me, yelling. Somewhere in the house, our dog whimpered. I would have to leave him, too. Leave our dog, leave the car, leave the clothes, leave the CDs and books, lose the opera, and *La Bohème* was next. Of course, it would have to be *La Bohème*. It was always *La Bohème*. The fact is, I'd even have to lose my toothbrush. He was watching me that closely now. I'd be lucky to get out of the house with my own skin.

I did the only thing I knew to do: I capitulated. I asked for his forgiveness. I brought him the bourbon bottle and he poured me a glass of my favorite wine, a Chardonnay he usually mocked for its lack of subtlety. We drank silently, pretending a truce. We crawled into bed and watched one of his favorite DVDs, a Sergio Leone Western. I would start to doze off, then pretend to be wide awake when he asked if I was sleeping. He didn't like me to fall asleep with the television on. He resented the ease with which I slipped into sleep each night.

On our television, a boy stood beneath his brother, who had a noose around his neck. If the boy moved, his brother would die. Henry Fonda stuck a harmonica in his mouth. "Play," he said, "play for your ever-lovin' brother." Of course he couldn't stand there forever, harmonica in mouth, hands tied behind his back. He staggered forward, and his brother died.

By the time the sun came up, I realized an unpredicted snow had been falling all night, and the streets were near impassable, even for a brand-new Volvo.

But I had to go to work or be docked a day's pay, snow or no snow, binge or no binge, Sergio Leone or no Sergio Leone. I said good-bye to my husband's slumbering form and headed out the door. I wore jeans, snow boots, a black turtleneck, the new winter coat, suede gloves, and a felt hat. I turned the key in the lock. I wanted to take it from my ring and throw it in the nearest drift, but I knew I couldn't. I'd have to come back. I walked to the train. I did my work. And that night, when the train stopped at our station, I wasn't on it. I was at my sister's house. She wasn't approving, but she was sympathetic. She listened as I called and told him, in a choked voice, that I was never coming back. He didn't say anything. The line went dead in my hand.

He didn't have a gun, after all, so there was no blood on the walls. But there was all that booze, and all those pills, his and mine, squirreled away for the sleeplessness we had never tried to cure. Because I didn't go back for forty-eight hours, things were pretty bad. The dog, luckily, had survived, and without resorting to anything desperate or disgusting. I had filled his kibble dish the morning I left. Still, it was bad, and everyone felt sorry for me, wanted to ease my guilt. So sorry that the suburban police said it must be an accident, and the coroner agreed, and the insurance company gave up fighting after a while, so the mortgage was paid off in one fell swoop, with the life insurance. There was no suicide note. And while there were all those threats, dutifully reported to all those mental health professionals, they proved nothing. He had mixed booze with pills, despite warnings. True, it was suspicious he had taken so many pills, but I was able to report in all honesty that he had often ignored dosage advice, taking two, three times what was recommended. He also had an amazing capacity for liquor.

It never occurred to anyone that he was probably dead the morning I left, that my phone call home that night, overheard by my sister, had been completely for show. Or that the pills had been chopped up and dissolved in his bourbon bottle days ago, in hopes such an all-nighter would come again, and soon. It had been hard, waiting, but it was worth it. I had not noticed the snow falling because I was lying in bed, listening to his heart stop.

He always said he would kill himself if I left. All I did was hold him to his word.

# Dear Penthouse Forum
# (A First Draft)

You won't believe this, but this really did happen to me just last fall, and all because I was five minutes late, which seemed like a tragedy at the time. "It's only five minutes," that's what I kept telling the woman behind the counter, who couldn't be bothered to raise her gaze from her computer screen and make eye contact with me. Which is too bad, because I don't need much to be charming, but I need *something* to work with. Why did they make so many keystrokes, anyway, these ticket clerks? What's in the computer that makes them frown so? I had the printout for my e-ticket, and I kept shoving it across the counter, and she kept pushing it back to me with the tip of a pen, the way I used to do with my roommate Bruce's dirty underwear, when we were in college. I'd rounded it up with a hockey stick and stashed it in the corner, just to make a pathway through our dorm room. Bruce was a goddamn slob.

"I'm sorry," she said, stabbing that one key over and over. "There's just nothing I can do for you tonight."

"But I had a reservation. Andrew Sickert. Don't you have it?"

"Yes," she said, hissing the *s* in a wet, whistling way, like a middle-school girl with new braces. God, how did older men do it? I just can't see it, especially if it really is harder to get it up as you get older, not that I can see that either. But if it does get more difficult, wouldn't you need a *better* visual?

"I bought that ticket three weeks ago." Actually, it was two, but I was seeking any advantage, desperate to get on that plane.

"It says on your printout that it's not guaranteed if you're not at the gate thirty minutes ahead of departure." Her voice was oh-so-bored, the tone of a person who's just loving your pain. "We had an overbooked flight earlier in the evening and a dozen people were on the standby list. When you didn't check in by nine twenty-five, we gave your seat away."

"But it's only nine forty now, and I don't have luggage. I could make it, if the security line isn't too long. Even if it's the last gate, I'd make it. I just have to get on that flight. I have . . . I have . . ." I could almost feel my imagination trying to stretch itself, jumping around inside my head, looking for something this woman would find worthy. "I have a wedding."

"You're getting married?"

"No!" She frowned at the reflexive shrillness in my voice. "I mean, no, of course not. If it were my wedding, I'd be there, like, a week ago. It's my, uh, brother's. I'm the best man."

The "uh" was unfortunate. "Is the wedding in Providence?"

"Boston, but it's easier to fly into Providence than Logan."

"And it's tomorrow, Friday?"

Shit, no one got married on Friday night. Even I knew that. "No, but there's the rehearsal dinner, and, you know, all that stuff."

More clicks. "I can get you on the seven A.M. flight if you promise to check in ninety minutes ahead of time. You'll be in Providence by eight thirty. I have to think that's plenty of time. For the rehearsal and stuff. By the way, that flight is thirty-five dollars more."

"Okay," I said, pulling out a Visa card that was dangerously close to being maxed out, but I was reluctant to give up my cash, which I would need in abundance Friday night. "I guess that's enough time."

And now I had nothing but time to spend in the dullest airport, Baltimore-Washington International, in the dullest suburb, Linthicum, on the whole eastern seaboard. Going home was not an option. Light Rail had stopped running, and I couldn't afford the $30 cab fare back to North Baltimore. Besides, I had to be in line at 5:30 A.M. to guarantee my seat, and that meant getting up at 4:00. If I stayed here, at least I couldn't miss my flight.

I wandered through the ticketing area, but it was dead, the counters all on the verge of closing down. I nursed a beer, but last call was 11:00 P.M., and I couldn't get to the stores and restaurants on the other side of the metal detectors because I didn't have a boarding pass. I stood by the stairs for a while, watching the people emerge from the terminals, their faces exhausted but happy because their journeys were over. It was almost as if there were two airports—"Departures," this ghost town where I was trapped, and "Arrivals," with people streaming out of the gates and onto the escalators, fighting for their baggage and then throwing themselves into the gridlocked lanes on the lower level, heading home, heading out. I should be doing the same thing myself, four-hundred-some miles away. My plane would be touching down by now, the guys would be looking for me, ready to go. I tried to call them, but my cell was dead. That was the kind of night I was having.

I stretched out on one of the padded benches opposite my ticket counter and essayed a little catnap, but some old guy was pushing a vacuum cleaner right next to my head, which seemed a little hostile. Still, I closed my eyes and tried not to think of what I was missing in Boston. The guys would probably be at a bar by now, kicking back some beers. At least I'd make it to the major festivities the next night. It hadn't been a complete lie, the wedding thing. I was going to a friend's bachelor party, even though I wasn't invited to the wedding proper, but that's just because there's bad blood between the bride and me. She tells Bruce I'm a moron, but the truth is we had a little thing, when they were sorta broken up junior year, and she's terrified I'm going to tell him. And, also, I think, because she liked it, enjoyed ol' Andy, who brought a lot more to the enterprise than Bruce ever could. I'm not slagging my friend, but I lived with the guy for four years. I know the hand he was dealt, physiologically.

Behind my closed eyes, I thought about that week two years ago, how she had come to my room when she knew Bruce was at work, and locked the door behind her, and, without any preamble, just got down on her knees, and—

"Are you stranded?"

I sat up with a start, feeling as if I had been caught at something, but luckily I wasn't too disarranged down there. There was a woman standing over me, older, somewhere between thirty and forty, in one of those no-nonsense suits and smoothed-back hairdos, toting a small rolling suitcase. From my low vantage point, I couldn't help noticing she had nice legs, at least from ankle to knee. But the overall effect was prim, preternaturally old-ladyish.

"Yeah. They overbooked my flight, and I can't get another one until morning, but home's too far."

"No one should have to sleep on a bench. A single night could throw your back out of alignment for life. Do you need money? You probably could get a room in one of the airport motels for as little as fifty dollars. The Sleep Inn is cheap."

She fished a wallet out of her bag, and while I'm not strong on these kinds of details, it looked like an expensive purse to me, and the billfold was thick with cash. Most of the time, I don't angst over money—I'm just twenty-three, getting started in the world, I'll make my bundle soon enough—but it was hard, looking at all those bills and thinking about the gap between us. Why shouldn't I take fifty dollars? She clearly wouldn't feel it.

But for some reason I couldn't. "Naw. Because I'd never repay you. I mean, I could, I've got a job. But I know myself. I'll lose your address or something, never get it back to you."

She smiled, which transformed her features. Definitely between thirty and forty, but closer to the thirty end now that I studied her. Her eyes were gray, her mouth big and curvy, fuller on top than on the bottom, so her teeth poked out just a little. I go for that overbite thing. And the suit was a kind of camouflage, I realized, in a good way. Most women dress to hide their flaws, but a few use clothes to cover up their virtues. She was trying to hide her best qualities, but I could see the swells beneath her outfit—both on top and in the back, where her ass rose up almost in defiance of the tailored jacket and straight skirt. You can't keep a good ass down.

"Don't be so gallant," she said. "I'm not offering a loan. I'm doing a good deed. I like to do good deeds."

"It just doesn't seem right." I don't know why I was so firm on this, but I think it was because she was basically sweet. I couldn't help thinking we'd meet again, and I wouldn't want to be remembered as the guy who took fifty dollars from her.

"Well . . ." That smile again, bigger this time. "We have a stand-off."

"Guess so. But you better get down to that taxi stand if you want to get home tonight. The line's twenty deep." We glanced out the windows, down to the level below, which was just chaos. Up here, however, it was quiet and private, the man with the vacuum cleaner having finally moved on, the counters all closed.

"I'm lucky. I have my own car."

"I think the lucky person is the man who's waiting at home for you."

"Oh." She was flustered, which just made her sexier. "There's no one—I mean—well, I'm single."

"That's hard to believe." The automatic bullshit thing to say, yet I was sincere. How could someone like that ticket-clerk crone have a ring on her finger, while this woman was running around loose?

"It's a chicken-or-egg problem."

"Huh?"

"Am I single because I'm a workaholic, or am I a workaholic because I'm single?"

"Oh, that's easy. It's the first one. No contest."

Her faced seemed to light up and I swear I saw her eyes go filmy, as if she were about to cry. "That's the nicest thing anyone's ever said to me."

"You need to hang out with better people, then."

"Look—" She put her hand on mine, and it was cool and soft, the kind of hand that gets slathered in cream on a regular basis, the hand of a woman who's taking care of every part of herself. I knew she'd be waxed to a fine finish beneath that conservative little suit, with painted toenails and nothing but good smells. "I have a two-bedroom apartment on the south side of the city, just a few blocks from the big hotels. You can spend the night in my guest room, catch the first airport shuttle from the Hyatt at five. It's only fifteen dollars, and you'll get where you're going rested and unkinked."

Funny, but I felt protective of her. It was almost as if I were two people—a guy who wanted to keep her from a guy like me, and the guy who wanted to get inside her apartment and rip that suit off, see what she was keeping from the rest of the world.

"I couldn't do that. That's an even bigger favor than giving me fifty dollars for a hotel room."

"I don't know. It seems to me there are ways you could pay me back, if you put your mind to it."

She didn't smile, or arch an eyebrow, or do a single thing with her face to acknowledge what she had just offered. She simply turned and began pulling her bag toward the sliding glass doors. But I was never more certain in my life that a woman wanted me. I got up, grabbed my own suitcase, and followed her, our wheels thrumming in unison. She led me to a black BMW in the short-term lot. Neither one of us said a word, we could barely look at each other, but I had her skirt half-way up her thigh even as she handed the parking lot attendant two bucks. He never even bothered to look down, just handed her the change, bored with his life. It's amazing what people don't see, but after all, people didn't see her, this amazing woman. Because she was small and modest, she passed through the world without acknowledgment. I was glad I hadn't made the mistake of not seeing what was there.

Her apartment was only twenty minutes away, and if it had been twenty-five, I think I would have made her pull over to the side of the road or risked bursting. I had her skirt above her waist now, yet she kept control of the car and leveled her eyes straight ahead, which just made me wilder for her. Once she parked, she didn't bother to pop the trunk, and by that time I wasn't too worried about my suitcase. I wasn't going to need any clothes until the morning. She ran up the stairs and I followed.

The apartment building was a little shabby, and in an iffier neighborhood than I expected, but those warehouse lofts usually are in odd parts of town. She pulled me into the dark living room and locked the door behind me, throwing on the deadbolt as if I might change my mind, but there was no risk of that.

I didn't have the time or the inclination to take in my surroundings, although I did notice that the room was sparsely furnished—nothing more than a sofa, a desk with an open laptop, and this huge credenza of jars with gleaming gold tops, which looked sort of like those big things of peppers you see at some delis, although not quite the same. I couldn't help thinking it was a project of hers, that maybe they were vases distorted by the moonlight.

"You an artist?" I asked as she backed away and began pulling her clothes off, revealing a body that was even better than I had hoped.

"I'm in business."

"I mean, as a hobby?" I inclined my head toward the credenza, as I was trying to get my trousers off without tripping.

"I'm a pickler."

"What?" Not that I really cared about the answer, as I had my hands on her now. She let me kiss and touch what I could reach, then sank to her knees, as if all she cared about was pleasing me. Well, she had said she was into good deeds, and I had done pretty well by her in the car.

"A pickler," she said, her breath warm and moist. "I put up fruits and vegetables and other things as well, so I can enjoy them all winter long." And then she stopped talking because she had—

**Maureen stops**, frowning at what she has written. Has she mastered the genre? This is her sixth letter, and while the pickups are getting easier, the prose is becoming harder. Part of the problem is that the men bring so little variation to their end of the bargain, forcing her to be ever more inventive about their lives and their missions. Even when they do tell her little pieces of their backstories, like this one, Andy, it's so boring, so banal. Late to the airport, a missed connection, not enough money to do anything but sleep on a bench, blah, blah, blah. Ah, but she doesn't have the luxury of picking them for material. She has to find the raw stuff and mold it to her needs.

So far, the editors of *Penthouse* haven't printed any of her letters—too much buildup, she supposes, which is like too much foreplay as far as she's concerned. Ah, but that's the difference between men and women, the unbridgeable gap. One wants seduction, the other wants action. It's why her scripts never sell, either. Too much buildup, too much narrative. And, frankly, she knows her sex scenes suck. Part of the problem is that in real life Maureen almost never completes the act she's trying to describe in her fiction; she's too eager to get to her favorite part. So, yes, she has her own foreplay issues.

No, there are definitely voice problems in this piece. Would a young man remember that whistling sound that braces make, or is she simply giving too much away about her own awkward years? Would a twenty-three-year-old man recognize an expensive purse? Or use the word "preternaturally"? Also, she probably should be careful about being too factual. The $2 parking fee—a more astute person, someone who didn't have his hand up a woman's skirt, fumbling around as if he's looking for spare change beneath a sofa cushion, might wonder why someone returning from a business trip paid for only an hour of parking. She should recast her apartment as well, make it more glamorous, the same way she upgraded her Nissan Sentra to a gleaming black BMW. Speaking of which, she needs to get the car to Wax Works, just in case, and change Andy's name in the subsequent drafts. She doesn't worry that homicide detectives read *Penthouse* Forum for clues to open cases, but they almost certainly read it. Meanwhile, his suitcase is gone, tossed in a Dumpster behind the Sleep Inn near the airport, and Andy's long gone, too.

Well—she looks up at the row of gleaming jars, which she needs to lock away again behind the credenza's cupboards, but they're so pretty in the moonlight, almost like homemade lava lamps. Well, she reminds herself. Most of Andy is long gone.

# The Babysitter's Code

The rules, the real ones, have seldom been written down, yet every girl knows them. (The boys who babysit don't, by the way. They eat too much, they leave messes, they break vases while roughhousing with the kids, but the children adore the boys who babysit, so they still get invited back.) The rules are intuitive, as are most things governing the behavior of teenage girls. Your boyfriend may visit unless it's explicitly forbidden, but the master bedroom is always off-limits, just as it would be in your own house. Eat what you like, but never break the seal on any bag or box. Whatever you do, try to erase any evidence of your presence in the house by evening's end. The only visible proof of your existence should be a small dent on a sofa cushion, preferably at the far end, as if you were too polite to stretch across its entire length. Finally, be careful about how much food you consume. No parent should come home and peer into the Pringles can—or the Snackwell's box or the glass jar of the children's rationed Halloween candy—and marvel at your capacity. There is nothing ruder than a few crumbs of chips at the bottom of a bag, rolled and fastened with one of those plastic clips, or a single Mint Milano resting in the last paper cup.

Terri Snyder, perhaps the most in-demand babysitter in all of River Run, knew and followed all these rules. Once when she was at the Morrows' house, she discovered a four-pound can of pistachio nuts and got a little carried away. And while the canister was so large that it provided cover for her gluttony, the shells in the trash can left no doubt as to how much she had eaten. To conceal the grossness of her appetite, she packed those shells in her knapsack and the pockets of her ski jacket. Riding home in the front seat of Ed Morrow's Jeep Cherokee, she realized she was rattling softly, but Mr. Morrow seemed to think it was the car's heater. The next time she babysat for the Morrows, she found another canister of pistachios, a sure sign of trust.

But then, the Morrows were among the most generous clients in Terri's circle. Most families, even the rich ones, hid what they considered precious—not just liquor, which interested Terri not at all, but also expensive chocolates and macadamia nuts and the asiago cheese dip from Cross Street Wine & Cheese in Baltimore. The last was especially dear, a souvenir from the parents' hip, carefree lives, when they lived where they wanted, with no worries about school districts, much less backyards and soccer leagues. The asiago dip was like the tiny little treasures that pioneer families kept in their sod houses—a single silver spoon, a pair of diamond earrings, a china-head doll. Almost laughable, yet touching somehow, a symbol of a foreign land from which they had chosen to exile themselves for some vague dream of betterment.

Terri always found these forbidden snacks but left them undisturbed, obeying another unwritten rule: you may snoop all you like, but you must not move or in any way tamper with the secrets of the houses left in your care. Read the dirty books and magazines by all means, catalog the couple's birth control (or lack thereof), poke through medicine cabinets and those mother lodes known as nightstands, but make sure everything and everyone is tucked in its respective bed before the parents return home.

The fathers' cluelessness is understandable, but why would mothers, most of them former babysitters, leave so many embarrassments to be discovered? Yet

Terri never stopped to wonder about this. Like most teenagers, she assumed her generation had invented depravity—and she was not entirely off the mark. Her clients remembered their pasts as one might remember a dream—hazy, incoherent, yet vaguely satisfying. Indulged in their youth, they had little need for rebellion in adulthood, and even less energy for it. Those who know the gin-soaked suburbs described in Cheever and Updike would be disappointed in River Run, where there was so much money and so little imagination. Sure, there was a sex toy here, a prescription for Viagra there, but Terri's systematic sleuthing did not uncover anything truly shocking—not until the day she found the beautiful little handgun, no bigger than a toy, nestled in Mrs. Delafield's lingerie drawer.

Now the Delafields had been considered odd from their arrival in the community two years ago. Mrs. Delafield ("Call me Jakkie, it's short for Jakarta, can you believe it? My mom was nuts") was very young, so young that even an incurious teenager such as Terri could see she did not belong in this overdone, overlarge, grown-up house in River Run's Phase V development. Local gossip put her at no more than twenty-five, which was worth gossiping about because Mr. Delafield was fifty-two. He was divorced, of course, with children in college, and now he had

Mrs. Delafield and the baby, a shockingly large child of sixteen months, a child so big that he was having trouble walking. Hugo's short, chubby legs simply could not propel his mass forward, and he continued to crawl, when he deigned to move at all. It was hard, looking at Mrs. Delafield, to figure out how such a huge child had come out of this lanky size 2, with hips narrower than most of the boys in the River Run freshmen class. No one knew what Mrs. Delafield had been before she was Mrs. Delafield. The one time Terri had dared to ask, Mrs. Delafield must not have understood the question because she said: "Oh, I was at my height when I met Mr. Delafield. You have no idea. I can't bear to look at the photographs because I'm such a mess now." Her hands shook, she chewed her nails when she thought no one was looking, and her hair was an odd shade of yellow. She was the most beautiful woman Terri had ever seen outside a magazine.

No one knew why the Delafields had chosen River Run, not at first. For while River Run was an extremely desirable place to live—great school district, beautiful countryside, and convenient to I-83, that was the locals' litany—not even its biggest boosters expected billionaires in their midst. The grandest house in Phase V could not compete with the waterfront estates outside Annapolis, or even the rambling mansions on Baltimore's north side. Plus, Hugo was so young, and the Delafields so very rich, they didn't have to worry about public schools.

The mystery was explained when Mr. Delafield's corporate helicopter landed with a great, ear-shattering roar in a clearing behind his property, acreage dedicated as permanent open space according to the master plan for River Run. The community and the River Run board fought the helicopter, of course. Mr. Delafield insisted he had been promised use of the land, that he would not have purchased the house otherwise. Yet the Delafields decided to stay in the house even after a zoning judge decided Mr. Delafield could not use the land. The corporate headquarters for his pharmaceutical company were in Harrisburg, Pennsylvania, no more than an hour's drive away. His chauffeur-driven Town Car pulled out of the quarter-mile driveway promptly at seven every weekday morning and returned thirteen hours later. Mrs. Delafield, who did not work, was left at home with Hugo and a live-in housekeeper, who apparently terrified her. She hired Terri to come on Tuesdays, the housekeeper's day off, and spell her for exactly four hours, from three to seven, for $5 an hour. Finding something to do with those four hours was a terrible chore for Mrs. Delafield. She tried tennis, but she wasn't coordinated. She tried shopping, but she found the nearest stores disappointing, preferring to purchase her clothes on seasonal excursions to New York. She signed up for ceramics class, but she didn't like what it did to her acrylic nails. Still, she was strict with herself, throwing herself into her Porsche SUV every Tuesday as if it were a grim duty.

She always returned promptly at seven, sometimes stepping out of her clothes as she crossed the threshold—whatever she had been in her past life, it had left her without modesty. She then handed Terri $25 and fixed a drink. Terri wasn't sure if the extra five dollars was a tip or a math error, and she didn't ask Mrs. Delafield for fear of embarrassing her. Mrs. Delafield was shy about her lack of education, to which she made vague, sinister references. "When I had to leave school . . . ," or "I wish I could have stayed for prom, but there was just no way." Sometimes she examined Terri's armload of textbooks, as if just touching them might convey the knowledge she had failed to acquire. "Is algebra hard? When they say European history, do they mean all the countries, even the little-bitty ones? Why would they want to you to study psychics?" The last was a misreading of "physics," but Terri didn't have the heart to correct her. Instead, she told Mrs. Delafield that River Run

High School had been founded at a time when there were a lot of alternative theories about education—perfectly true—and that it still retained a certain touchy-feely quality. Also true, although parents such as Terri's, who had known the original River Run, were always complaining it had become a ruthless college factory.

Given that the Delafields' house, like the Delafields' baby, was so huge, it had taken Terri a while to inventory its contents. Still, the wonders of Mrs. Delafield's underwear drawer were well known to her long before she found the gun. Drawers, really, because Mrs. Delafield had an entire bureau just for underwear and nightgowns. The bureau was built into the wall of a walk-in closet, one of two off the master bedroom, both almost as big as Terri's bedroom, but her family lived in a Phase II house. Terri had been through those drawers several times, so she was certain that the elegant little handgun she found there one March afternoon was a new addition, along with the rather nasty-looking tap pants of transparent blue gauze, with a slit where the crotch should be. Terri did not try on the tap pants, which she considered gross, but she did ease an emerald-green nightgown over her bra and panties. Small and compact, with thin legs and rather large breasts, Terri could not have looked less like Mrs. Delafield. Still, she rather liked the effect.

It never occurred to her to touch the gun, not at first. In fact, she was petrified just reaching around it to pick out various bits of lingerie. She treated it as if it were an explosive sachet. To Terri's knowledge, guns were like coiled snakes, always ready to strike. Didn't everyone know about the Shellenberg brothers, perhaps River Run's greatest tragedy? Not to mention that scene in *Pulp Fiction*.

But as time went by, and Terri kept returning to the lingerie drawers, the gun began to seem integral to the clothes she found there, an accessory, no different than the shoes and purses arrayed on the nearby shelves. It was so . . . pretty, that little silver gun, small and ladylike. Such a gun would never go off heedlessly. One Tuesday afternoon, Terri pulled on a black lace nightgown, one that was probably loose and flowing on Mrs. Delafield. On her, it bunched around the upper part of her body and tangled around her ankles. She slipped on a pair of Mrs. Delafield's high heels so she wouldn't trip on the hem, picked up the gun in her right hand, and posed for the full-length mirror at the back of the closet. The gun really made the outfit. She went into all the poses she knew from films—the straight-up-and-down Clint Eastwood glare, the wrist prop, the crouch. Each was better than the last.

A trio of quick, high beeps sounded, the signal that the front door had been opened and closed. Mrs.

Delafield always turned the alarm off when she went out because she didn't know how to program it. Terri, frozen in front of her reflection, wondered what she should do. Call out to the intruder that someone was home? Announce that she had a gun? But the front door had been locked, she was sure of that. Only someone with a key could have entered. Mrs. Delafield? But she never came back early. The housekeeper? It was her day off. Someone was coming up the stairs with a heavy, tired tread. Wildly, Terri glanced around the walk-in closet. The door was ajar; the soft overhead lights, so kind to her reflection, were on. She could lock herself in, but her clothes were folded on an armchair in the Delafields' bedroom. She could make a run for them, or array herself in some of Mrs. Delafield's oversize sweats, shove the gun back in the drawer, or—

"What the fuck?" asked Mr. Delafield, and, at that moment, Terri hated every adult in River Run who had fought his helicopter, even her own parents. If Mr. Delafield still had his helicopter, she would have heard him coming from a long way off.

"I'm the babysitter. Terri." She fought the impulse to cross her arms against her chest, as that would only draw attention to the gun in her hand.

"Oh," said the blond man with a ruddy face—it was impossible for him to turn even redder, yet Terri thought he seemed embarrassed. For her or himself?

"And—that? Do you bring that to all your babysitting jobs?"

She glanced down at the sweet silver gun, held at her hip as if it were a small purse. "No. No, that's not mine. It's yours."

"Not mine. You mean it's Jakkie's? Jakkie has a gun? Son of a bitch. Why would Jakkie have a gun?"

Terri shrugged, not wanting to tell Mr. Delafield that she had always assumed it was because his wife feared him, with his big, shambling body and red, red face. Now she wondered if he feared his wife, if she had overlooked some menace in Mrs. Delafield's ditziness.

"Where did you find it?" Terri's right hand, the one holding the gun, gestured loosely toward the open drawer, and he ducked his head, as if expecting it to go off. "With her pretty little panties, huh? Well, no wonder I never saw it."

The situation was so surreal, to use a word of which Terri was particularly fond at the time, that she couldn't figure out how to behave. She put the gun on top of the built-in bureau and slipped on Mrs. Delafield's most prosaic robe.

"I was just looking at it," she said, as if that explained everything. "No one I know owns a gun."

"Well, I didn't know anyone I knew had a gun, either." He laughed, and Terri joined him, a little nervously.

"You looked nice," he said, as if he didn't mean it but wanted to be polite. "In the gown, I mean."

"It doesn't really fit right."

"Oh. Well, you can get stuff altered, right? Jakkie does it all the time."

Did he not know that the gown was his wife's? Or was hepretending to think otherwise, to spare Terri the humiliation of being caught in violation of almost every rule of good babysitting? Or was it possible that he really liked how Terri looked? Terri was terrified that he might come toward her, or touch her in some way. She was terrified he wouldn't.

"Hugo's asleep," she offered, reminding him of who she was and why she was here.

"Hugo," he said. "You know, I have no idea where she got that name. Maybe from Baby Huey. He has too many chromosomes. Or not enough. If I had married what my daughters call an age-appropriate woman, someone thirty-five or forty, she would have had amnio, and we would have known before he was born. Or we wouldn't have kids at all. But Jakkie was only twenty-three when she got pregnant, and Hugo's a freak. He won't live past the age of five."

"He's just big."

"He is. Huge Hugo. But he's screwed up, too. I don't know what Jakkie's going to do when he dies. I wonder if that's why she bought the gun." He shook his head, disagreeing with himself. "No, she'll go in a slow, catatonic decline, refusing to eat, wandering around the house in her robe. In that robe. All these clothes, and she spends most of her time in that robe."

"Oh." Terri had grabbed it because the blue flannel looked so ordinary, the antidote to the expensive lingerie she had probably damaged, stretching it to fit her so-very-different proportions. "I'm sorry, I'll—"

"It's okay." Waving his hands in front of his face, fanning himself, as if it were a summer's day instead of a late-winter one. "It's no big deal. You should keep it. She'll never miss it. Keep it."

She knew, from the River Run Self-Esteem Project, that this was how such things began. Men gave you gifts or money, then asked for favors in return. Teachers, coaches, neighbors—the girls at River Run had been taught to assume they were all potential predators, far more sex-crazed than their male peers.

"I couldn't possibly," she demurred.

"Suit yourself. Put, um, everything back where you found it."

And with that, he was gone. Terri listened to him leave the room and walk downstairs, then waited another minute before going into the bedroom to change. She then returned to the closet and made sure everything was where it belonged. She assumed Mr. Delafield would tell Mrs. Delafield what she had done, and she would lose this weekly gig, an easy $25 by anyone's standards. But losing her job did not bother her as much as the encounter itself. It was not unlike a dream she had from time to time. A man, an older one—one taller and darker than Mr. Delafield—found her alone somewhere and just . . . took over. It was at once a scary and comforting dream, one that always ended a little too soon. That was what she was feeling now—relieved, yet desirous of knowing what might have happened if Mr. Delafield had kept going. Would he have been more insistent with a different kind of girl—someone truly beautiful, like Katarina Swann, or someone weak and shy, like Bennie Munson? It was Terri's lot to fall in the middle of that continuum— pretty enough, but not a raving beauty. Nor was she like Bennie, someone who all but begged to be used and abused by the world.

Mrs. Delafield came home at seven, as always, and seemed indifferent to Terri's news that Mr. Delafield was in his den, watching television while working out on his elliptical machine. No one, not even Terri, stopped to wonder why he hadn't sent Terri home and assumed Hugo's care. For the next six days, Terri waited for Mrs. Delafield to call and say she wouldn't be needing Terri anymore, but the call never came. She went back at three P.M. the following week and everything was as it always was—the quiet house, the listless baby (who now seemed more precious to Terri because he was doomed), the gun in the lingerie drawer. Caught once, Terri knew she should turn over a new leaf, but she found herself in the walk-in closet within twenty minutes, modeling lingerie and holding the gun. This time she moved on to Mrs. Delafield's evening dresses, which she had never dared touch before. She listened for the door to beep, refusing to admit to herself that her ears were straining toward that sound because she wanted to hear it. She had started a diet—for senior prom, she assured her mother, who grudgingly allowed it. Terri's mom hated diets. But it was working already, she could tell. Mrs. Delafield's things were not so tight in the waist this week.

Mr. Delafield did not come home early that day, or the next week, or the week after. He never came home early again. In April, he stopped coming home at all. His absence, like most absences, took time to register. First a neighbor realized the Town Car had stopped gliding in and out of the driveway at its usual hours. Then Terri noticed the pile of bundled-up *Wall Street Journals* in the three-car garage, placed in a basket, as if Mr. Delafield might return and want to work through two weeks, three weeks, an entire month of business news. It was only when Mrs. Delafield put out the whole collection for recycling—on the wrong day, in the wicker basket, and still bundled in their plastic wrappers, in violation of every protocol—that Terri realized Mr. Delafield was never coming back. The following Tuesday, Mrs. Delafield paid her $20 instead of the usual $25 and Terri finally understood that the extra five dollars had always been a tip, one Mrs. Delafield had decided she could no longer afford.

On the third Tuesday in May, Terri arrived to find the house full of boxes and Mrs. Delafield flitting around with various lists, shouting into her portable phone as if the connection was bad. Yet she looked radiant, more beautiful than Terri had ever seen her, and her conversations seemed to hum with excitement. "I have so much to do," she told Terri with obvious delight. "Lawyers, Realtors, moving companies—oh, it's all so complicated! But a week from now, Hugo and I will be gone, and this place will be on the market. We'll miss you!"

She headed out, full of true purpose for once, and Terri walked through the house. It was as if some careless, heedless babysitter had been here first, for all the drawers and closets were open, their contents tumbling out helter-skelter. Yet the little silver gun was still in its place of honor, lying on a bed of emerald-green silk. Terri picked it up, intending to do nothing more than hold it one more time. It fit her hand so well, looked so right. It wasn't her imagination: she was beautiful when she held this gun. Mr. Delafield had said as much. Take it, he had said, and she had assumed he meant the nightgown. Clearly, he meant the gun. He had been asking Terri to save him, to protect him from his crazy wife, who was capable of anything in her grief and anxiety over their damaged child. Terri had been Mr. Delafield's last hope, and when she failed him, he had no choice but to leave.

On what she would later claim was an impulse, Terri stuffed the gun in her knapsack, grabbing the emerald-green slip as an afterthought. After all, she needed something to muffle the sound of the metal. She couldn't afford the possibility that the gun might rattle when Mrs. Delafield took her home later this evening, or assume that Mrs. Delafield, like Mr. Morrow, would be polite enough to pretend that a mysterious sound was nothing more than a faulty car heater. She swaddled the gun with great tenderness, placing it in the outside pocket of her beat-up bag, assuring herself all the while that when something makes you beautiful, it should be yours to keep.

# Hardly Knew Her

S ofia was a lean, hipless girl, the type that older men still called a tomboy in 1975, although her only hoydenish quality was a love of football. In the vacant lot behind the neighborhood tavern, the boys welcomed her into their games. This was in part because she was quick, with sure hands. But even touch football sometimes ended in pile-ups, where it was possible to steal a touch or two and claim it was accidental. She tolerated this feeble groping most of the time, punching the occasional boy who pressed too hard too long, which put the others on notice for a while. Then they forgot, and it happened again—they touched, she punched. It was a price she was more than willing to pay for the exhilaration she felt when she passed the yew berry bushes that marked the end zone, a gaggle of boys breathless in her wake.

But for all the afternoons she spent at the vacant lot, she never made peace with the tricky plays—the faked handoffs, the double pumps, the gimmicky laterals. It seemed cowardly to her, a way for less gifted players to punish those with natural talent. It was one thing to spin and feint down the field, eluding grasping hands with a swivel of her nonhips. But to pretend the ball was somewhere it wasn't struck her as cheating, and no one could ever persuade her otherwise.

She figured it was the same with her father and cards. He knew the game was steeped in bluffing and lying, but he could never resign himself to the fact. He depended on good cards and good luck to get him through, and even Sofia understood that was no way to win at poker. But the only person her father could lie to with any success was himself.

"That your dad?" Joe, one of the regular quarterbacks, asked one Friday afternoon as they sprawled in the grass, game over, their side victorious again.

Sofia looked up to see her father slipping through the back door of the tavern, which people called Gordon's, despite the fact that the owner's name was Peter Papadakis. Perhaps someone named Gordon had owned it long ago, but it had been Mr. Papadakis's place as far back as Sofia could remember.

"Yeah."

"What's he doing, going through the back door?" That was a scrawny boy, Bob, one of the grabby ones.

Sofia shredded grass in her fingers, ignoring him. Joe said, "Poker."

"Poker? Poker? I hardly knew her." Bob was so pleased with his wit that he rolled back and forth, clutching his stomach, and some of the other boys laughed as if they had never heard this old joke before. Sofia didn't laugh. She hated watching her father disappear in the back room of the tavern, from which he would not emerge until early Saturday. But it was better than running into him on the sidewalk between here and home. He always pretended surprise at seeing her, proclaiming it the darnedest coincidence, Sofia on Brighton Avenue, same as him. On those occasions, he would stop and make polite inquiries into her life, but he would be restless all the while, shifting his weight from one foot to another, anxious as a little kid on the way to his own birthday party.

"How's it going, Fee?" That was her family nickname, and she was just beginning to hate it.

"S'all right, I guess."

"School okay?"

"Not bad. I hate algebra."

"It'll come in handy one day."

"How?"

"If you get through high school, maybe go on to community college, you won't be stuck here in Dundalk, breathing air you can see."

"I like it here." She did. The water was nearby and although it wasn't the kind you could swim in—if you fell in, you were supposed to tell your mom so she could take you for a tetanus shot, but no one ever told—the view from the water's edge made the world feel big, yet comprehensible. Dundalk wasn't Baltimore, although the map said it was. Dundalk was a country unto itself, the Republic of Bethlehem Steel. And in 1975, Beth Steel was like the Soviet Union. You couldn't imagine either one not being there. So the families of Dundalk breathed the reddish air, collected their regular paychecks, and comforted one another when a man was hurt or killed, accepting those accidents as the inevitable price for a secure job. It was only later, when the slow poison of asbestosis began moving from household to household, that the Beth Steel families began to question the deal they had made. Later still, the all-but-dead company was sold for its parts and the new owner simply ended it all—pensions, health care, every promise ever made. But in 1975, in Dundalk, a Beth Steel family was still the best thing to be, and the children looked down on those whose fathers had to work for any other company.

"Go home and do your homework," her father told Sofia.

"No homework on Fridays," she said. "But I want to eat supper and wash the dishes before *Donny and Marie* comes on."

They never spoke of his plans for the evening, much less the stakes involved, but after such encounters Sofia went home and hid whatever she could. She longed to advise her mother to do the same, but it was understood that they never spoke of her father's winning and losing, much less the consequences for the household.

"I bought it for you, didn't I?" her father had told her younger brother, Brad, wheeling the ten-speed bicycle with the banana seat out of the garage. Brad had owned the shiny Schwinn for all of a month. "Why'd I ever think we needed fancy candlesticks like these?" her father grumbled, taking the grape-bedecked silver stems from the sideboard, as if his only problem was a sudden distaste for their ornate style. One Saturday morning, he came into Sofia's room and tried to grab her guitar, purchased a year earlier after a particularly good Friday, but something in her expression made him put it back.

Instead he sold the family dog, a purebred collie, or so her father had said when he brought the puppy home three months ago. It turned out that Shemp had the wrong kind of papers, some initials other than AKC. The man who agreed to buy Shemp from them had lectured her father, accusing him of being taken in by the Mennonite puppy mills over the state line. He gave her father twenty-five dollars, saying: "People who can't be bothered to do the most basic research probably shouldn't have a dog, anyway."

Sofia, sitting in the passenger seat of her father's car—she had insisted on accompanying him, thinking it would shame her father, but in the end she was the one who was ashamed that she had chosen her guitar over Shemp—chewed over this fact. Her father was so gullible that he could be duped by Mennonites. She imagined them ringed around a poker table, solemn bearded faces regarding their cards. Mennonites would probably be good at poker if God let them play it.

Her father spoke of his fortune as if it were the weather, a matter of temperature outside his control. "I was hot," her father crowed coming through the door Saturday morning, carrying a box of doughnuts. "I've never seen a colder deck," he'd say, heading out Saturday afternoon after a long morning nap on the sofa. "I couldn't catch a break."

You just can't bluff, Sofia thought. But then, neither could she. Perhaps it was in her genes. That was why she had to outrun the boys on the other team. Go long and I'll hit you, Joe told her, and that's what she did, play after play. She outran her competition or she didn't, but she never tried to fool the other players or faulted anyone else when she failed to catch a ball that was thrown right at her. She didn't think of herself as hot or cold, or try to blame the ball for what she failed to do. A level playing field was not a figure of speech to Sofia. It was all she knew. She made a point of learning every square inch of the vacant lot—the slight depressions where you could turn an ankle if you came down wrong, the sections that stayed mushy long after the rain, the slope in one of their improvised end zones that made it tricky to set up for the pass. With just a little homework, Sofia believed, you could control for every possibility.

Sofia's stubborn devotion to football probably led to the onslaught of oh-so-girly gifts on her next birthday—a pink dress, perfume, and a silver necklace with purplish jewels that her mother said were amethysts. "Semiprecious," she added. There were three of them, one large oval guarded by two small ones, set in a reddish gold. The necklace was the most beautiful thing that Sofia had ever seen.

"Maybe you'll go to the winter dance up at school, Fee," her mother suggested hopefully, fastening the necklace around her neck.

"Someone has to ask you first," Sofia said, pretending not to be impressed by her own reflection.

"Oh, it's okay to go with a group of girls, too," her mother said.

Sofia didn't know any girls, actually. She was friendly with most of them, but not friends. The girls at school seemed split about her: some thought her love of football was genuine, if odd, while others proclaimed it an awfully creative way to be a tramp. This second group of girls whispered that Sofia was fast, fast in the bad way, that football wasn't the only game she played with all those boys in the vacant lot behind Gordon's Tavern. What would they say if she actually danced with one, much less let him walk her home?

"I'd be scared to wear this out of the house," she said, placing a tentative finger on the large amethyst. "Something might happen to it."

"Your aunt would want you to wear it and enjoy it," her mother said. "It's an heirloom. It belonged to Aunt Polly, and her aunt before her, and their grandmother before that. But Tammy didn't have any girls, so she gave it to me a few years ago, said to put it away for a special birthday. This one's as special as any, I think."

"What if I lost it?"

"You can't," her mother said. "It has a special catch—see?"

But Sofia wasn't worried about the catch. Or, rather, she was worried about the other catch, the hidden rules that were always changing. She was trying to figure out if the necklace qualified as a real gift, one that her father couldn't reclaim. It hadn't been purchased in a store. It had come from her father's side of the family. And although it was a birthday gift, it hadn't been wrapped up in paper and ribbons. She put it back in its box, a velvety once-black rectangle that was all the more beautiful for having faded to gray. Where would her father never look for it?

Three weeks later, Sofia awoke one Saturday to find her father standing over her guitar. Her father must not have known how guitar strings were attached because he cut them with a pocketknife, sliced them right down the middle and reached into the hole to extract the velvet box, which had been anchored in a tea towel at the bottom, so it wouldn't make an obvious swishing noise if someone picked up the guitar and shook it. How had he known it was there? Perhaps he had reached for the guitar again and felt the extra weight. Perhaps he simply knew Sofia too well, a far more disturbing thought. At any rate, he held the velvet box in his hand.

"I'll buy you new ones," he said.

He meant the strings, of course, not the necklace or the amethysts.

"But you can't sell it," she said, groping for the word her mother had invoked so lovingly. "It's a hair-loom."

"Oh, Fee, it's nothing special. I'll buy you something much better when my luck changes."

"Take something else, anything else. Take the guitar."

"Strings cut," he said, as if he had found it that way and believed it beyond repair. "Besides, I told this fellow about it and he said he'll take it in lieu of . . . in lieu of debts owed, if he finds it satisfactory. I don't even have to go to the trouble of pawning it."

"But if you don't pawn it, we can't ever get it back."

"Honey, when did we ever redeem a pawnshop ticket?"

This was true, but at least the pawnshop held open the promise of recovering things. If the necklace went to a person, it would be gone as Shemp. Sofia imagined it on the neck of a smug girl, like one of the ones who whispered about her up at school. A girl who would say: Oh, my father bought me this at the pawnshop. It's an antique. My father said the people who owned it probably didn't know it was valuable. But Sofia did and her mother did. It was only her father who didn't value it, except as a way to cover his losses.

"Please don't take it," she said. She tried to make her face do whatever it had done the day he had backed down before, but it was dim in her room and her father was resolved. He pocketed the beautiful box and left.

But he didn't leave the house right away. He never did, not on the glum Saturdays that followed his bad nights, the ones that came and went without doughnuts. He went down to the breakfast table and wolfed down a plate of fried eggs. Sofia followed him down to the table, staring at him silently, but he refused to meet her gaze. Her mother might intervene if she told her, but Sofia didn't feel that she had earned anyone's help. She had sat by while the candlesticks left, turned her back when Brad cried over his bicycle. She was on her own.

Her father took a long nap on the sofa, opening his eyes from time to time to comment on whatever television program was drifting by. "Super Bowl's going to be a snorer this year." "Wrestling's fixed, everyone knows that." It was going on three by the time he left the house and Sofia followed behind, shadowing him in the alleys that ran parallel to Brighton Avenue. She thought she might show up at the last minute, shaming her father, then remembered that hadn't worked with Shemp. Instead, she crouched behind a row of yew bushes at the end of the property that bordered the vacant lot. She had retrieved many a mis-thrown football from these bushes, so she knew how thick and full they were. She also knew that the red berries were poison, a piece of vital information that had been passed from child to child as long as anyone in the neighborhood could remember. *Don't eat them little red berries. They look like cherries, but one bite will kill you.* When she was little, when she was still okay with being Fee, she had gathered berries from the bushes and used them in her Hi Ho! Cherry-O game at home. For some reason it had been far more satisfying, watching these real-if-inedible berries tumble out of the little plastic bucket. She was always careful to make sure that Brad didn't put any in his mouth, schooling him as she had been schooled.

A man was waiting for her father behind Gordon's place. He held himself as if he thought he was good looking, and maybe he was. He wore a leather jacket with the collar turned up and didn't seem to notice that the day was too cold for such a light jacket. When he opened the velvet box, he nodded and pocketed it with a shrug. But he clearly didn't appreciate the thing of beauty before him and that bothered Sofia more than anything. At least Shemp had gone to a man who thought he was a good dog deserving of a good home. This man wasn't worthy of her necklace.

She watched him get into a red car, a Corvette that Joe and the other boys had commented on enviously whenever it appeared in Gordon's parking lot. He wasn't an every-weeker, not like her dad, but he came around quite a bit. Now that she was paying attention, it seemed to her that she had seen the car all over the neighborhood—up and down Brighton Avenue, outside the snowball stand in spring and summer, in the parking lot over to Costas Inn, at the swim club. He came around a lot. Maybe Joe knew his name, or his people.

Three months later. The clocks had been turned forward and the days were milder. There was another dance at school and Sofia was going this time. Things had changed. She had changed.

"Why isn't Joe picking you up?" her mother asked.

"We're meeting there," Sofia said. "He's not a *boyfriend*-boyfriend."

"I thought he was. You've been going to the movies together on weekends, almost every Saturday since St. Patrick's Day."

"Just matinees. Things are different now. We're just friends. This isn't a date. But he'll walk me home, so you don't have to worry. Okay?"

"What time does the dance end?"

"Eleven."

"And you'll come straight home." A command, not a question.

"Sure."

Sofia shouldn't have agreed so readily; it made her mother suspicious. She studied her daughter's face, trying to figure out the exact nature of the lie. Reluctantly, she let Sofia go, yanking her dress down in the back as if she could extend the cloth. Sofia had grown some since her birthday and the pink dress was a little short, but short was the fashion of the day, as were the platform shoes she clattered along in. She had practiced in them off and on for two weeks, and they still felt like those Dutch shoes, big as boats around her skinny ankles, Olive Oyl sandals. Thank God they had ankle straps or she would have fallen out of them in less than a block.

Two blocks down, where she should have crossed the boulevard to go up to the school, she turned right instead, heading for the tavern. She didn't go in, of course, but waited by the back door, which was just a back door on Saturday nights, nothing more. Within five minutes, a red Corvette pulled into the parking lot.

"Hey," said the man in the driver's seat, a man she now knew as Brian. He wore his leather jacket with the collar turned up, although the night was a little warm for it.

"Hey," she said, getting into the car and pulling her dress so it didn't bunch up around her.

"Never seen you in a skirt before, Gino." That was his joke, calling her "Gino" after Gino Marchetti.

"And I've never seen you in anything but that leather jacket."

"Well, technically, this is our first date. There's a lot we don't know about each other, isn't there?"

Sofia smiled in what she hoped was a mysterious and alluring way.

"Maybe we should get to know each other better. What do you think?"

She nodded.

"My place okay?"

She nodded again. It had taken her three months to get to this point—three months of careful conversation in Gordon's parking lot, which began when she threw the ball at the red Corvette, presumably in a fit of celebration upon scoring a touchdown. Brian, who had just pulled up, got out and started screaming, but he settled down fast when Sofia apologized, prettily and tearfully. Plus, she hadn't damaged the car, not a bit. After that afternoon, he would stand in the lot for a few minutes, watching them play. Watching *her* play, she was sure of it. He brought sodas for everyone. He asked if they wanted to go for ice cream. He took them, one at a time, on rides around the block. Sofia always went last. The rides were short, no more than five minutes, but a lot can happen in five minutes. He told her that he managed a Merry-Go-Round clothing store, offered to get her a discount. She told him she was bored with school and thinking about dropping out. He said he had been married for a while, but he was single now. "I'm single, too," Sofia said, and he laughed as if it were the funniest thing in the world.

"Maybe we should go out sometimes, us both being single and all," he said. That had been yesterday.

The date made, it was understood that he would not come to her house, shake hands with her father, and make small talk with her mother while Sofia turned a round brush in her hair, trying to feather her bangs. Other things were understood, too. That it would not be a movie date or a restaurant date. Sofia knew what she was signing up for. Her only concern was that he might want to drive someplace, stay in the Corvette, when she wanted to see where he lived.

So she said as much, when he asked what she wanted to do. "Why don't we just go to your place?"

His eyebrows shot up. "Why not?" He passed her a brown bag that he had held between his legs as he drove and she took a careful sip. It wasn't her first drink, but she recognized that this was something sweet, liquor overlaid with a peppermint flavor, a girly drink for someone assumed to be inexperienced. Thoughtful of him.

Brian lived out Essex way, in some new apartments advertising move-in specials and a swimming pool. She hoped it wouldn't take too long because she had only so much time, but she was surprised at just how fast it happened. One minute they were kissing, and it wasn't too bad. She almost liked it. Then all of a sudden he was hovering above her, asking if she was fixed up, a question she didn't understand right away. When she did, she shook her head, and he said, "Shit," but pulled a rubber over himself, rammed into her and yelled at her to come, as if he were a coach or a gym teacher, exhorting her to do something difficult but not impossible.

"I . . . don't . . . do that," she panted out.

He took that as permission to do what he needed. Once finished, he pulled away quickly, if apologetically.

"Sorry, but if you're not on the Pill, I can't afford to hang around, you know? One little sperm gets out and my life is over. I've already got one kid to pay for."

That detail had not come up in their rides around the block.

"Uh-huh."

"You ready to go back?"

"Can't we watch some television, maybe try again?"

"Didn't get the feeling that you cared for it."

"I'm just . . . quiet. I liked it." She placed a tentative hand on his chest, which was narrow and a little sunken once out of the leather jacket. "I liked it a lot."

He chose the wrestling matches on channel 45, then arranged the covers over them and put his arm around her.

"You know, wrestling's fixed," she said.

"Who says?"

"Everybody." She didn't want to mention her father.

"So? It's the only decent thing on."

"Just seems like cheating," she said. "I don't like games like that. Like, for example . . . poker."

"Poker? I hardly knew her." He gave her rump a friendly pat and laughed. She tried to laugh, too.

"Still," she said, gesturing at the television. "It doesn't seem right. Pretending."

"Well, I guess that's why you don't do it."

"Wrestle?"

"Fake it. You know, it wouldn't hurt you to act like you liked it, just a little. If you're frigid, you're frigid, but why should a guy be left feeling like he didn't do right by you?"

"I'll try," she said. "I can do better. Maybe if there could be more kissing first."

He tried, she had to give him that. He slowed down, kissed her a lot, and she could see how it might be better. She still didn't feel moved, but she took his advice, shuddering and moaning like the women in the movies, the R-rated ones she and Joe had been sneaking into this spring. At any rate, whatever she did wore him out, and he fell asleep.

She didn't bother to put on her clothes, although she did carry her purse with her as she moved from room to room. When she didn't find the velvet box right away, she found herself taking other things in her panic and anger—a Baltimore Orioles ashtray, a pair of purple candles, a set of coasters, a Bachman-Turner Overdrive eight-track, an unused bar of Ivory soap in the bathroom. Her clunky sandals off, she was quiet and light on her feet, and he didn't stir at all until she tried a small drawer in his dresser. The drawer stuck a little and Sofia gave it a wrenching pull to force it open. He whimpered in his sleep and she froze, certain she was about to be caught, but he didn't do anything but roll over. It was the velvet box that had made the drawer stick, wedged against the top like peanut butter on the roof of someone's mouth. But when snapped it open, the box was empty. In her grief and frustration, she gave a little cry.

"What the—"

He was out of bed in an instant, grabbing her wrist and pushing her face into the pea-green carpet, crunchy with dirt and food and other things.

"Put it back, you thievin' whore, or I'll—"

She grabbed one of her shoes and hit him with it, landing a solid blow on his ear. He roared and fell back, but only for a minute, grabbing her ankle as she tried to crawl away and gather her clothes.

"Look," she said, "I'm thirteen."

He didn't let go of her ankle, but his grip loosened. "Bullshit. You told me you were in high school."

"I'm thirteen," she repeated. "Call the police. They'll believe me, I'm pretty sure. I'm thirteen and you just raped me. I never had sex before tonight."

"No way I'm your first. You didn't bleed, not even a little."

"Not everybody does. I play a lot of football. And maybe you're not big enough to make a girl bleed."

He slapped her for that and she returned his open-hand smack with her shoe, hitting him across the head so hard that he fell back and didn't get back up. Still, she kept hitting him, her frustration over the long-gone necklace driving her. She struck him for everything that had been lost, for every gift that had come and gone and couldn't be retrieved. For Brad's bicycle, for her mother's candlesticks, for Shemp. She pounded the shoe against his head again and again, as if she were a child throwing a tantrum, and in a way she was. Eventually, she fell back, her breath ragged in her chest. It was only then that she realized how still Brian was.

She put her ear to his chest. She was pretty sure his heart was still beating, that he was still breathing. Pretty sure. She put on her clothes and grabbed her macramé purse, still full of the trophies she had taken. She checked her watch, a confirmation gift. There was no way she could get home in time without a ride. She helped herself to money from Brian's wallet, and it turned out he had quite a bit. "I'll meet you outside," she told the taxi dispatcher in a whisper, although Brian didn't appear to be conscious.

It was almost midnight when she came up the walk and both parents were waiting for her.

"Where were you?"

"At the dance."

"Don't lie to us."

"I was at the dance," she repeated.

"Where's Joe? Why did you come home alone, in a cab?"

"He came with another girl, a real date. Another boy, someone I didn't know, offered to walk me home. He got . . . fresh." She pointed to the red mark on her face.

"Who was he?" her father demanded, grabbing her by the arm. "Where does he live?"

"All I know is that he was called Steve and when I wouldn't . . ." She shrugged, declining to put a name to the thing she wouldn't do. "At any rate, he put me out of the car on Holabird Avenue and I had to hail a cab. I'm sorry. I know it was wrong of me. I won't ever take a ride with a stranger again."

"You could have been killed," her mother said, clutching her to her chest. Sofia's father simply stared at her. When she went up to her room, he followed her.

"You telling the truth?" he asked.

"Yes." It seemed to Sofia that her father's eyes were boring into her macramé bag, as if he could see the stolen treasures inside, including Brian's cash. Even after the cab ride all the way from Essex, there was quite a bit left over. But maybe all he was seeing was another object that he would raid, the next time he was caught short.

"Daddy?"

"What?"

"Don't take any more of my stuff, okay?"

"You don't have any stuff, missy. Everything in this house belongs to me."

"You take any more of my stuff, I'll run away. I'll go to California and do drugs and be a hippie." This was about the worst fate that any parent could imagine for a child, back in Dundalk in 1975. True, the Summer of Love was long past, but time moved slowly in Dundalk, and they were still worried about hippies and LSD.

"You wouldn't."

"I would."

"I'll drag you home and make you sorry."

"I'll make you sorrier."

"The hell you say."

"I'll go to the police and tell them about the game at Gordon's, in the back room."

"You wouldn't."

"I would. I'll do it this very Friday night. But if you promise to leave me and my stuff alone, I'll leave you alone. Deal?"

He didn't shake on it, or even nod his head. But when her father left her room that night, Sofia knew he would never enter it again.

That was the spring that Sofia learned to bluff, and once she started, she found it hard to stop. She would never have called the cops on her father because it would have killed her mother. She was sixteen, not thirteen, but she knew that she could pass for thirteen. All of a sudden, Sofia could bluff, pretend, plan, plot, trick, cheat, cajole, threaten, blackmail. Even steal if she chose, for while the necklace belonged to her and she would have been within her rights to take it back if she had found it, she had no claim on the other things she had grabbed. Brian hadn't stolen from her, after all. He knew nothing about the necklace or who owned it or what it was worth, except in the most literal terms. He had probably pawned it soon after accepting it for payment, or given it to another girl who went for rides in that red Corvette. For several days, Sofia checked the paper worriedly, reading deep into the local section to see if a man had been found dead from a beating in an Essex apartment. She even considered getting rid of her shoes but decided that was a greater sacrifice than she needed to make. Whatever happened to Brian, his red Corvette was no longer seen up and down Brighton Avenue.

She used part of his money to buy a padlock for her bedroom door, a fancy one with a key. She used the balance to buy a lava lamp from Spencer's at East Point Mall. At night, her homework done, she watched the reddish-orange blobs break apart and rearrange themselves. Even within that narrow glass, there seemed to be no limit to the forms they could take. Her father stewed and steamed about the lock, saying she had no right to lock a room in his house. He also criticized the lava lamp, saying it proved she was on drugs because what sober, right-minded person could be entertained by such a thing.

But for all he complained, he never tried to breach the lock, although it would have been a simple thing to pry it off with a hammer, not much harder than slicing through a set of guitar strings. He was scared of her now, just a little, and incapable of concealing that fear no matter how he might try.

It was a new sensation, having someone scared of her. Sofia liked it.

# Femme Fatale

This is true: there comes a time in the life of a beautiful woman, or even an attractive one with an abundance of charm, when she realizes that she can no longer rely on her looks. If she is unusually, exceedingly self-aware, the realization is a timely one. But, more typically, it lags the physical reality by several years, like a thunderclap when a lightning storm is passing by. One one thousand, two one thousand, three one thousand, four one thousand . . . boom. One one thousand, two one thousand, three one thousand, four one thousand, five one thousand. *Boom.* The lightning is moving out, away, which is a good thing in nature, but not in the life of a beautiful woman.

That's how it happened for Mona. A gorgeous woman at twenty, a stunning woman at thirty, a striking woman at forty, a handsome woman at fifty, she was pretty much done by sixty—but only if one knew what she had been, once upon a time, and at this point that knowledge belonged to Mona alone. A sixty-eight-year-old widow when she moved into LeisureWorld, she was thought shy and retiring by her neighbors in the Creekside Condos, Phase II. She was actually an incurious snob who had no interest in the people around her. People were overrated, in Mona's opinion, unless they were men and they might be persuaded to marry you. *This is not my life,* she thought, walking the trails that wound through the pseudo-city in suburban Maryland. *This is not what I anticipated.*

Mona had expected . . . well, she hadn't thought to expect. To the extent that she had been able to imagine her old age at all, she had thought her sunset years might be something along the lines of Eloise at the Plaza—a posh place in a city center, with twenty-four-hour room service and a concierge. Such things were available—but not to those with her resources, explained the earnest young accountant who reviewed the various funds left by Mona's husband, her fourth, although Hal Wickham had believed himself to be her second.

"Mr. Wickham has left you with a conservative, diversified portfolio that will cover your costs at a comfortable level—but it's not going to allow you to live in a hotel," the accountant had said a little huffily, almost as if he were one of Hal's children, who had taken the same tone when they realized how much of their father's estate was to go to Mona. But she was his wife, after all, and not some fly-by-night spouse. They had been married fifteen years, her personal best.

"But there's over two million, and the smaller units in that hotel are going for less than a million," she said, crossing her legs at the knee and letting her skirt ride up, just a bit. Her legs were still quite shapely, but the accountant's eyes slid away from them. A shy one. These bookish types killed her.

"If you cash out half of the investments, you earn half as much on the remaining principal, which isn't enough to cover your living expenses, not with the maintenance fees involved. Don't you see?"

"I'd be paying cash," she said, leaning forward, so her breasts rested on her elbows. They were still quite impressive. Bras were one wardrobe item that had improved in Mona's lifetime. Bras were amazing now, what they did with so little fabric.

"Yes, theoretically. But there would be taxes to pay on the capital gains of the stocks acquired in your name, and your costs would outpace your earnings. You'd have to dip into your principal, and at that rate, you'd be broke in"—he did a quick calculation on his computer—"seven years. You're only sixty-eight now—"

"Sixty-one," she lied reflexively.

"All the more reason to be careful," he said. "You're going to live a long, long time."

But to Mona, now ensconced in Creekside Condos, Phase II, it seemed only that it would feel that way. She didn't golf, so she had no use for the two courses at LeisureWorld. She had never learned to cook, preferring to dine out, but she loathed eating out alone and the delivery cuisine available in the area was not to her liking. She watched television, took long walks, and spent an hour a day doing vigorous isometric exercises that she had learned in the late sixties. This was before Jane Fonda and aerobics, when there wasn't so much emphasis on sweating. The exercises were the closest thing that Mona had to a religion and they had been more rewarding than most religions, delivering exactly what they promised—and in this lifetime, too. Plus, all her husbands, even the ones she didn't count, had benefited from the final set of repetitions, a series of pelvic thrusts done in concert with vigorous yogic breathing.

One late fall day, lying on her back, thrusting her pelvis in counterpoint to her in-and-out breaths, it occurred to Mona that her life would not be much different in the posh, downtown hotel condo she had so coveted. It's not as if she would go to the theaters or museums; she had only pretended interest in those things because other people seemed to expect it. Museums bored her and theater baffled her—all those people talking so loudly, in such artificial sentences. Better restaurants wouldn't make her like eating out alone, and room service was never as hot as it should be. Her surroundings would be a considerable improvement, with truly top-of-the-line fixtures, but all that would have meant is that she would be lying on a better-quality carpet right now. Mona was not meant to be alone and if she had known that Hal was going to die only fifteen years in, she might have chosen differently. Finding a husband at the age of sixty-eight, even when one claimed to be sixty-one, had to be harder than finding a job at that age. With Hal, Mona had consciously settled. She wondered if he knew that. She wondered if he had died just to spite her.

There was a Starbucks in LeisureWorld plaza and she sometimes ended her afternoon walks there, curious to see what the fuss was about. She found the chairs abominable—had anyone over fifty ever tried to rise from these low-slung traps?—but she liked what a younger person might call the vibe. (Mona didn't actually know any young people and had been secretly glad that Hal's children loathed her so, as it gave her an excuse to have nothing to do with them or the grand-children.) She treated herself to sweet drinks, choco-late drinks, drinks with whipped cream. Mona had been on a perpetual diet since she was thirty-five, and while the discipline, along with her exercises, had kept her body hard, it had made her face harder still. The coffee drinks and pastries added weight, but no more than five or six pounds, and it was better than Botox, plumping and smoothing Mona's cheeks. She sipped her drink, stared into space, and listened to the curious non-music on the sound system. It wasn't odd to be alone in Starbucks, quite the opposite. When parties of two or three came in, full of conversation and pri-vate jokes, they were the ones who seemed out of place. The regulars all relaxed a little when those interlopers finally left.

"I hate to intrude, but I just had to say—ma'am? Ma'am?"

The man who stood next to her was young, no more than forty-five. At first glance, he appeared handsome, well put together. At second, the details betrayed him. There was a stain on his trench coat, flakes of dandruff on his shoulders and down the front of his black turtleneck sweater.

Still, he was a man and he was talking to her.

"Yes?"

"You're . . . someone, aren't you? I'm bad with names, but I don't forget faces and you—well, you were a model, right? One of the new-wave ones in the sixties, when they started going for that coltish look."

"No, you must think—"

"My apologies," he said. "Because you were better known for the movies, those avant-garde ones you did before you chucked it all and married that guy, although you could have been as big as any of them. Julie Christie. She was your only serious competition."

It took Mona a second to remember who Julie Christie was, her brain first detouring through memories of June Christie but then landing on an image of the actress. She couldn't help being pleased, if he was confusing her with someone who was serious competition for Julie Christie. Whoever he thought she was must have been gorgeous. Mona felt herself preening, even as she tried to deny the compliment. He thought she was even younger than she pretended to be.

"I'm not—"

"But you are," he said. "More beautiful than ever. Our culture is so confused about its . . . aesthetic values. I'm not talking about the veneration of age as wisdom, or the importance of experience, although those things are to the good. You are, objectively, more beautiful now than you were back then."

"Perhaps I am," she said lightly. "But I'm not whoever you think I was, so it's hard to know."

"Oh. Gosh. My apologies. I'm such an idiot—"

He sank into the purple velvet easy chair opposite her, twisting the brim of his hat nervously in his hands. She liked the hat, the fact of it. So few men bothered nowadays, and as a consequence, fewer men could pull them off. Mona was old enough, just, to remember when all serious men wore hats.

"I wish you could remember the name," she said, teasing him, yet trying to put him at ease, too. "I'd like to know this stunner that you say I resemble."

"It's not important," he said. "I feel so stupid. Fact is—I bet she doesn't look as good today as you do."

"Mona Wickham," she said, extending her hand. He bowed over it. Didn't kiss it, just bowed, a nice touch. Mona was vain of her hands, which were relatively unblemished. She kept her nails in good shape with weekly manicures and alternated her various engagement rings on the right hand. Today it was the square-cut diamond from her third marriage. Not large, but flawless.

"Bryon White," he said. "With an O, like the poet, only the R comes first."

"Nice to meet you," she said. Two or three seconds passed, and Bryon didn't release her hand and she didn't take it back. He was studying her with intense, dark eyes. Nice eyes, Mona decided.

"The thing is, you could be a movie star."

"So some said, when I was young." Which was, she couldn't help thinking, a good decade before the one in which this Bryon White thought she had been a model and an actress.

"No, I mean now. Today. I could see you as, as— Catherine, the Russian empress."

Mona frowned. Wasn't that the naughty one?

"Or, you know, Lauren Bacall. I think she's gorgeous."

"I didn't like her in that movie with Streisand."

"No, but with Altman—with Altman, she was magnificent."

Mona wasn't sure who Altman was. She remembered a store in New York, years ago, B. Altman's. After her first marriage, she had changed into a two-piece going-away suit purchased there, a dress with matching jacket. She remembered it still, standing at the top of the staircase in that killingly lovely suit, in a houndstooth check of fuchsia and black, readying to throw the bouquet. She remembered thinking: *I look good, but now I'm married, so what does it matter?* Mona's first marriage had lasted two years.

Bryon picked up on her confusion. "In *Prêt à Porter.*" This did not clear things up for Mona. "I'm sorry, it translates to—"

"I know the French," she said, a bit sharply. "I used to go to the Paris collections, buy couture." That was with her second husband, who was rich, rich, rich, until he wasn't anymore. Until it turned out he never really was. Wallace just had a high tolerance for debt, higher than his creditors, as it turned out. Mona didn't leave because he filed for bankruptcy, but it didn't make the case for staying, either.

"It was a movie a few years back. The parts were better than the whole, if I can be so bold as to criticize a genius. The thing is, I'm a filmmaker myself."

Mona hadn't been to a movie in ten years. The new ones made her sleepy. She fell asleep, woke up when something blew up, fell back asleep again. "Have you—"

"Made anything you've heard of? No. I'm an indie, but, you know, you keep your vision that way. I'm on the festival circuit, do some direct-to-video stuff. Digital has changed the equation, you know?"

Mona nodded as if she did.

"Look, I don't want to get all Schwab's on you—"

Finally, a reference that Mona understood.

"—but I'm working on something right now and you would be so perfect. If you would consider reading for me, or perhaps, even, a screen test . . . there's not much money in it, but who knows? If you photograph the way I think you will, it could mean a whole new career for you."

He offered her his card, but she didn't want to put her glasses on to read it, so she just studied it blindly, pretending to make sense of the brown squiggles on the creamy background. The paper was of good stock, heavy and textured.

"In fact, my soundstage isn't far from here, so if you're free right now—"

"I'm on foot," she said. "I walked here from my apartment."

"Oh, and you wouldn't want to get in a car with a strange man. Of course."

Mona hadn't been thinking of Bryon as strange. In fact, she had assumed he was gay. What kind of man spoke so fervently of models and old-time movie stars? But now that he said it—no, she probably shouldn't, part of her mind warned. But another part was shouting her down, telling her such opportunities come along just once. Maybe she looked better than she realized. Maybe Mona's memory of her younger self had blinded her to how attractive she still was to someone meeting her for the first time.

"I'll tell you what. I'll call you a cab, give the driver the address. Tell him to wait, with the meter running, all on me."

"Don't be silly." Mona clutched the arms of the so-called easy chair and willed herself to rise as gracefully as possible. Somehow she managed it. "Let's go."

She was not put off by the fact that Bryon's sound-stage was a large locker in one of those storage places. "A filmmaker at my level has to squeeze every nickel until it hollers," he said, pulling the garage-type door behind them. She wasn't sure how he had gotten power rigged up inside, but there was an array of professional-looking lights. The camera was a battery-powered camcorder, set up on a tripod. He even had a "set"—a three-piece 1930s-style bedroom set, with an old-fashioned vanity and bureau to match the ornately carved bed.

He asked Mona to sit on the padded stool in front of the vanity and address the camera directly, saying whatever came into her head.

"Um, testing one, two, three. Testing."

"You look great. Talk some more. Tell me about yourself."

"My name is Mona—" She stumbled for a second, forgetting the order of her surnames. After all, she had five.

"Where did you grow up, Mona?"

"Oh, here, there, and everywhere." Mona had learned long ago to be stingy with the details. They dated one so.

"What were you like as a young woman?"

"Well, I was the . . . bee's knees." An odd expression for her to use, one that pre-dated her own birth by quite a bit. She laughed at its irrelevance and Bryon laughed, too. She felt as if she had been drinking brandy Alexanders instead of venti mochas. Felt, in fact, the way she had that first afternoon with her second husband, when they left the bar at the Drake Hotel and checked into a room. She had been only thirty-five then, and she had let him keep the drapes open, proud of how her body looked in the bright daylight bouncing off Lake Michigan.

"I bet you were. I bet you were. And all the boys were crazy about you."

"I did okay."

"Oh, you did more than okay, didn't you, Mona?"

She smiled. "That's not for me to say."

"What did you wear, Mona, when you were driving those boys crazy? None of those obvious outfits for you, right? You were one of those subtle ones, like Grace Kelly. Pretty dresses, custom fit."

"Right." She brightened. Clothing was one of the few things that interested her. "That's what these girls today don't get. I had a bathing suit, a one-piece, strapless. As modest as it could be. But it was beige, just a shade darker than my own skin, and when it got wet . . ." She laughed, the memory alive to her, the effect of that bathing suit on the young men around the pool at the country club in Atlanta.

"I wish you still had that bathing suit, Mona."

"I'd still fit into it," she said. It would have been true two months ago, before she discovered Starbucks.

"I bet you would. I bet you would." Bryon's voice seemed thicker, lower, slower.

"I never let myself go, the way some women do. They say it's metabolism and menopause"—oh, she wished she could take that word back, one should never even allude to such unpleasant facts of life—"but it's just a matter of discipline."

"I sure wish I could see you in that suit, Mona."

She laughed. She hadn't had this much fun in ages. He was flirting with her, she was sure of it. Gay or not, he liked her.

"I wish I could see you in your *birthday* suit."

"Bryon!" She was on a laughing jag now, out of control.

"Why can't I, Mona? Why can't I see you in your birthday suit?"

Suddenly, the only sound in the room was Bryon's breath, ragged and harsh. It was hard to see anything clearly, with the lights shining in her eyes, but Mona could see that he was steadying the camera with just one hand.

"You want to see me naked?" she asked.

Bryon nodded.

"Just . . . see?"

"That's how we start, usually. Slow like. Everyone has his or her own comfort zone."

"And the video—is that for your eyes only?"

"I told you, I'm an independent filmmaker. Direct to video. A growing market."

"People pay?"

Another shy nod. "It's sort of a . . . niche within the industry."

"Niche."

"It's my niche," he said. "It's what I like. I make other films about, um, things I don't like so much. But I love watching truly seasoned women teach young men about life."

"And you'd pay for this?"

"Of course."

"How much?"

"Some. Enough."

"Just to look? Just to see me, as I am?"

"A little for that. More for . . . more."

"How much?" Mona repeated. She was keen to know her worth.

He came around from behind the camera, retrieved a laminated card from the drawer in the vanity table, then sat on the bed and patted the space next to him. Why laminated? Mona decided not to think about that. She moved to the bed and studied the card, not unlike the menu of services and prices at a spa. She could do that. And that. Not that, but definitely that and that. The fact was, she had done most of these things, quite happily.

"Let me make you a star, Mona."

"Are you my leading man?"

"Our target demographic prefers to see younger men with the women. I just need to get some film of you to take to my partner so he'll underwrite it. I have a very well-connected financial backer."

"Who?"

"Oh, I'll never say. He's very discreet. Anyway, he likes to know that the actresses are . . . up to the challenges of their roles. Usually a striptease will do, a little, um, self-stimulation. But it's always good to have extra footage. I make a lot of films, but these are the ones I like best. The ones I watch."

"Well, then," Mona said, unbuttoning her blouse. "Let's get busy."

*Fetish,* Mona said to herself as she shopped in the Giant. *Fetish,* she thought as she retrieved her mail from the communal boxes in the lobby. *I am a fetish.* This was the word that Bryon used to describe her "work," which, two months after their first meeting, comprised four short films. She had recoiled at the word at first, feeling it marked her as a freak, something from a sideshow. "Niche" had been so much nicer. But Bryon assured her that the customers who bought her videos were profoundly affected by her performance. There was no irony, no belittling. She was not the butt of the joke, she was the object of their, um, affection.

"Different people like different things," he said to her in Starbucks one afternoon. She was feeling a little odd, as she always did when a film was completed. It was so strange to spend an afternoon having sex and not be taken shopping afterward, just given a cashier's check. "Our cultural definitions of sexuality are simply too narrow."

"But your other films, the other tastes you serve"— Mona by now had familiarized herself with Bryon's catalog, which included the usual whips and chains, but also a surprisingly successful series of films that featured obese women sitting on balloons—"they're sick."

"There you go, being judgmental," Bryon said. "Children is wrong, I'll give you that. Because children can't consent. Everything else is fair game."

"Animals can't consent."

"I don't do animals, either. Adults and inanimate objects, that's my credo."

It was an odd conversation to be having in her Starbucks at the LeisureWorld Plaza, that much was sure. Mona looked around nervously, but no one was paying attention. The other customers probably thought Mona and Bryon were a mother and son, although she didn't think she looked old enough to be Bryon's mother.

"By the way"—Byron produced a small stack of envelopes—"we've gotten some letters for you."

"Letters?"

"Fan mail. Your public."

"I'm not sure I want to read them."

"That's up to you. Whatever you do—don't make the mistake of responding to them, okay? The less they know about Sexy Sadie, the better. Keep the mystery." He left her alone with her public.

Keep the mystery. Mona liked that phrase. It could be her credo, to borrow Bryon's word. Then she began to think about the mysteries that Bryon was keeping. If she had already received—she stopped to count, touching the envelopes gingerly—eleven pieces of fan mail, then how many fans must she have? If eleven people wrote, then hundreds—no, thousands—must watch and enjoy what she did.

So why was she getting paid by the job, with no percentage, no profit-sharing? God willing, her health assured, she could really build on this new career. After all, they actually had to make her look older, dressing her in dowdy dresses, advising her to make her voice sound more quavery than it was. Bryon had the equipment, Bryon had the distribution—but only Mona had Mona. How replaceable was she?

**"Forget it,"** Bryon said when she broached the topic on the set a few weeks later. "I was up-front with you from the start. I pay you by the act. By the piece, if you will. No participation. You signed a contract, remember?"

Gone was the rapt deference from that first day at Starbucks. True, Mona had long ago figured out that it was an act, but she had thought there was a germ of authenticity in it, a genuine respect for her looks and presence. How long had Bryon been stalking her? she wondered now. Had he approached her because of her almost lavender eyes, or because she looked vulnerable and lonely? Easy, as they used to say.

"But I have fans," she said. "People who like me, specifically. That ought to be worth a renegotiation."

"You think so? Then sue me in Montgomery County courts. Your neighbors in LeisureWorld will probably love reading about that in the suburban edition of the *Washington Post*."

"I'll quit," she said.

"Go ahead," Bryon said. "You think you're the only lonely old lady who needs a little attention? I'll put the wig and the dress on some other old bag. My films, my company, my concept."

"Some concept," Mona said, trying not to let him see how much the words hurt. So she was just a lonely old lady to him, a mark. "I sit in a room, a young man rings my doorbell, I end up having sex with him. So far, it's been a UPS man, a delivery boy for a florist, a delivery boy for the Chinese restaurant, and a young Mormon on a bicycle. What's next, a Jehovah's Witness peddling the *Watchtower*?"

"That's not bad," Bryon said, pausing to write a quick note to himself. "Look, this is the deal. I pay you by the act. You don't want to do it, you don't have to. I'm always scouting new talent. Maybe I'll find an Alzheimer's patient, who won't be able to remember from one day to the next what she did, much less try to hold me up for a raise. You old bitches are a dime a dozen."

It was the "old bitches" part that hurt.

**When Mona's** second husband's fortune had proved to be largely smoke and mirrors, she had learned to be more careful about picking her subsequent husbands. That was in the pre-Internet days, when determining a person's personal fortune was much more labor-intensive. She was pleased to find out from a helpful librarian how easy it was now to compile what was once known as a Dun and Bradstreet on someone, how to track down the silent partner in Bryon White's LLC.

Within a day, she was having lunch with Bernard Weinman, a dignified gentleman about her own age. He hadn't wanted to meet with her, but as Mona detailed sweetly what she knew about Bernie's legitimate business interests—more information gleaned with the assistance of the nice young librarian—and his large contributions to a local synagogue, he decided they could meet after all. He chose a quiet French restaurant in Bethesda, and when he ordered white wine with lunch, Mona followed suit.

"I have a lot of investments," he said. "I'm not hands-on."

"Still, I can't imagine you want someone indiscreet working for you."

"Indiscreet?"

"How do you think I tracked you down? Bryon talks. A lot."

Bernie Weinman bent over his onion soup, spilling a little on his tie. But it was a lovely tie, expensive and well made. For this lunch meeting, he wore a black suit and crisp white shirt with large gold cuff links.

"Bryon's very good at . . . what he does. His mail-order business is so steady it's almost like an annuity. I get a very good return on my money, and I've never heard of him invoking my name."

"Well, he did. All I did was make some suggestions about how to"—Mona groped for the odd business terms she had heard on television—"how to grow your business, and he got very short with me, said you had no interest in doing things differently. And when I asked if I might speak to you, he got very angry, threatened to expose me. If he would blackmail me, a middle-class widow with no real money, imagine what he might do to you."

"Bryon knows me well enough not to try that," Bernie Weinman said. After a morning at the Olney branch of the Montgomery County Public Library, Mona knew him pretty well, too. She knew the rumors that had surrounded the early part of his career, the alleged but never proven ties to the numbers runner up in Baltimore. Bernie Weinman had built his fortune from corner liquor stores in Washington,

D.C., which eventually became the basis for his chain of party-supply stores. But he had clearly never lost his taste for the recession-proof businesses that had given him his start—liquor, gambling, prostitution. All he had done was live long enough and give away enough money that people were willing to forget his past. Apparently, the going price of redemption in Montgomery County was five million dollars to the capital fund at one's synagogue.

"Does Bryon know you so well that he wouldn't risk keeping two sets of books?"

"What?"

"I know what I get paid. I know how cheaply the product is made and produced, and I know how many units are moved. He's cheating you."

"He wouldn't."

"He would—and brag about it, too. He said you were a stupid old man who was no longer on top of his game."

"He said that?"

"He said much worse."

"Tell me."

"I c-c-can't," Mona whispered, looking shyly into her salade niçoise as if she had not made four adult films under the moniker "Sexy Sadie."

"Paraphrase."

"He said . . . he said there was no film in the world that could, um, incite you. That you were . . . starchless."

"That little SOB."

"He laughs at you, behind your back. He practically brags about how he's ripping you off. I've put myself in harm's way, just talking to you, but I couldn't let this go on."

"I'll straighten him out—"

"No! Because he'll know it was me and he'll—he's threatened me, Bernie." This first use of his name was a calculated choice. "He says no one will miss me and I suppose he's right."

"You don't have any children?"

"Just stepchildren, and I'm afraid they're not very kind to me. It was hard for them, their father remarrying, even though he had been a widower for years." Divorced for two years, and Mona had been the central reason, but the kids wouldn't have liked her under any circumstances. "No, no one would miss me. Except my fans."

She let the subject go then, directing the conversation to Bernie and his accomplishments, the legitimate ones. She asked questions whose answers she knew perfectly well, touched his arm when he decided they needed another bottle of wine, and, although she drank only one glass to his every two, declared herself unfit to drive home. She was going to take a taxi, but Bernie insisted on driving her, and accompanying her to the condo door, to make sure she was fine, and then into her bedroom, where he further assessed her fineness. He was okay, not at all starchless, somewhere between a sturdy baguette and a loaf of Wonder bread. She'd had worse. True, he felt odd, after the series of hard-bodied young men that Bryon had hired for her. But this, at least, did not fall under the category of fetish. He was seventy-three and she was sixty-eight-passing-for-sixty-one. This was normal. This was love.

Bryon White was never seen again. He simply disappeared, and there was no one who mourned him or even really noticed. And while Bernie Weinman was happily married, he had strong opinions about how his new mistress should spend her time. Mona took over the business but had to retire from performing, at least officially, although she sometimes auditioned the young men, just to be sure. Give Bryon credit, Mona thought, now that she had to scout the coffee shops and grocery stores, recruiting the new talent. It was harder than it looked and Bryon's instincts had been unerring, especially when it came to Mona. She really was a wonderful actress.

# One True Love

His face didn't register at first. Probably hers didn't either. It wasn't a face-oriented business, strange to say. In the early days, on the streets, she had made a point of studying the men's faces as a means of protection. Not because she thought she'd ever be downtown, picking someone out of a lineup. Quite the opposite. If she wasn't careful, if she didn't size them up beforehand, she'd be on a gurney in the morgue and no one would give a shit. Certainly not Val, although he'd be pissed in principle at being deprived of anything he considered his property. And while Brad thought he loved her, dead was dead. Who needed postmortem devotion?

So she had learned to look closely at her potential customers. Sometimes just the act of that intense scrutiny was enough to fluster a man and he moved on, which was the paradoxical proof that he was okay. Others stared back, welcoming her gaze, inviting it. That kind really creeped her out. You wanted nervous, but not too nervous; any trace of self-loathing was a big tip. In the end, she had probably walked away from more harmless ones than not, guys whose problems were nothing more than a losing card in the great genetics lottery—dry lips, a dead eye, or that bad skin that always seemed to signal villainy, perhaps because of all the acne-pitted bad guys in bad movies. Goes to show what filmmakers knew; Val's face couldn't be smoother. Still, she never regretted her vigilance, although she had paid for it in the short run, taking the beatings that were her due when she didn't meet Val's quotas. But she was alive and no one raised a hand to her anymore, not unless they paid handsomely for that privilege. She had come a long way.

Twenty-seven miles, to be precise, for that was the distance from where her son had been conceived in a motel that charged by the hour and the suburban soccer field where he was now playing forward for the Sherwood Forest Robin Hoods. He was good, and not just motherly pride good, but truly skilled, fleet and lithe. Over the years, she had persuaded herself that he bore no resemblance to his father, an illusion that allowed her to enjoy unqualified delight in his long limbs, his bright red hair and freckles. Scott was Scott, hers alone. Not in a smothering way, far from it. But when he was present, no one else mattered to her. At these weekend games, she stayed tightly focused on him. It was appalling, in her private opinion, that some other mothers and fathers barely followed the game, chatting on their cell phones or to one another. And during the breaks, when she did try to make conversation, it was unbearably shallow. She wanted to talk about the things she read in the *Economist* or heard on NPR, things she had to know to keep up with her clientele. They wanted to talk about aphids and restaurants. It was a relief when the game resumed and she no longer had to make the effort.

She never would have noticed the father on the other side of the field if his son hadn't collided with Scott, one of those heart-stopping, freeze-frame moments in which one part of your brain insists it's okay, even as another part helpfully supplies all the worst-case scenarios. Stitches, concussion, paralysis. Play was suspended and she went flying across the still-dewy grass. Adrenaline seemed to heighten all her senses, taking her out of herself, so she was aware of how she looked. She was equally aware of the frumpy, overweight blond mother who commented to a washed-out redhead:

"Can you believe she's wearing Tod's loafers and Prada slacks to a kids' soccer game?" But she wasn't the kind to go around in yoga pants and tracksuits, although she actually practiced yoga and ran every morning.

Scott was all right, thank God. So was the other boy. Their egos were more bruised than their bodies, so they staggered around a bit, exaggerating their injuries for the benefit of their teammates. It was only polite to introduce herself to the father, to stick out her hand and say: "Heloise Lewis."

"Bill Carroll," he said. "Eloise?"

"Heloise. As in hints from."

He shook her hand. She had recognized him the moment he said his name, for he was a credit card customer, William F. Carroll. He had needed a second more, but then he knew her as Jane Smith. Not terribly original, but it did the job. Someone had to be named Jane Smith, and it was so bogusly fake that it seemed more real as a result.

"Heloise," he repeated. "Well, it's very nice to meet you, Heloise. Your boy go to Dunwood?"

His vowels were round with fake sincerity, a bad sign. Most of her regulars were adequate liars; they had to be to juggle the compartmentalized lives they had created for themselves. And she was a superb liar. Bill Carroll wasn't even adequate.

"We live in Turner's Grove, but he goes to private school. Do you live—"

"Divorced," he said briefly. "Weekend warrior, driving up from D.C. every other Saturday, expressly for this tedium."

That explained everything. She hadn't screwed up. Her system simply wasn't as foolproof as she thought. Before Heloise's company took on a new client, she always did a thorough background check, looking up vehicle registrations, tracking down the home addresses. (And if no home address could be found, she refused the job.) A man who lived in her zip code, or even a contiguous one, was rejected out of hand, although she might assign him to one of her associates.

She hadn't factored in divorce. Perhaps that was an oversight that only the never-married could make.

"Nice to meet you," she said.

"Nice to meet you." He smirked.

This was trouble. What kind of trouble, she wasn't sure yet, but definitely trouble.

**When Heloise** decided to move to the suburbs, shortly after Scott was born, it had seemed practical and smart, even mainstream. Wasn't that what every parent did? She hadn't anticipated how odd it was for a single woman to buy a house on one of the best cul-desacs in one of the best subdivisions in Anne Arundel County, the kind of houses that newly single mothers usually sold post-divorce because they couldn't afford to buy out the husband's 50 percent stake in the equity. She had chosen the house for the land, almost an acre, which afforded the most privacy, never thinking of the price. Then she enrolled Scott in private school, another flag: what was the point of moving here if one could afford private school? The neighbors had begun to gossip almost immediately, and their speculation inspired the backstory she needed. A widow—yes. A terrible accident, one of which she still could not speak. She was grateful for her late husband's prag-matism and foresight when it came to insurance, but—she'd rather have him. Of course.

Of course, her new confidantes echoed back, al-though some seemed less than convinced. She could almost see their brains working it through: if I could lose the husband and keep the house, it wouldn't be so bad. It was the brass ring of divorced life in this cul-de-sac, losing the husband and keeping the house. (The Dunwood school district was less desir-able and therefore less pricy, which explained how Bill Carroll's ex maintained her life there.) Heloise simply hadn't counted on the scrutiny her personal life would attract.

She had counted on her ability to construct a story about her work that would quickly stupefy anyone who asked, not that many of these stay-at-home mothers seemed curious about work. "I'm a lobbyist," she said. "The Women's Full Employment Network. I work in Annapolis, Baltimore, and D.C. as necessary, advocating parity and full benefits for what is traditionally considered women's work. So-called pink-collar jobs."

"How about pay and benefits for what we do?" her neighbors inevitably asked. "Is there anyone who works harder than a stay-at-home mom?"

*Ditchdiggers,* she thought. Janitresses and custodians. Gardeners. Meter readers. The girl who stands on her feet all day next to a fryer, all for the glory of minimum wage. Day laborers, men who line up on street corners and take whatever is offered. Hundreds of people you stare past every day, barely recognizing them as human. Prostitutes.

"No one works harder than a mother," she always replied with an open, honest smile. "I wish there was some way I could organize us, establish our value to society in a true dollars-and-cents way. Maybe one day."

Parenting actually was harder than the brand of prostitution that she now practiced. She made her own hours. She made top-notch wages. She was her own boss and an excellent manager. With the help of an exceptionally nonjudgmental nanny, she had been able to arrange her life so she never missed a soccer game or a school concert. If sleeping with other women's husbands was what it took, so be it. She could not imagine a better line of work for a single mother.

For eight years, it had worked like a charm, her two lives never overlapping.

And then Scott ran into Bill Carroll's son at the soccer game. And while no bones cracked and no wounds opened up, it was clear to her that she would bear the impact of this collision for some time to come.

**"We have** to talk," said the message on her cell phone, a number that she never answered, a phone on which she never spoke. It was strictly for incoming messages, which gave her plausible deniability if a message was ever intercepted. His voice was clipped, imperious, as if she had annoyed him deliberately. "We have to talk ASAP."

No we don't, she thought. Let it go. I know and you know. I know you know I know. You know I know you know. Talking is the one thing we don't have to do.

But she called him back.

"There's a Starbucks near my office," he said. "Let's meet accidentally there in about an hour. You know—aren't you Scott's mom? Aren't you Billy Jr.'s dad? Blah, blah, blah, yadda, yadda, yadda."

"I don't think we really need to speak."

"I do." He was surprisingly bossy in his public life, given his preferences in his private one. "We need to straighten a few things out. And, who knows, if we settle everything, maybe I'll throw a little business your way."

"That's not how I work," she said. "You know that. I don't take referrals from clients. It's not healthy, clients knowing each other."

"Yeah, well, that's one of the things we're going to talk about. How you work. And how you're going to work from now on."

**He wasn't** the first bully in her life. That honor belonged to her father, who had beaten her when he got tired of beating her mother. "How do you stay with him?" she had asked her mother more than once. "You only have one true love in your life," her mother responded, never making it clear if her true love was Heloise's father or some long-gone man who had consigned her to this joyless fate.

Then there was Heloise's high school boyfriend, the one who persuaded her to drop out of college and come to Baltimore with him, where he promptly dumped her. She had landed a job as a dancer at one of the Block's nicer clubs, but she had gotten in over her head with debt, trying to balance work and college. That had brought Val into her life. She had worked for him for almost ten years before she had been able to strike out on her own, and there had been a lot of luck in that. A lot of luck and not a little deceit.

People who thought they knew stuff, people on talk shows, quack doctors with fake credentials, had lots of advice about bullies. Bullies back down if you stand up to them. Bullies are scared inside.

Bully-shit. If Val was scared inside, then his outsides masked it pretty well. He sent her to the hospital twice and she was pretty sure she would be out on the third strike if she ever made the mistake of standing up to him again. Confronting Val hadn't accomplished anything. Being sneaky, however, going behind his back while smiling to his face, had worked beautifully. That had been her first double life—Val's smiling consort, Brad's confidential informant. What she was doing now was kid stuff, compared to all that.

"Chai latte," she told the counterwoman at the Starbucks in Dupont Circle. The girl was beautiful, with tawny skin and green eyes. She could do much better for herself than a job at a coffee shop, even one that paid health insurance. Heloise offered health insurance to the girls who were willing to be on the books of the Women's Full Employment Network. She paid toward their health plans and Social Security benefits, everything she was required to do by law.

"Would you like a muffin with that?" Suggestive selling, a good technique. Heloise used it in her business.

"No thanks. Just the chai, tall."

"Heloise! Heloise Lewis! Fancy seeing you here."

His acting had not improved in the seventy-two hours since they had first met. He inspected her with a smirk, much too proud of himself, his expression all but announcing: I know what you look like naked.

She knew the same about him, of course, but it wasn't an image on which she wanted to dwell.

Heloise hadn't changed her clothes for this meeting. Nor had she put on makeup, or taken her hair out of its daytime ponytail. She was hoping that her Heloise garb might remind Bill Carroll that she was a mother, another parent, someone like him. She did not know him well, outside the list of preferences she had cataloged on a carefully coded index card. Despite his tough talk on the phone, he might be nicer than he seemed.

"The way I see it," he said, settling in an overstuffed chair and leaving her a plain wooden one, "you have more to lose than I do."

"Neither one of us has to lose anything. I've never exposed a client and I never will. It makes no sense as a business practice."

He looked around, but the Starbucks was relatively empty, and in any event, he didn't seem the type capable of pitching his voice low.

"You're a whore," he announced.

"I'm aware of how I make my living."

"It's illegal."

"Yes—for both of us. Whether you pay or are paid, you've broken the law."

"Well, you've just lost one paying customer."

Was that all he wanted to establish? Maybe he wasn't as big a dick as he seemed. "I understand. If you'd like to work with one of my associates—"

"You don't get it. I'm not paying anymore. Now that I know who you are and where you live, I think you ought to take care of me for free."

"Why would I do that?"

"Because if you don't, I'm going to tell everyone you're a whore."

"Which would expose you as my client."

"Who cares? I'm divorced. Besides, how are you going to prove I was a customer? I can out you without exposing myself."

"There are your credit card charges." American Express Business Platinum, the kind that accrued airline miles. She was better at remembering the cards than the men themselves. The cards were tangible, concrete. The cards were individual in a way the men were not.

"Business expenses. Consulting fees, right? That's what it says on the bill."

"Why would a personal injury lawyer need to consult with the Women's Full Employment Network?"

"To figure out how to value the lifelong earning power of women injured in traditional pink-collar jobs." His smile was triumphant, ugly and triumphant. He had clearly put a lot of thought into his answer and was thrilled at the chance to deliver it so readily. But then he frowned, which made his small eyes even smaller. It would be fair to describe his face as piggish, with those eyes and the pinkish nose, which was very broad at the base and more than a little upturned. "How did you know I was a personal injury lawyer?"

"I research my clients pretty carefully."

"Well, maybe it's time that someone researched *you* pretty carefully. Cops. A prosecutor hungry for a high-profile case. The call girl on the cul-de-sac. It would make a juicy headline. "

"Bill, I assure you I have no intention of telling anyone about our business relationship if that's what you're worried about."

"What I'm worried about is that you're expensive and I wouldn't mind culling you from my overhead. You bill more per hour than I do. Where do you get off, charging that much?"

"I get off," she said, "where you get off. You know, right at that moment I take my little finger—"

"Shut up." His voice was so loud that it broke through the dreamy demeanor of the counter girl, who started and exchanged a worried look with Heloise. A moment ago, Heloise had been pitying her, and now the girl was concerned about Heloise. That was how quickly things could change. "Look, this is the option. I get free rides for life or I make sure that everyone knows what you are. Everyone. Including your cute little boy."

He was shrewd, bringing Scott into the conversation. Scott was her soft spot, her only vulnerability. Before she got pregnant, when she was the only person she had to care for, she had done a pretty shitty job of it. But Scott had changed all that, even before he was a flesh-and-blood reality. She would do anything to protect Scott, anything. Ask Brad for a favor, if need be, although she hated leaning on Brad.

She might even go to Scott's father, not that he had any idea he was Scott's father, and she was never going to inform him of that fact. But she didn't like asking him for favors under any circumstances. Scott's father thought he was in her debt. She needed to maintain the equilibrium afforded by that lie.

"I can't afford to work for free."

"It won't be every week. And I understand I won't have bumping rights over the paying customers. I'm just saying that we'll go on as before, once or twice a month, but I don't pay for it anymore. It will be like dating, without all the boring socializing. What do the kids call it? A booty call."

"I have to think about this," she said.

"No you don't. See you next Wednesday."

He hadn't even offered to pay for her chai or buy her a muffin.

**She called** Brad first, but the moment she saw him, waiting in the old luncheonette on Eastern Avenue, she realized it had been a mistake. Brad had taken an oath to serve and protect, but the oath had been for those who obeyed the laws, not those who lived in flagrant disregard of them. He had already done more for her than she had any right to expect. He owed her nothing.

Still, it was hard for a woman, any woman, not to exploit a man's enduring love, not to go back to that well and see if you could still draw on it. Brad knew her and he loved her. Well, he thought he knew her and he loved the person he thought he knew. Close enough.

"You look great," he said, and she knew he wasn't being polite. Brad preferred daytime Heloise to the nighttime version, always had.

"Thanks."

"Why did you want to see me?"

*I need advice on how to get a shameless, grasping parasite out of my life.* But she didn't want to plunge right in. It was crass.

"It's been too long."

He placed his hands over hers, held them on the cool Formica tabletop, indifferent to the coffee he had ordered. The coffee here was awful, had always been awful. She was not one to romanticize these old diners. Starbucks was taking over the world by offering a superior product, changing people's perceptions about what they deserved and what they could afford. In her private daydreams, she would like to be the Starbucks of sex-for-hire, delivering guaranteed quality to business travelers everywhere. No, she wouldn't call it Starfucks, although she had seen that joke on the Internet. For one thing, it would sound like one of those celebrity impersonator services. Besides, it wasn't elegant. She wanted to take a word or reference that had no meaning in the culture and make it come to mean good, no-strings, quid pro quo sex. Like . . . "zephyr." Only not "zephyr," because it denoted quickness, and she wanted to market sex as a spa service for men, a day or night of pampering with a long list of services and options. So not "zephyr," but a word like it, one that sounded cool and elegant but whose real meaning was virtually unknown and therefore malleable in the public imagination. Amazon.com was another good example. Or eBay. Familiar yet new.

But that fantasy seemed more out of reach than ever. Now she would settle for keeping the life she already had.

"Seriously, Heloise. What's up?"

"I missed you," she said lamely, yet not inaccurately. She missed Brad's adoration, which never seemed to dim. For a long time she had expected him to marry someone else, to pursue the average family he claimed he wanted to have with her. But now that they were both pushing forty with a very short stick, she was beginning to think that Brad liked things just the way they were. As long as he carried a torch for a woman he could never have, he didn't have to marry or have kids. Back when Scott was born, Brad had dared to believe he was the father, had even hopefully volunteered to take a DNA test. She had to break it to him very gently that he wasn't, and that she didn't want him to be part of Scott's life under any circumstances, even as an uncle or Mommy's "friend." She couldn't afford for Scott to have any contact with her old life, no matter how remote or innocuous.

"Everyone okay? You, Scott? Melina?" Melina was her nanny, the single most important person in her employ. The girls could come and go, but Heloise could never make things work without Melina.

"We're all fine."

"So what's this meeting about?"

"Like I said, I missed you." She sounded more persuasive this time.

"Weezie, Weezie, Weezie," he said, using the pet name that only he was allowed. "Why didn't things work out between us?"

"I always felt it was because I wanted to continue working after marriage."

"Well, yeah, but . . . it's not like I was opposed to you working on principle. It was just—a cop can't be married to a prostitute, Weezie."

"It's my career," she said. It was her career and her excuse. No matter what she had chosen as her vocation, Brad would never have been the right man for her. He had taken care of her on the streets, asking nothing in return, and she had taken him to bed a time or two, grateful for all he did. But it had never been a big passion for her. It had, in fact, been more like a free sample, the kind of thing a corporation does to build up community goodwill. A free sample to someone she genuinely liked, but a freebie nonetheless, like one of those little boxes of detergent left in the mailbox. You might wash your clothes in it, but it probably didn't change your preferences in the long run.

They held hands, staring out at Eastern Avenue. They had been sweeping this area lately, Brad said, and the trade had dried up. But they both knew that was only temporary. Eventually the girls and the boys came back, and the men were never far behind. They all came back, springing up like mushrooms after a rain.

**Her meeting** with Scott's dad, in the visiting room at Supermax, was even briefer than her coffee date with Brad. Scott's father was not particularly surprised to see her; she had made a point of coming every few months or so, to keep up the charade that she had nothing to do with him being here. His red hair seemed duller after so many years inside, but maybe it was just the contrast with the orange DOC uniform. She willed herself not to see her boy in this man, to acknowledge no resemblance. Because if Scott was like his father on the outside, he might be like his father on the inside, and that she could not bear.

"Faithful Heloise," Val said, mocking her.

"I'm sorry. I know I should come more often."

"It takes a long time to put a man to death in Maryland, but they do get around to it eventually. Bet you'll miss me when I'm gone."

"I don't want you to be killed." Just locked up forever and forever. Please, God, whatever happens, he must never get out. One look at Scott and he'll know. He was hard enough to get rid of as a pimp. Imagine what he'll be like as a parent. He'll take Scott just because he can, because Val never willingly gave up anything that was his.

"Well, you know how it is when you work for yourself. You're always hustling, always taking on more work than you can handle."

"How are things? How many girls have you brought in?"

Unlike Brad, Val was interested in her business, perhaps because he felt she had gained her acumen from him. Then again, if he hadn't been locked up, she never would have been allowed to go into business for herself. That's what happened, when your loan shark became your pimp. You never got out from under. Figuratively and literally.

But now that Val couldn't control her, he was okay with her controlling herself. It was better than another man doing it.

"Things are okay. I figure I have five years to make the transition to full-time management."

"Ten, you continue taking care of yourself. You look pretty good for your age."

"Thanks." She fluttered her eyelashes automatically, long in the habit of using flirtation as a form of appeasement with him. "Here's the thing . . . there's a guy, who's making trouble for me. Trying to extort me. We ran into each other in real life and now he says he'll expose me if I don't start doing him for free."

"It's a bluff. It's fuckin' Cold War shit."

"What?"

"The guy has as much to lose as you do. He's all talk. It's like he's the USSR and you're the USA back in the 1980s. No matter who strikes first, you both go sky-high."

"He's divorced. And he's a personal injury lawyer, so I don't know how much he cares about his reputation. He might even welcome the publicity."

"Naw. Trust me on this. He's just fucking with you."

Val didn't know about Scott, of course, and never would if she could help it. The problem was, it was harder to make the case for how panicky she was if she couldn't mention Scott.

"I've got a bad feeling about this," she insisted. "He's a loose cannon. I always assumed that guys who came to me had to have a certain measure of built-in shame about what they did. He doesn't."

"Then give me his name and I'll arrange for things to happen."

"You can do that from in here?"

He shrugged. "I'm on death row. What have I got to lose?"

It was what she wanted, what she had come for. She would never ask for such a favor, but if Val volunteered—well, would that be so wrong? Yet the moment she heard him make the offer, she couldn't take it. She had tested herself, walked right up to the edge of the abyss that was Val, allowed him to tempt her with the worst part of himself.

Besides, if Val could have some nameless, faceless client killed from here, then he could—she didn't want to think about it.

"No. No. I'll think of something."

*Not my son's face,* she told herself as she bent to kiss his cheek. *Not my son's freckles. Not my son's father.* But he was, she could never change that fact. And while she visited Val, in part, to convince him that she had nothing to do with the successful prosecution that had been brought against him when undercover narc Brad Stone somehow found the gun used to kill a young man, she also came because she was grateful to him for the gift of Scott. She hated him with every fiber of her being, but she wouldn't have Scotty if it weren't for him. She wouldn't have Scott if it weren't for Val.

Maybe she did know something about divorce, after all.

**Five days** went by, days full of work. Congress was back in session, which always meant an uptick in business. She was beginning to resign herself to the idea of doing things Bill Carroll's way. He was not the USSR and she was not the USA. The time for Cold Wars was long past. He was a terrorist in a breakaway republic, determined to have the status he sought at any cost. He was a man of his word and his words were ugly, inflammatory, dangerous. She met with him at a D.C. hotel as he insisted, picking up the cost of the room, which was usually covered by her clients. He left two dollars on the dresser, then said: "For housekeeping, not for you," with a cruel laugh. Oh, he cracked himself up.

She treated herself to room service, then drove home in a funk, flipping on WTOP to check traffic, not that it was usually a problem this late. A body had just been discovered in Rock Creek Park, a young woman. Heloise could tell from the flatness of the report that it was a person who didn't matter, a homeless woman or a prostitute. She grieved for the young woman, for she sensed automatically that the death would never be solved. It could have been one of hers. It could have been her. You tried to be careful, but nothing was fool-proof. Look at the situation she was in with Bill Carroll. You couldn't prepare for every contingency. That was her mistake, thinking she could control everything.

Bill Carroll.

Once at home, she called her smartest girl, Trini, a George Washington University coed who took her money under the table and didn't ask a lot of questions. Trini learned her part quickly and well, and within an hour she was persuading police that she had seen a blue Mercedes stop in the park and roll the body out of the car. Yes, it was dark, but she had seen the man's face lighted by the car's interior dome and it wasn't a face one would forget, given the circumstances. Trini gave a partial plate—a full one wouldn't have worked, not in the long run—and it took police only a day to track down Bill Carroll and bring him in for question-ing. By then, Heloise had Googled him, found a photo on the Internet and e-mailed it to Trini, who subse-quently had no problem picking him out of a lineup.

From the first, Bill Carroll insisted that Heloise Lewis would establish his alibi, but he didn't mention that their assignation was anything more than two adults meeting for a romantic encounter. Which it technically was, after all. No money had exchanged hands, at his insistence. Perhaps he thought it would be a bad idea, confessing to a relationship with one prostitute while being investigated in the murder of another. At any rate, Heloise corroborated his version. She told police that they had a date in a local hotel. No, the reservation was in her name. Well, not her name, but the name of "Jane Smith." She was a single mother, trying to be careful. Didn't Dr. Laura always say that single parents needed to keep their kids at a safe distance from their relationships? True, hers was the only name on the hotel register. He had wanted it that way. No, she wasn't sure why. No, she didn't think anyone on the staff had seen him come and go; she had ordered a cup of tea from room service after he left, which was why she was alone in the room at 11 P.M. She spoke with many a hesitation and pause, always telling the truth, yet never sounding truthful. That's how good a liar Heloise was. She could make the truth sound like a lie, a lie sound like the truth.

Still, her version was strong enough to keep police from charging him. After all, there was no physical evidence in his car and they had only two letters from the plate. Witnesses did make mistakes, even witnesses as articulate and positive as the wholesome young GW student. That was when Heloise told Bill she was prepared to recant everything, go to the police and confess that she had lied to cover up for a longtime client.

"I'll tell them it was all made up, that I did it as a favor to you, unless you promise to leave me alone from now on." They were meeting in the Starbucks on Dupont Circle again, but the beautiful girl had the day off. That, or she had moved on.

"But then they'll know you're a whore."

"A whore who can provide your alibi."

"I didn't do anything." His voice was whiny, put-upon. Then again, he was being framed for a crime he didn't commit, so his petulance was earned.

"I heard there's a police witness who picked you out of the lineup, put you at the scene. And once I out myself as a whore—well, then it's an established fact that you traffic in whores. That's not going to play very well for you. In fact, I'll tell the police that you wanted me to do something that I didn't want to do, an act so degrading and hideous I can't even speak of it, and we argued and you went slamming out of the room, angry and frustrated. Maybe that poor dead girl paid the price for your aggression and hostility."

He very quickly came to see it her way. He muttered and complained, but once he left the Starbucks, she was sure she would never see him again. Not even back in the suburbs, for she had signed Scott up for travel soccer, having ascertained that Bill Carroll's son was not skilled enough to make the more competitive league. It was a lot more time, but then—she had always had time for Scott. She had set up her life so she was always there for her son. If there was a better gig for a single mother, she had yet to figure it out.

Her only regret was the dead girl. Heloise's debts to the dead seemed like bad karma, mounting up in a way that would have to be rectified one day. There had been that boy Val had killed for no crime greater than laughing at his given name—Valery. She had told the boy, a drug dealer, Val's big secret and the boy had let it slip, so Val killed him. Killed him, then driven off in the boy's car, just because it was there and he could, but it was the theft of the car that made it a death penalty crime in Maryland. And even as Heloise had soothed Val and carted shoeboxes of money to various lawyers, skimming as much as she had dared, she was giving Brad the information they needed to lock him up forever. She had used a dead boy to create a new life for herself, and she had never looked back.

And now there was this anonymous girl, someone not much different from herself, whose death remained unsolved. If it had been Baltimore, Heloise could have leaned on Brad a little, pressed to know what leads the department had. But it was D.C. and she had no connections there, not in law enforcement, and Congress's relationship with the city was notoriously rocky. The Women's Full Employment Network offered a reward for any information leading to an arrest in the case, but nothing came of it.

Finally, there were all those little deaths, as the French called them, all those sighing, depleted men, slumping back against the bed—or the carpet, or the chair, or the bathtub—temporarily sated, briefly safe, for there was no one more harmless than a man who had just orgasmed. Even Val had been safe for a few minutes in the aftermath. How many men had there been now, after eight years with Val and nine years on her own? She did not want to count. She left her work at the office, and when she came home, she stood in her son's doorway and watched him sleep, grateful to have found her one true love.

# PART TWO

# Other Cities, Not My Own

# Pony Girl

She was looking for trouble and she was definitely going to find it. What was the girl thinking when she got dressed this morning? When she decided—days, weeks, maybe even months ago—that this was how she wanted to go out on Mardi Gras day? And not just out, but all the way up to the interstate and Ernie K-Doe's, where this kind of costume didn't play. There were skeletons and Mardi Gras Indians and baby dolls, but it wasn't a place where you saw a lot of people going for sexy or clever. That kind of thing was for back in the Quarter, maybe outside Café Brasil. It's hard to find a line to cross on Mardi Gras day, much less cross it, but this girl had gone and done it. In all my years—I was nineteen then, but a hard nineteen—I'd seen only one more disturbing sight on a Mardi Gras day and that was a white boy who took a Magic Marker, a thick one, and stuck it through a piercing in his earlobe. Nothing more to his costume than that, a Magic Marker through his ear, street clothes, and a wild gaze. Even in the middle of a crowd, people granted him some distance, let me tell you.

The Mardi Gras I'm talking about now, this was three years ago, the year that people were saying that customs mattered, that we had to hold tight to our traditions. Big Chief Tootie Montana was still alive then, and he had called for the skeletons and the baby dolls to make a showing, and there was a pretty good turnout. But it wasn't true old school, with the skeletons going to people's houses and waking up children in their beds, telling them to do their homework and listen to their mamas. Once upon a time, the skeletons were fierce, coming in with old bones from the butcher's shop, shaking the bloody hanks at sleeping children. Man, you do that to one of these kids today, he's as like to come up with a gun, blow the skeleton back into the grave. Legends lose their steam, like everything else. What scared people once won't scare them now.

Back to the girl. Everybody's eyes kept going back to that girl. She was long and slinky, in a champagne-colored body stocking. And if it had been just the body stocking, if she had decided to be Eve to some boy's Adam, glued a few leaves to the right parts, she wouldn't have been so . . . disrupting. Funny how that goes, how pretending to be naked can be less inflaming than dressing up like something that's not supposed to be sexy at all. No, this one, she had a pair of pointy ears high in her blond hair, which was pulled back in a ponytail. She had pale white-and-beige cowboy boots, the daintiest things you ever seen, and—this was what made me fear for her—a real tail of horsehair pinned to the end of her spine, swishing back and forth as she danced. Swish. Swish. Swish. And although she was skinny by my standards, she managed the trick of being skinny with curves, so that tail jutted out just so. Swish. Swish. Swish. I watched her, and I watched all the other men watching her, and I did not see how anyone could keep her safe if she stayed there, dancing into the night.

Back in school, when they lectured us on the straight and narrow, they told us that rape is a crime of violence. They told us that a woman isn't looking for something just because she goes out in high heels and a halter and a skirt that barely covers her. Or in a champagne-colored body stocking with a tail affixed. They told us that rape has nothing to do with sex. But sitting in Ernie K-Doe's, drinking a Heineken, I couldn't help but wonder if rape started as sex and then moved to violence when sex was denied. *Look at me, look at me, look at me,* the tail seemed to sing as it twitched back and forth. Yet Pony Girl's downcast eyes, refusing to make eye contact even with her dancing partner, a plump cowgirl in a big red hat, sent a different message. *Don't touch me, don't touch me, don't touch me.* You do that to a dog with a steak, he bites you, and nobody says that's the dog's fault.

Yeah, I wanted her as much as anyone there. But I feared for her even more than I wanted her, saw where the night was going and wished I could protect her. Where she was from, she was probably used to getting away with such behavior. Maybe she would get away with it here, too, if only because she was such an obvious outsider. Not a capital-T tourist, not some college girl from Tallahassee or Birmingham who had gotten tired of showing her titties on Bourbon Street and needed a new thrill. But a tourist in these parts, the kind of girl who was so full of herself that she thought she always controlled things. She was counting on folks to be rational, which was a pretty big count on Mardi Gras day. People do odd things, especially when they's masked.

I saw a man I knew only as Big Roy cross the threshold. Like most of us, he hadn't bothered with a costume, but he could have come as a frog without much trouble. He had the face for it—pop eyes, wide, flat mouth. Big Roy was almost as wide as he was tall, but he wasn't fat. I saw him looking at Pony Girl, long and hard, and I decided I had to make my move. At worst, I was out for myself, trying to get close to her. But I was being a gentleman, too, looking out for her. You can be both. I know what was in my heart that day, and while it wasn't all-over pure, it was something better than most men would have offered her.

"Who you s'posed to be?" I asked, after dancing awhile with her and her friend. I made a point of making it a threesome, of joining them, as opposed to trying to separate them from each other. That put them at ease, made them like me.

"A horse," she said. "Duh."

"Just any horse? Or a certain one?"

She smiled. "In fact, I am a particular horse. I'm Misty of Chincoteague."

"Misty of where?"

"It's an island off Virginia," she was shouting in my ear, her breath warm and moist. "There are wild ponies, and every summer, the volunteer firemen herd them together and cross them over to the mainland, where they're auctioned off."

"That where you from?"

"Chincoteague?"

"Virginia."

"My family is from the Eastern Shore of Maryland. But I'm from here. I go to Tulane."

The reference to college should have made me feel a little out of my league, or was supposed to, but somehow it made me feel bolder. "Going to college don't you make you from somewhere, any more than a cat born in an oven can call itself a biscuit."

"I love it here," she said, throwing open her arms. Her breasts were small, but they were there, round little handfuls. "I'm never going to leave."

"Ernie K-Doe's?" I asked, as if I didn't know what she meant.

"Yes," she said, playing along. "I'm going to live here forever. I'm going to dance until I drop dead, like the girl in the red shoes."

"Red shoes? You wearing cowboy boots."

She and her friend laughed, and I knew it was at my expense, but it wasn't a mean laughter. Not yet. They danced and they danced, and I began to think that she had been telling a literal truth, that she planned to dance until she expired. I offered her cool drinks, beers and sodas, but she shook her head; I asked if she wanted to go for a walk, but she just twirled away from me. To be truthful, she was wearing me out. But I was scared to leave her side because whenever I glanced in the corner, there was Big Roy, his pop eyes fixed on her, almost yellow in the dying light. I may have been a skinny nineteen-year-old in blue jeans and a Sean John T-shirt—this was back when Sean John was at its height—but I was her self-appointed knight. And even though she acted as if she didn't need me, I knew she did.

Eventually she started to tire, fanning her face with her hands, overheated from the dancing and, I think, all those eyes trained on her. That Mardi Gras was cool and overcast, and even with the crush of bodies in Ernie K-Doe's, it wasn't particularly warm. But her cheeks were bright red, rosy, and there were patches of sweat forming on her leotard—two little stripes beneath her barely-there breasts, a dot below her tail and who knows where else.

Was she stupid and innocent, or stupid and knowing? That is, did she realize the effect she was having and think she could control it, or did she honestly not know? In my heart of hearts, I knew she was not an innocent girl, but I wanted to see her that way because that can be excused.

Seeing her steps slow, anticipating that she would need a drink now, Big Roy pressed up, dancing in a way that only a feared man could get away with, a sad little hopping affair. Not all black men can dance, but the ones who can't usually know better than to try. Yet no one in this crowd would dare make fun of Big Roy, no matter how silly he looked.

Except her. She spun away, made a face at her cowgirl, pressing her lips together as if it was all she could do to keep from laughing. Big Roy's face was stormy. He moved again, placing himself in her path, and she laughed out loud this time. Grabbing her cowgirl's hand, she trotted to the bar and bought her own Heineken.

"Dyke," Big Roy said, his eyes fixed on her tail.

"Yeah," I said, hoping that agreement would calm him, that he would shake off the encounter. Myself, I didn't get that vibe from her at all. She and Cowgirl were tight, but they weren't like that, I didn't think.

When Pony Girl and Cowgirl left the bar, doing a little skipping step, Big Roy wasn't too far behind. So I followed Big Roy as he followed those girls, wandering under the freeway, as if the whole thing were just a party put on for them. These girls were so full of themselves that they didn't even stop and pay respect to the Big Chiefs they passed, just breezed by as if they saw such men every day. The farther they walked, the more I worried. Big Roy was all but stalking them, but they never looked back, never seemed to have noticed. And Big Roy was so fixed on them that I didn't have to worry about him glancing back and seeing me behind him. Even so, I darted from strut to strut, keeping them in my sights. Night was falling.

They reached a car, a pale blue sedan—theirs, I guess—and it was only when I watched them trying to get into it that I began to think that the beers they had drunk had hit them hard and fast. They weren't big girls, after all, and they hadn't eaten anything that I had seen. They giggled and stumbled, Cowgirl dropping her keys—after all, Pony Girl didn't have no place to keep keys—their movements wavy and slow. The pavement around the car was filthy with litter, but that didn't stop Pony Girl from going down on her knees to look for the keys, sticking her tail high in the air. Even at that moment, I thought she had to know how enticing that tail was, how it called attention to itself.

It was then that Big Roy jumped on her. I don't know what he was thinking. Maybe he assumed Cowgirl would run off, screaming for help—and wouldn't find none for a while, because it took some time for screams to register on Mardi Gras day, to tell the difference between pleasure and fear. Maybe he thought rape could turn to sex, that if he just got started with Pony Girl, she'd like it. Maybe he meant to hurt them both, so it's hard to be sorry for what happened to him. I guess the best answer is that he wasn't thinking. This girl had made him angry, disrespected him, and he wanted some satisfaction for that.

But whatever Big Roy intended, I'm sure it played different in his head from what happened. Cowgirl jumped on his back, riding him, screaming and pulling at his hair. Pony Girl rolled away, bringing up those tiny boots and thrusting them at just the spot, so he was left gasping on all fours. They tell women to go for the eyes if they's fighting, not to count on hitting that sweet spot, but if you can get it, nothing's better. The girls had all the advantage they needed, all they had to do was find those keys and get out of there.

Instead, the girls attacked him again, rushing him, crazy bitches. They didn't know the man they were dealing with, the things he'd done just because he could. Yet Big Roy went down like one of those inflatable clowns you box with, except he never popped back up. He went down and . . . I've never quite figured out what I saw just then, other than blood. Was there a knife? I tell you, I like to think so. If there wasn't a knife, I don't want to contemplate how they did what they did to Big Roy. Truth be told, I turned my face away after seeing that first spurt of blood geyser into the air, the way they pressed their faces and mouths toward it like greedy children, as if it were a fire hydrant being opened on a hot day. I crouched down and prayed that they wouldn't see me, but I could still hear them. They laughed the whole time, a happy squealing sound. Again, I thought of little kids playing, only this time at a party, whacking at one of those papier-mâché things. A piñata, that's what you call it. They took Big Roy apart as if he were a piñata.

Their laughter and the other sounds died away, and I dared to look again. Chests heaving, they were standing over what looked like a bloody mound of clothes. They looked quite pleased with themselves. To my amazement, Pony Girl peeled her leotard off then and there, so she was wearing nothing but the tights and the boots. She appeared to be about to start on them, when she yelled out, in my direction:

"What are you looking at?"

Behind the highway's strut, praying I couldn't be seen, I didn't say anything.

"Is this what you wanted to see?" She opened her arms a little, did a shimmying dance so her breasts bounced, and Cowgirl laughed. I stayed in my crouch, calculating how hard it would be to get back to where the crowds were, where I would be safe. I could outrun them easy. But if they got in the car and came after me, I wouldn't have much advantage.

The girls waited, as if they expected someone to come out and congratulate them. When I didn't emerge, they went through Big Roy's pockets, took the cash from his wallet. Once the body, if you could call it that, was picked clean of what little it had, Pony Girl popped the trunk of the car. She stripped the rest of the way, so she was briefly naked, a ghostly glow in the twilight. She stuffed her clothes, even her ears and her tail, in a garbage bag, then slipped on jeans, a T-shirt, and a pair of running shoes. Cowgirl didn't get all the way naked, but she put her red hat in the garbage bag, swapped her full skirt for a pair of shorts. They drove off, but not at all in a hurry. They drove with great deliberation, right over Big Roy's body—and right past me, waving as they went.

I suppose they's smart. I suppose they watch those television shows, know they need to get rid of every little scrap of clothing, that there's no saving anything, not even those pretty boots, if they don't want it to be traced back to them. I suppose they've done this before, or at least had planned it careful-like, given how prepared they were. I think they've done it since then, at least once or twice. At least, I've noticed the little stories in the *Times-Picayune* this year and last—a black man, found dead on Mardi Gras day, pockets turned out. But the newspaper is scanty with the details of how the man got dead. Not shot, they say. A suspicious death, they say. But they don't say whether it was a beating or a cutting or a hot shot or what. Makes me think they don't know how to describe what's happened to these men. Don't know how, or don't feel it would be proper, given that people might be eating while they's reading.

Just like that, it's become another legend, a story that people tell to scare the little ones, like the skeletons showing up at the foot of your bed and saying you have to do your homework and mind your parents. There are these girls, white devils, go dancing on Mardi Gras, looking for black men to rob and kill. The way most people tell the story, the girls go out dressed as demons or witches, but if you think about it, that wouldn't play, would it? A man's not going to follow a demon or a witch into the night. But he might be lured into a dark place by a fairy princess, or a cat—or a Cowgirl and her slinky Pony Girl, with a swatch of horsehair pinned to the tailbone.

# ARM and the Woman

Sally Holt was seldom the prettiest woman in the room, but for three decades now she had consistently been one of the most sought-after for one simple fact: she was a wonderful listener. Whether it was her eight-year-old son or her eighty-year-old neighbor or some male in between, Sally rested her chin in her palm and leaned forward, expression rapt, soft laugh at the ready—but not too ready, which gave the speaker a feeling of power when the shy, sweet sound finally bubbled forth, almost in spite of itself. In the northwest corner of Washington, where overtly decorative women were seen as suspect if not out-and-out tacky, a charm like Sally's was much prized. It had served her well, too, helping her glide into the perfect marriage to her college sweetheart, a dermatologist, then allowing her to become one of Northwest Washington's best hostesses, albeit in the amateur division. Sally and her husband, Peter, did not move in and did not aspire to the more rarefied social whirl, the one dominated by embassy parties and pink-faced journalists who competed to shout pithy things over one another on cable television shows. They lived in a quieter, in some ways more exclusive world, a charming, old-fashioned neighborhood comprised of middle-class houses that now required upper-class incomes to own and maintain.

And if, on occasion, in a dark corner at one of the endless parties Sally and Peter hosted and attended, her unwavering attention was mistaken for affection, she managed to deflect the ensuing pass with a graceful shake of her auburn curls. "You wouldn't want me," she told the briefly smitten men. "I'm just another soccer mom." The husbands backed away, sheepish and relieved, confiding in each other what a lucky son of a bitch Peter Holt was. Sally Holt had kept her figure, hadn't allowed herself to thicken into that androgynous khaki-trousered—let's be honest, downright dykish—mom so common in the area, which did have a lot of former field hockey players gone to seed. Plus, she was so great to talk to, interested in the world, not forever prattling about her children and their school.

Sally's secret was that she didn't actually hear a word that her admirers said, just nodded and laughed at the right moments, cued by their inflections as to how to react. Meanwhile, deep inside her head, she was mapping out the logistics of her next day. Just a soccer mom, indeed. To be a stay-at-home mother in Northwest D.C. was to be nothing less than a general, the Patton of the car pool, the Eisenhower of the HOV lane. Sally spent most of her afternoons behind the wheel of a Porsche SUV, moving her children and other people's children from school to lessons, from lessons to games, from games to home. She was ruthlessly efficient with her time and motion, her radio always tuned to WTOP to catch the traffic on the eights, her brain filled with alternative routes and illegal shortcuts, her gaze at the ready to thaw the nastiest traffic cop. She could envision her section of the city in a three-dimensional grid, her house on Morrison and the Dutton School off Nebraska the two fixed stars in her universe. Given all she had to do, you really couldn't blame her for not listening to the men who bent her ear, a figure of speech that struck her as particularly apt. If she allowed all those words into her head, her ears would be bent—as crimped, tattered, and chewed-up looking as the old tomcat she had owned as a child, a cat who could not avoid brawls even after he was neutered.

But when Peter came to her in the seventeenth year of their marriage and said he wanted out, she heard him loud and clear. And when his lawyer said their house, mortgaged for a mere $400,000, was now worth $1.8 million, which meant she needed $700,000 to buy Peter's equity stake, she heard that, too. For as much time as she spent behind the wheel of her car, Sally was her house, her house was Sally. The 1920s stucco two-story was tasteful and individual, with a kind of perfection that a decorator could never have achieved. She was determined to keep the house at all costs, and when her lawyer proposed a way it could be done, without sacrificing anything in child support or her share of Peter's retirement funds, she had approved it instantly and then, as was her habit, glazed over as the details were explained.

"What do you mean, I owe a million dollars on the house?" she asked her accountant, Kenny, three years later.

"You refinanced your house with an interest-only balloon mortgage to buy Peter out of his share. Now it's come due."

"But I don't have a million dollars," Sally said, as if Kenny didn't know this fact better than anyone. It was April, he had her tax return in front of him.

"No biggie. You get a new mortgage. Unfortunately, your timing sucks. Interest rates are up. Your monthly payment is going to be a lot bigger—just as the alimony is ending. Another bit of bad timing."

Kenny relayed all this information with zero emotion. After all, it didn't affect *his* bottom line. It occurred to Sally that an accountant should have a much more serious name. What was she doing, trusting someone named Kenny with her money?

"What about the equity I've built up in the past three years?"

"It was an interest-only loan, Sally. There is no additional equity." Kenny, a square-jawed man who bore a regrettable resemblance to Frankenstein, sighed. "Your lawyer did you no favors, steering you into this deal. Did you know the mortgage broker he referred you to was his brother-in-law? And that your lawyer is a partner in the title company? He even stuck you with PMI."

Sally was beginning to feel as if they were discussing sexually transmitted diseases instead of basic financial transactions.

"I thought I got an adjustable-rate mortgage. ARMs have conversion rates, don't they? And caps? What does any of this have to do with PMI?"

"ARMs do. But you got a balloon and balloons come due. All at once, in a big lump. Hence the name. You had a three-year grace period, in which you had an artificially low rate of 3.25 percent, with Peter's three thousand in rehabilitative alimony giving you a big cushion. Now it's over. In today's market, I recommend a thirty-year fixed, but even that's not the deal it was two years ago. According to today's rates the best you can do is . . ."

Frankennystein used an old-fashioned adding machine, the kind with a paper roll, an affectation Sally had once found charming. He punched the keys and the paper churned out, delivering its noisy verdict.

"A million financed at thirty-year fixed rates— you're looking at $7,000 a month, before taxes."

It was an increase of almost $4,000 a month over what she had been paying for the last three years and that didn't take into account the alimony she was about to lose.

"I can't cover that, not with what I get in child support. Not and pay my share of the private school tuition, which we split fifty-fifty."

"You could sell. But after closing costs and paying the real estate agent's fee, you'd walk away with a lot less cash than you might think. Maybe eight hundred thousand. "

Eight hundred thousand dollars. She couldn't buy a decent three-bedroom for that amount, not in the neighborhood, not even in the suburbs. There, the schools would be free at least, but the Dutton School probably mattered more to Sally than it did to the children. It had become the center of her social life since Peter had left, a place where she was made to feel essential. Essential and adored, one of the parents who helped out without becoming a fearsome buttinsky or know-it-all.

"How long do I have to figure this out?" she asked Kenny.

"The balloon comes due in four months. But the way things are going, you'll be better off locking in sooner rather than later. Greenspan looked funny the last time the Fed met."

"Funny?"

"Constipated, like. As if his sphincter was the only thing keeping the rates down."

"Kenny," she said with mock reproach, her instinctive reaction to a man's crude joke, no matter how dull and silly. Already, her mind was miles away, flying through the streets of her neighborhood, trying to think who might help her. There was a father who came to Sam's baseball games, often straight from work, only to end up on his cell, rattling off percentages. He must be in real estate.

**"I own** a title company," Alan Moore said. "Which, I have to say, is like owning a mint these days. The

money just keeps coming. Even with the housing sup-
ply tight as it is, people always want to refinance."

"If only I had thought to talk to you three years
ago," Sally said, twisting the stalk of a gone-to-seed
dandelion in her hand. They were standing along the
first-base line, the better to see both their sons—Sam,
adorable if inept in right field, and Alan's Duncan, a
wiry first baseman who pounded his glove with great
authority, although he had yet to catch a single throw
to the bag.

"The thing is—" Alan stopped as the batter made
contact with the ball, driving it toward the second
baseman, who tossed it to Duncan for the out. There
was a moment of suspense as Duncan bobbled it a bit,
but he held on.

"Good play, son!" Alan said, and clapped, then
looked around. "I didn't violate the vocalization rule,
did I?"

"You were perfect," Sally assured him. The league
in which their sons played did, in fact, have strict
rules about parents' behavior, including guidelines on
how to cheer properly—with enthusiasm, but without
aggression. It was a fine line.

"Where was I? Oh, your dilemma. The thing is, I
can hook you up with someone who can help you find
the best deal, but you might want to consider taking
action against your lawyer. He could be disbarred for

what he did, or at least reprimanded. Clearly a conflict of interest."

"True, but that won't help me in the long run." She sighed, then exhaled on the dandelion head, blowing away the fluff.

"Did you make a wish?" Alan asked. He wasn't handsome, not even close. He looked like Ichabod Crane, tall and thin, with a pointy nose and no chin.

"I did," Sally said with mock solemnity.

"For what?"

"Ah, if you tell, they don't come true." She met his eyes, just for a moment, let Alan Moore think that he was her heart's desire. Later that night, her children asleep, a glass of white wine at her side, she plugged figures into various mortgage calculators on the Internet, as if a different site might come up with a different answer. She charted her budget on Quicken—*if she traded the Porsche for a Prius, if she stopped buying organic produce at Whole Foods, if she persuaded Molly to drop ballet.* But there were not enough sacrifices in the world to cover the looming shortfall in their monthly bills. They would have to give up everything to keep the house—eating, driving, heat and electricity.

And even if she did find the money, found a way to make it work, her world was still shrinking around her. When Peter first left, it had been almost a relief to be free of him, grouchy and cruel as he had become in midlife. She had been glad for an excuse to avoid parties as well. Now that she was divorced, the husbands behaved as if a suddenly single woman was the most unstable molecule of all in their social set. But Alan Moore's gaze, beady as it was, had reminded her how nice it was to be admired, how she had enjoyed being everyone's favorite confidante once upon a time, how she had liked the hands pressed to her bare spine, the friendly pinch on her ass.

She should marry again. It was simple as that. She left the Internet's mortgage calculators for its even more numerous matchmakers, but the world she glimpsed was terrifying, worse than the porn she had once found cached on Peter's laptop. She was old by the standards enumerated in these online wish lists. Worse, she had children, and ad after ad specified that that would just not do. She looked at the balding, pudgy men, read their demands—no kids, no fatties, no over-forties—and realized they held the power to dictate the terms. No, she would not subject herself to such humiliation. Besides, Internet matches required writing, not listening. In a forum where she could not nod and laugh and gaze sympathetically, Sally was at a disadvantage. Typing "LOL" in a chat room simply didn't have the same impact.

Now a man with his own children, that would be ideal. A widower or a divorcee who happened to have custody, rare as that was. She mentally ran through the Dutton School directory, then pulled it from the shelf and skimmed it. No, no, no—all the families she knew were disgustingly intact, the divorced and reblended ones even tighter than those who had stayed with their original mates. Didn't anyone die anymore? Couldn't the killers and drug dealers who kept the rest of Washington in the upper tier of homicide rates come up to Northwest every now and then, take out a housewife or two?

Why not?

**In a** school renowned for dowdy mothers, Lynette Moore was one of the dowdiest, gone to seed in the way only a truly preppy woman can. She had leathery skin and a Prince Valiant haircut, which she smoothed back from her face with a grosgrain ribbon headband. Her laugh was a loud, annoying bray, and if someone failed to join in her merriment, she clapped the person on the back as if trying to dislodge a lump of food. On this particular Thursday afternoon, Lynette stood on the sidewalk, speaking animatedly to one of the teachers, punching the poor woman at intervals. Sally, waiting her turn in the car pool lane, thought how easily a foot could slip, how an accelerator could jam. The SUV would surge forward, Lynette would be pinned against the column by the school's front door. So sad, but no one's fault, right?

No, Sally loved the school too much to do that. Besides, an accident would take out Ms. Grayson as well, and she was an irreplaceable resource when it came to getting Dutton's graduates into the best colleges.

Three months, according to her accountant. She had three months. Maybe Peter would die; he carried enough life insurance to pay off the mortgage, with plenty left over for the children's education. No, she would never get that lucky. Stymied, she continued to make small talk with Alan Moore at baseball games but began to befriend Lynette as well, lavishing even more attention on her in order to deflect any suspicions she might harbor about Sally's kindness to Alan. Lynette was almost pathetically grateful for Sally's attention, adopting her with the fervor that adolescent girls bring to new friendships. Women appreciate good listeners, too, and Sally nodded and smiled over tea and, once five o'clock came around, glasses of wine. Lynette had quite a bit to say, the usual litany of complaints. Alan worked all the time. There was zero romance in their marriage. She might as well be a single mom—"Not that a single mom is a bad thing to be," she squealed, clapping a palm over her large, unlipsticked mouth.

"You're a single mom without any of the advantages," Sally said, pouring her another glass of wine. *Drive home drunk. What do I care?*

"There are advantages, aren't there?" Lynette leaned forward and lowered her voice, although Molly was at a friend's and Sam was up in his room with Lynette's Duncan, playing *The Sims.* "No one ever says that, but it's true."

"Sure. As long as you have the money to sustain the standard of living you had, being single is great."

"How do you do that?" Asked with specificity, as if Lynette believed that Sally had managed just that trick. Sally, who had long ago learned the value of the nonreply, raised her eyebrows and smiled serenely, secretly.

"I think Alan cheats on me," Lynette blurted out.

"I would leave a man who did that to me."

Lynette shook her head. "Not until the kids are grown and gone. Maybe then. But I'll be so old. Who would want me then?"

*Who would want you now?*

"Do what you have to do." Another meaningless response, perfected over the years. Yet no one ever seemed to notice how empty Sally's sentiments were, how vapid. She had thought it was just men who were fooled so easily, but it was turning out that women were equally foolish.

"Alan and I never have sex anymore."

"That's not uncommon," Sally said. "All marriages have their ups and downs."

"I love your house." Logical sequences of thought had never been Lynette's strength, but this conversation was abrupt and odd even by her standards. "I love you."

Lynette put a short stubby hand over Sally's, who fought the instinctive impulse to yank her own away. Instead, it was Lynette who pulled back in misery and confusion.

"I don't mean that way," she said, staring into her wineglass, already half empty.

Sally took a deep breath. "Why not?"

Lynette put her hand back over Sally's. "You mean . . . ?"

Sally thought quickly. No matter how far Sam and Duncan disappeared into their computer world, she could not risk taking Lynette to the master bedroom. She had a hunch that Lynette would be loud. But she also believed that this was her only opportunity. In fact, Lynette would shun her after today. She would cut Sally off completely, ruining any chance she had of luring Alan away from her. She would have to see this through or start over with another couple.

"There's a room, over our garage. It used to be Peter's office."

She grabbed the bottle of wine and her glass. She was going to need to be a little drunk, too, to get through this. Then again, who was less attractive in the large scheme of things, Alan or Lynette? Who would be more grateful, more giving? Who would be more easily controlled? She was about to find out.

**Lynette may** not have been in love when she blurted out that sentiment in Sally's kitchen, but she was within a week. Lynette being Lynette, it was a loud, unsubtle love, both behind closed doors and out in public, and Sally had to chide her about the latter, school her in the basics of covert behavior, remind her not to stare with those cowlike eyes or try to monopolize Sally at public events, especially when Alan was present. They dropped their children at school at 8:30 and Lynette showed up at Sally's house promptly at 8:45, bearing skim-milk lattes and scones. Lynette's idea of the perfect day, as it turned out, was to share a quick latte upon arriving, then bury her head between Sally's legs until 11 A.M., when she surfaced for the Hot Topics segment on *The View*. Then it was back to devouring Sally, with time-outs for back rubs and baths. Lynette's large, eager mouth turned out to have its uses. Plus, she asked for only the most token attention in return, which Sally provided largely through a handheld massage tool from the Sharper Image.

Best of all, Lynette insisted that, as much as she loved Sally, she could never, ever leave Alan, not until the children were grown and out of the house. She warned Sally of this repeatedly, and Sally would nod sadly, resignedly. "I'll settle for the little bit I can have," she said, stroking Lynette's Prince Valiant bob.

"If Alan ever finds out . . ." Lynette said glumly.

"He won't," Sally assured her. "Not if we're careful. There. No—there." Just as her attention drifted away in conversation, she found it drifting now, floating toward an idea, only to be distracted by Lynette's insistent touch. Later. She would figure everything out later.

**"You're not** going to believe this," Sally told Lynette at the beginning of their third week together, during one of the commercial breaks on *The View.* "Peter found out about us."

"Ohmigod!" Lynette said. "How?"

"I'm not sure. But he knows. He knows everything. He's threatening to take the children away from me."

"Ohmigod."

"And—" She turned her face to the side, not trusting herself to tell this part. "And he's threatening to go to Alan."

"Shit." In her panic, Lynette got up and began putting on her clothes, as if Peter and Alan were outside the door at this very moment.

"He hasn't yet," Sally said quickly. "But he will, if I fight the change in the custody order. He's given me a week to decide. I give up the children or he goes to Alan."

"You can't tell. You can't."

"I don't want to, but—how can I lose my children?"

Lynette understood, as only another mother could. They couldn't tell the truth, but she couldn't expect Sally to live with the consequences of keeping the secret. Lynette would keep her life while Sally would lose hers. No woman could make peace with such blatant unfairness.

"Would he really do this?"

"He would. Peter—he's not the nice man everyone thinks he is. Why do you think we got divorced? And the thing is, if he gets the kids—well, it was one thing for him to do the things he did to me. But if he ever treated Molly or Sam that way . . ."

"What way?"

"I don't want to talk about it. But if it should happen—I'd have to kill him."

"The pervert." Lynette was at once repelled and fascinated. The dark side of Sally's life was proving as seductive to her as Sally had been.

"I know. If he had done what he did to a stranger, he'd be in prison for life. But in a marriage, such things are legal. I'm stuck, Lynette. I won't ruin your life for anything. You told me from the first that this had to be a secret."

"There has to be a way . . ."

"There isn't. Not as long as Peter is a free man."

"Not as long as he's alive."

"You can't mean—"

Lynette put a finger to Sally's lips. These had been the hardest moments to fake, the face-to-face encounters. Kissing was the worst. But it was essential not to flinch, not to let her distaste show. She was so close to getting what she wanted.

"Trust me," Lynette said.

Sally wanted to. But she had to be sure of one thing. "Don't try to hire someone. It seems like every time someone like us tries to find someone, it's always an undercover cop. Remember Ruth Ann Aron." A politician from the Maryland suburbs, she had done just that. But her husband had forgiven her, even testified on her behalf during the trial. She had been found guilty anyway.

"Trust me," Lynette repeated.

"I do, sweetheart. I absolutely do."

**Dr. Peter Holt** was hit by a Jeep Cherokee, an Eddie Bauer limited edition, as he crossed Connecticut Avenue on his way to Sunomono, a place where he ate lobster pad thai every Thursday evening. The driver told police that her children had been bickering in the backseat over what to watch on the DVD player and she turned her head, just a moment, to scold them. Distracted, she had seen Holt and tried to stop but hit the accelerator instead. Then, as her children screamed for real, she had driven another hundred yards in panic and hysteria. If the dermatologist wasn't dead on impact, he was definitely dead when the SUV finally stopped. But the only substance in her blood was caffeine, and while it was a tragic, regrettable accident, it was clearly an accident. Really, investigators told Holt's stunned survivors, his ex-wife and two children, it was surprising that such things didn't happen more often, given the congestion in D.C., the unwieldy SUVs, the mothers' frayed nerves, the nature of dusk, with its tricky gray-green light. It was a macabre coincidence, their children being classmates, the parents being superficial friends on the sidelines of their sons' baseball games. But this part of D.C. was like a village unto itself, and the accident had happened only a mile from the school.

At Peter's memorial service, Lynette Moore sought a private moment with Sally Holt and those who watched from a distance marveled at the bereaved woman's composure and poise, the way she comforted her ex-husband's killer. No one was close enough to hear what they said.

"I'm sorry," Lynette said. "It didn't occur to me that after—well, I guess we can't see each other anymore."

"No," Sally lied. "It didn't occur to me, either. You've sacrificed so much for me. For Molly and Sam, really. I'm in your debt forever. It will always be our secret."

And she patted Lynette gently on the arm, the last time the two would ever touch.

Peter's estate went to the children—but in trust to Sally, of course. She determined that it would be in the children's best interest to pay off the balloon mortgage in cash and his brother, the executor, agreed. Peter would have wanted the children to have the safety and sanctity of home, given the emotional trauma they had endured.

No longer needy, armored with a widow's pre-rogatives, Sally found herself invited to parties again, where solicitous friends attempted to fix her up with the rare single men in their circles. Now that she didn't care about men, they flocked around her and Sally did what she had always done. She listened and she laughed, she laughed and she listened, but she never really heard anything—unless the subject was money. Then she paid close attention, even writing down the advice she was given. The stock market was so turgid, everyone complained. The smart money was in real estate.

Sally nodded.

# Honor Bar

He took all his girlfriends to Ireland, as it turned out. "All" being defined as the four he had dated since Moira, the inevitably named Moira, with the dark hair and the blue eyes put in with a dirty finger. (This is how he insisted on describing her. She would never have used such a hackneyed phrase in general and certainly not for Moira, whose photographic likeness, of which Barry happened to have many, showed a dark-haired, pale-eyed girl with hunched shoulders and a sour expression.)

When he spoke of Moira, his voice took on a lilting quality, which he clearly thought was Irish, but which sounded to her like the kind of singsong voice used on television shows for very young children. She had dark HAIR and pale BLUE eyes put in with a

DIRTY FINGER. Really, it was like listening to one of the Teletubbies wax nostalgic, if one could imagine Po (or Laa-Laa or Winky-Dink, or whatever the faggoty purple one was named) hunched over a pint of Guinness in a suitably picturesque Galway bar. Without making contact, Barry explained how he had conceived this trip to exorcise the ghost of Moira, only to find that it had brought her back in full force (again) and he was oh so sorry, but it was just not to be between them and he could not continue this charade for another day.

So, yes, the above—the triteness of his speech, its grating quality, his resemblance to a Guinness-besotted Teletubby—was what she told herself after-ward, the forming scab over the hurt and humiliation of being dumped two weeks into a three-week tour of the Emerald Isle. (Guess who called it that.) After her first, instinctive outburst—"You asshole!"—she set-tled down and listened generously, without recrimina-tions. It had not been love between them. He was rich and she was pretty, and she had assumed it would play out as most of her relationships did. Twelve to twenty months, two or three trips, several significant pieces of jewelry. He was pulling the plug prematurely, that was all, and Ireland barely counted as a vacation in her opinion. It had rained almost every day and the shopping was shit.

Still, she nodded and interjected at the proper moments, signaling the pretty waitress for another, then another, but always for him. She nursed her half pint well into the evening. At closing time, she slipped the waitress twenty euros, straight from his wallet, and the young woman obligingly helped to carry Barry through the streets to the Great Southern. His eyes gleamed a bit as she and the waitress heaved him on the bed, not that he was anywhere near in shape for the award he was imagining. (And how did his mind work, she wondered in passing, how did a man who had just dumped a woman two weeks into a three-week trip persuade himself that the dumpee would then decide to honor him with a going-away threesome? True, she had been a bit wild when they first met. That was how a girl got a man like Barry, with a few decadent acts that suggested endless possibilities. But once you had landed the man, you kept putting such things off, suggested that the blow job in the cab would follow the trip to Tiffany, not vice versa, and pretty soon he was reduced to begging for the most ordinary favors.)

No, they tucked Barry in properly and she tipped the waitress again, sending her into the night. Once the girl was gone, she searched his luggage and selected several T-shirts of which he was inordinately fond. These she ripped into strips, which she then used to bind his wrists and ankles to the four-poster bed. She debated with herself whether she needed to gag him—he might awaken and start to struggle—and decided it was essential. She disconnected the phone, turned the television on so it would provide a nice steady hum in the background, then helped herself to his passport, Visa card, and all the cash he had. Then, as Barry slept the rather noisy sleep of the dead-drunk, she raided the minibar—wine, water, cashews. She was neither hungry nor thirsty, but the so-called honor bar was the one thing that Barry was cheap about. "It's the principle," he said, but his indignation had a second-hand feel to it, something passed down by a parent. Or, perhaps, a girlfriend. Moira, she suspected. She opened a chocolate bar but rejected it. The chocolate wasn't quite right here.

They were e-ticketed to Dublin, but that was a simple matter. She used the room connection to go online, and never mind the cost, rearranging both their travel plans. Barry was now booked home via Shannon, while she continued on to Dublin, where she had switched hotels, choosing the Merrion because it sounded expensive and she wanted Barry to pay. And pay and pay and pay. Call it severance. She wouldn't have taken up with Barry if she hadn't thought he was good for at least two years.

It had been Barry's plan to send her home, to continue to Dublin without her, where he would succumb to a mounting frenzy of Moira-mourning. That's what he had explained in the pub last night. And he still could, of course. But she thought there might be a kernel of shame somewhere inside the man, and once he dealt with the missing passport and the screwed-up airline reservations, he might have the good sense to continue home on the business-class ticket he had offered her. ("Yes, I brought you to Ireland only to break up with you, but I am sending you home business class.") He was not unfair, not through and through. His primary objective was to be rid of her, as painlessly and guiltlessly as possible, and she had now made that possible. He wouldn't call the police or press charges, or even think to put a stop on the credit card, which she was using only for the hotel and the flight back.

Really, she was very fair. Honorable, even.

"**Mr. Gardner** will be joining me later," she told the clerk at the Merrion, pushing the card toward him, and it was accepted without question.

"And did you want breakfast included, Mrs. Gardner?"

"Yes." She wanted everything included—breakfast and dinner and laundry and facials, if such a thing were available. She wanted to spend as much of Barry's money as possible. She congratulated herself for her cleverness, using the American Express card, which had no limit. She could spend as much as she liked at the hotel, now that the number was on file.

It was time, as it turned out, that was harder to spend. For all Barry's faults—a list that was now quite long in her mind—he was a serious and sincere traveler, the kind who made the most of wherever he landed. He was a tourist in the best sense of the word, a man determined to wring the most experience from travel. While in Galway, they had rented a car and tried to follow Yeats's trail, figuratively and literally, driving south to see his castle and the swans at Coole, driving north to Mayo and his final resting place, in the shadow of Ben Bulben. She had surprised Barry with her bits of knowledge about the poet, bits usually gleaned seconds earlier from the guidebook, which she skimmed covertly while pretending to look for places to eat lunch. Skimming was a great skill, much under-rated, especially for a girl who was not expected to be anything but decorative.

Of course, it had turned out that Yeats's trail was also Moira's. She had been a literature major in college and she had a penchant for the Irish and a talent, apparently, for making clever literary allusions at the most unlikely moments. On Barry and Moira's infamous trip, which had included not just Ireland but London and Edinburgh, Moira had treated Barry to a great, racketing bit of sex after seeing an experimental production of *Macbeth* at the Festival, one set in a Texas middle school. And while the production came off with mixed results, it somehow inspired a most memorable night with Moira, or so Barry had confided, over all those pints in Galway. She had brought him to a great shuddering climax, left him spent and gasping for breath, then said without missing a beat: "Now go kill Duncan." (When the story failed to elicit whatever tribute Barry thought its due—laughter, amazement at Moira's ability to make Shakespearean allusions after sex—he had added: "I guess you had to be there." "No thank you," she had said.)

She did not envy Moira's education. Education was highly overrated. A college dropout, she had supported herself very well throughout her twenties, moving from man to man, taking on the kinds of jobs that helped her to meet them—galleries, catering services, film production offices. Now she was thirty—well, possibly thirty-one, she had been lying about her age for so long, first up, then down, that she got a little confused. She was thirty or thirty-one, maybe even thirty-two, and while going to Dublin had seemed like an inspired bit of revenge against Barry, it was not the place to find her next position, strong euro be damned. Paris, London, Zurich, Rome, even Berlin—those were the kinds of places where a beautiful woman could meet the kind of man who would take her on for a while. Who was she going to meet in Dublin? Bono? But he was married and always prattling about poverty, a bad sign.

So, alone in Dublin, she wasn't sure what to do, and when she contemplated what Barry might have done, she realized it was what Moira might have done, and she wanted no part of that. Still, somehow—the post office done, Kilcommon done, the museums done— she found herself in a most unimpressive townhouse, studying a chart that claimed to explain how parts of *Ulysses* related to the various organs of the human body.

"Silly, isn't it?" asked a voice behind her, startling her, not only because she had thought herself alone in the room, but also because the voice expressed her own thoughts so succinctly. It was an Irish voice, but it was a sincere voice, too, the beautiful vowels without all the bullshit blarney, which had begun to tire her. She could barely stand to hail a cab anymore because the drivers exhausted her so, with their outsize personalities and long stories and persistent questions. She couldn't bear to be alone, but she couldn't bear all the conversation, all the yap-yap-yap-yap-yap that seemed to go with being Irish.

"It's a bit much," she agreed.

"I don't think any writer, even Joyce, thinks things out so thoroughly before the fact. If you ask me, we just project all this symbolism and meaning onto books to make ourselves feel smarter."

"I feel smarter," she said, "just talking to you." It was the kind of line in which she specialized, the kind of line that had catapulted her from one safe haven to the next, like Tarzan swinging on a vine.

"Rory Malone," he added, offering his hand, offering the next vine. His hair was raven black, his eyes pale blue, his lashes thick and dark. Oh, it had been so long since she had been with anyone good looking. Perhaps Ireland was a magical place after all.

"Bliss," she said, steeling herself for the inane things that her given name inspired. Even Barry, not exactly quick on the mark, had a joke at the ready when she provided her name. But Rory Malone simply shook her hand, saying nothing. A quiet man, she thought to herself. Thank God.

**"How long** are you here for?"

They had just had sex for the first time, a most satisfactory first time, which is to say it was prolonged, with Rory extremely attentive to her needs. It had been a long time since a man had seemed so keen on her pleasure. Oh, other men had tried, especially in the beginning, when she was a prize to be won, but their best-intentioned efforts usually fell a little short of the mark and she had grown so used to faking it that the real thing almost caught her off guard.

"How long are you staying here?" he persisted. "In Dublin, I mean."

"It's . . . open-ended." She could leave in a day, she could leave in a week. It all depended on when Barry would cut off her credit. How much guilt did he feel? How much guilt should he feel? She was beginning to see that she might have gone a little over the edge where Barry was concerned. He had brought her to Ireland and discovered he didn't love her. Was that so bad? If it weren't for Barry, she never would have met Rory, and she was glad she had met Rory.

"Open-ended?" he said. "What do you do, that you have such flexibility?"

"I don't really have to worry about work," she said.

"I don't worry about it, either," he said, rolling to the side and fishing a cigarette from the pocket of his jeans.

That was a good sign—a man who didn't have to worry about work, a man who was free to roam the city during the day. "Let's not trade histories," she said. "It's tiresome."

"Good enough. So what do we talk about?"

"Let's not talk so much, either."

He put out his cigarette and they started again. It was even better the second time, better still the third. She was sore by morning, good sore, that lovely burning feeling on the inside. It would probably lead to a not-so-lovely burning feeling in a week or two and she ordered some cranberry juice at breakfast that morning, hoping it could stave off the mild infection that a bout of sex brought with it.

"So Mr. Gardner has finally joined you," the waiter said, used to seeing her alone at breakfast.

"Yes," she said.

"I'll have a soft-boiled egg," Rory said. "And some salmon. And some of the pancakes?"

"Slow down," she said, laughing. "You don't have to try everything at one sitting."

"I have to keep my strength up," he said, "if I'm going to keep my lady happy."

She blushed and, in blushing, realized she could not remember the last time she had felt this way.

**Show me** the real Dublin," she said to Rory later that afternoon, feeling bold. They had just had sex for the sixth time, and if anything, he seemed to be even more intent on her needs.

"This is real," he said. "The hotel is real. I'm real. How much more Dublin do you need?"

"I'm worried there's something I'm missing."

"Don't worry. You're not."

"Something authentic, I mean. Something the tourists never see."

He rubbed his chin. "Like a pub?"

"That's a start."

So he took her to a pub, but she couldn't see how it was different from any other pub she had visited on her own. And Rory didn't seem to know anyone, although he tried to smoke and professed great surprise at the new antismoking laws. "I smoke here all the time," he bellowed in more or less mock outrage, and she laughed, but no one else did. From the pub, they went to a rather sullen restaurant, and when the check arrived, he was a bit slow to pick it up.

"I don't have a credit card on me," he said at last—sheepishly, winningly—and she let Barry pay.

Back in bed, things were still fine. So they stayed there more and more, although the weather was perversely beautiful, so beautiful that the various hotel staffers who visited the room kept commenting on it.

"You've been cheated," said the room service waiter. "Ask for your money back. It's supposed to rain every day, not pour down sunlight like this. It's unnatural, that's what it is."

"And is there no place you'd like to go, then?" the chambermaid asked when they refused her services for the third day running, maintaining they didn't need a change of sheets or towels.

Then the calls began, gentle but firm, running up the chain of command until they were all but ordered out of the room, so the staff could have a chance to freshen it. They went, blinking in the bright light, sniffing suspiciously at the air, so fresh and light after the recirculated air of their room, which was now a bit thick with smoke. After a few blocks, they went into a department store, where he fingered the sleeves of soccer jerseys. Football, she corrected herself. Football jerseys.

"Where do you live?" she asked Rory, but only because it seemed that someone should be saying something.

"I have a room."

"A bed-sit?" She had heard the phrase somewhere, perhaps in a British novel, and was proud of being able to use it. Although, come to think of it, Ireland and Great Britain were not the same, so the slang might not apply.

"What?"

"Never mind." She must have used it wrong.

"I like this one." He indicated a red-and-white top. She had the distinct impression that he expected her to buy it for him. Did he think she was rich? That was understandable, given the hotel room, her easy way with room service, not to mention the minibar over the past few days. All on Barry, but Rory didn't know that.

Still, it seemed a bit cheesy to hint like this, although she had played a similar game with Barry in various stores and her only regret was that she hadn't taken him for more, especially when it came to jewelry. Trips and meals were ephemeral and only true high-fashion clothing—the classics, authentic couture—increased in value. She was thirty-one. (Or thirty, possibly thirty-two.) She had only a few years left in which to reap the benefits of her youth and her looks. Of course, she might marry well, but she was beginning to sense she might not. She did not inspire matrimony, not that she had been trying. Then again, it was when you didn't care that men wanted to marry you. What would happen as thirty-five closed in? Would she regret not accepting the proposals made, usually when she was in a world-class sulk? Marriage to a man like Barry had once seemed a life sentence. But what would she do instead? She really hadn't thought this out as much as she should.

"Let's go back to the room," she said abruptly. "They must have cleaned it by now."

They hadn't, not quite, so they sat in the bar, drinking and waiting. It was early to drink, she realized, but only by American standards. In Rory's company, she had been drinking at every meal except breakfast and she wasn't sure she had been completely sober for days.

Back in the room, Rory headed for the television set, clicking around with the remote control, then throwing it down in disgust. "I can't get any scores," he said.

"But they have a crawl—"

"Not the ones I want, I mean." He looked around the room, restless and bored, and seemed to settle on her only when he had rejected everything else—the mini-bar, the copy of that morning's *Irish Times*, a glossy magazine. Even then, his concentration seemed to fade midway through and he patted her flank. She pretended not to understand, so he patted her again, less gently, and she rolled over. Rory was silent during sex, almost grimly so, but once her back was to him, he began to grunt and mutter in a wholly new way and when he finished, he breathed a name into the nape of her neck.

Trouble was, it wasn't hers. She wasn't sure whose it was, but she recognized the distinct lack of her syllables— no "Bluh" to begin, no gentle hiss at the end.

"What?" she asked. It was one thing to be a stand-in for Barry, when he was footing the bills, to play the ghost of Moira. But she would be damned before she would allow a freeloader such as Rory the same privilege.

"What?" he echoed, clearly having no idea what she meant.

"Whose name are you saying?"

"Why, Millie. Like in the novel *Ulysses*. I was pretending you were Millie and I was Bloom."

"It's Molly, you idiot. Even I know that."

"Molly. That's what I said. A bit of playacting. No harm in that."

"Bullshit. I'm not even convinced that it was a woman's name you were saying."

"Fuck you. I don't do guys."

His accent had changed—flattened, broadened. He now sounded as American as she did.

"Where are you from?"

He didn't answer.

"Do you live in Dublin?"

"Of course I do. You met me here, didn't you?"

"Where do you live? What do you do?"

"Why, here. And this." He tried to shove a hand beneath her, but she felt sore and unsettled, and she pushed him away.

"Look," he said. "I've made you happy, haven't I? Okay, so I'm not *Irish*-Irish. But my, like, ancestors were. And we've had fun, haven't we? I've treated you well. I've earned my keep."

Bliss glanced in the mirror opposite the bed. She thought she knew what men saw when they looked at her. She had to know; it was her business, more or less. She had always paid careful attention to every aspect of her appearance—her skin, her hair, her body, her clothes. It was her only capital and she had lived off the interest, careful never to deplete the principle. She exercised, ate right, avoided drugs, and, until recently, drank only sparingly—enough to be fun, but not enough to wreck her complexion. She was someone worth having, a woman who could captivate desirable men—economically desirable men, that is— while passing hot hors d'oeuvres or answering a phone behind the desk at an art gallery.

But this was not the woman Rory had seen, she was realizing. Rory had not seen a woman at all. He had seen clothes. He had seen her shoes, high-heeled Christian Lacroixs that were hell on the cobblestones. And her bag, a Marc Jacobs slung casually over the shoulder of a woman who could afford to be casual about an $800 bag because she had far more expensive ones back home. Only "home" was Barry's apartment, she realized, and lord knows what he had done with her things. Perhaps that was why he hadn't yet alerted the credit card company, because he was back in New

York, destroying all her things. He would be pissed about the T-shirts, she realized somewhat belatedly. They were authentic vintage ones, not like the fakes everyone else was wearing now, purchased at Fred Segal last January.

And then she had brought Rory back to this room, this place of unlimited room service and the sumptuous breakfasts and the "Have-whatever-you-like-from-the-minibar" proviso. She had even let him have the cashews.

"You think I'm rich," she said.

"I thought you looked like someone who could use some company," Rory said, stretching and then rising from the bed.

"How old are you?"

"Twenty-four."

He was she, she was Barry. How had this happened? She was much too young to be an older woman and nowhere near rich enough.

"What do you do?"

"Like I said, I don't worry about work too much." He gave her his lovely grin, although she was not quite as charmed by it.

"Was I . . . work?"

"Well, as my dad said, do what you love and you'll love what you do."

"But you'd prefer to do men, wouldn't you. Men for fun, women for money."

"I told you I'm no cocksucker," he said, and landed a quick, smart backhand on her cheek. The slap was professional, expert, the slap of a man who had ended more than one argument this way. Bliss, who had never been struck in her life—except on the ass, with a hairbrush, by an early boyfriend who found that exceptionally entertaining—rubbed her cheek, stunned. She was even more stunned to watch Rory proceed to the minibar and crouch on all fours before it, inspecting its restocked shelves.

"Crap wine," he said. "And I am sick to hell of Guinness and Jameson."

The first crack of the door against his head was too soft; all it did was make him bellow. But it was hard enough to disorient him, giving Bliss the only advantage she needed. She straddled his back and slammed the door repeatedly on his head and his neck. Decapitation occurred to her as a vague goal and she barely noticed his hands reaching back, scratching and flailing, attempting to dislodge her. She settled for motionlessness and silence, slamming the door on his head until he was still.

But still was not good enough. She wrestled a corkscrew from its resting place—fifteen euros—and went to work. Impossible. Just as she was about to despair, she spied a happy gleam beneath the bedspread, a steak knife that had fallen to the floor and somehow gone undetected. She finished her work, even as the hotel was coming to life around her—the telephone ringing, footsteps pounding down the corridors. She should probably put on her robe. She was rather . . . speckled.

"**How old** are you, then?" the police officer—they called them gardai here—asked Bliss.

"How old do I look?"

"You look about twenty-five, but the records require more specific data." He was still being kind and solicitous, although Bliss sensed that the fading mark on her cheek had not done much to reconcile the investigators to the scene they had discovered. They were gallant and professed horror that she had been hit and insulted. But their real horror, she knew, was for Rory.

"Really? Twenty-five? You're not just saying that?"

"I'd be surprised if you could buy a drink legally in most places."

Satisfied, she gave her real age, although it took a moment of calculation to get it right. Was she thirty, thirty-one? Thirty, she decided. Thirty.

difficult to shop for. And as the accessories began to flow—golf books, golf-themed clothing, golf gloves, golf hats, golf highball glasses—Charlie inevitably learned quite a bit about golf. He watched tournaments on television and spoke knowingly of "Tiger" and "Singh," as well as the quirks of certain U.S. Open courses. He began to think of himself as a golfer who simply didn't golf. Which, as he gleaned from his friends who actually pursued the sport, might be the best of all possible worlds. Golf, they said, was their love and their obsession, and they all wished they had never taken it up.

**At any** rate, this continued for two years and everyone—Charlie, Marla, and Sylvia, his former administrative assistant—was very happy with this arrangement. But then Sylvia announced she wanted to go from mistress to wife. And given that Sylvia was terrifyingly good at making her pronouncements into reality, this was a rather unsettling turn of events for Charlie. After all, she had been the one who had engineered the affair in the first place, and even come up with the golf alibi. As he had noted on her annual evaluation, Sylvia was very goal-oriented.

"Look, I want to fuck you," Sylvia had said out of the blue, about six months after she started working

# A Good Fuck Spoiled

It began innocently enough. Well, if not innocently—and Charlie Drake realized that some people would refuse to see the origins of any extramarital affair as innocent—it began with tact and consideration. When Charlie Drake agreed to have an affair with his former administrative assistant, he began putting golf clubs in the trunk of his car every Thursday and Saturday, telling his wife he was going to shoot a couple holes. Yes, he really said "a couple holes," but then, he knew very little about golf at the time.

Luckily, neither did his wife, Marla. But she was enthusiastic about Charlie's new hobby, if only because it created a whole new category of potential gifts, and her family members were always keen for Christmas and birthday ideas for Charlie, who was notoriously for him. Okay, not totally out of the blue. She had tried a few more subtle things—pressing her breasts against his arm when going over a document, touching his hand, asking him if he needed her to go with him to conferences, even volunteering to pay her own way when told there was no money in the budget for her to attend. "We could even share a room," she said. It was when Charlie demurred at her offer that she said: "Look, I want to fuck you."

Charlie was fifty-eight at the time, married thirty-six years, and not quite at ease in the world. He remembered a time when nice girls didn't—well, when they didn't do it so easily and they certainly didn't speak of it this way. Marla had been a nice girl, someone he met at college and courted according to the standards of the day, and while he remembered being wistful in the early days of his marriage, when everyone suddenly seemed to be having guilt-free sex all the time, AIDS had come along and he decided he was comfortable with his choices. Sure, he noticed pretty girls and thought about them, but he had never been jolted to act on those feelings. It seemed like a lot of trouble, frankly.

"Well, um, we can't," he told Sylvia.

"Why? Don't you like me?"

"Of course I like you, Sylvia, but you work for me. They have rules about that. Anita Hill and all."

"The point of an affair is that it's carried on in secret."

"And the point of embezzlement is to get away with stealing money, but I wouldn't put my job at risk that way. I plan to retire from this job in a few years."

"But you feel what I'm feeling, right? This incredible force between us?"

"Sure." It seemed only polite.

"So if I find a job with one of our competitors, then there would be nothing to stop us, right? This is just about the sexual harassment rules?"

"Sure," he said, not thinking her serious. Then, just in case she was: "But you can't take your Rolodex, you know. Company policy."

A month later, he was called for a reference on Sylvia and he gave her the good one she deserved, then took her out to lunch to wish her well. She put her hand on his arm.

"So can we now?"

"Can we what?"

"Fuck?"

"Oh." He still wasn't comfortable with that word. "Well, no. I mean, as of this moment, you're still my employee. Technically. So, no."

"What about next week?"

"Well, my calendar is pretty full—"

"You don't have anything on Thursday." Sylvia did know his calendar.

"That's true."

"We can go to my apartment. It's not far."

"You know, Sylvia, when you're starting a new job, you really shouldn't take long lunches. Not at first."

"So it's going to be a long lunch." She all but growled these words at him, confusing Charlie. He was pretty sure that he hadn't committed himself to anything, yet somehow Sylvia thought he had. He had used the company's sexual harassment policy as a polite way to rebuff her, and now it turned out she had taken his excuse at face value. The thing was, he did not find Sylvia particularly attractive. She had thick legs, far too thick for the short skirts she favored, and she was a little hairy for his taste. Still, she dressed as if she believed herself a knockout and he did not want to disabuse her of this notion.

(And did Charlie, who was fifty-six, with thinning hair and a protruding stomach, ever wonder what Sylvia saw in him? No.)

"I'm not sure how I could get away," he said at last.

"I've already thought that out. If you told people you were playing golf, you could get away Thursdays at lunch. You know how many men at the company play golf. And then we could have Saturdays, too. Long Saturdays, with nothing but fucking."

He winced. "Sylvia, I really don't like that word."

"You'll like the way I do it."

He did, actually. Sylvia applied herself to being Charlie's mistress with the same brisk efficiency she had brought to being his administrative assistant, far more interested in his needs than her own. He made a few rules, mostly about discretion—no e-mails, as few calls as possible, nothing in public, ever—but otherwise he let Sylvia call the shots, which she did with a lot of enthusiasm. Before he knew it, two years had gone by, and he was putting his golf clubs in his car twice a week (except when it rained, which wasn't often, not in this desert climate) and he thought everyone was happy. In fact, Marla even took to bragging a bit that Charlie seemed more easygoing and relaxed since he had started golfing, but he wasn't obsessive about it like most men. So Marla was happy and Charlie was happy and Sylvia—well, Sylvia was not happy, as it turned out.

"When are you going to marry me?" she asked abruptly one day, right in the middle of something that Charlie particularly liked, which distressed him, as it dimmed the pleasure, having it interrupted, and this question was an especially jarring interruption, being wholly unanticipated.

"What?"

"I'm in love with you, Charlie. I'm tired of sneaking around like this."

"We don't sneak around anywhere."

"Exactly. For two years, you've been coming over here, having your fun, but what's in it for me? We never go anywhere outside this apartment, I don't even get to go to lunch with you, or celebrate my birthday. I want to marry you, Charlie."

"You do?"

"I loooooooooooove you." Sylvia, who clearly was not going to finish tending to him, threw herself across her side of the bed and began to cry.

"You do?" Charlie rather liked their current arrangement, and given that Sylvia had more or less engineered it, he had assumed it was as she wanted it.

"Of course. I want you to leave Marla and marry me."

"But I don't—" He had started to say he didn't want to leave Marla and marry Sylvia, but he realized this was probably not tactful. "I just don't know how to tell Marla. It will break her heart. We've been together thirty-eight years."

"I've given it some thought." Her tears had dried with suspicious speed. "You have to choose. For the next month, I'm not going to see you at all. In fact, I'm not going to see you again until you tell Marla what we have."

"Okay." Charlie laid back and waited for Sylvia to continue.

"Starting now, Charlie."

"Now? I mean, I'm already here. Why not Saturday?"

"Now."

Two days later, as Charlie was puttering around the house, wondering what to do with himself, Marla asked: "Aren't you going to play golf?"

"What?" Then he remembered. "Oh, yeah. I guess so." He put on his golf gear, gathered up his clubs, and headed out. But to where? How should he kill the next five hours? He started to go to the movies, but he passed the club on his way out to the multiplex and thought that it looked almost fun. He pulled in and inquired about getting a lesson. It was harder than it looked, but not impossible, and the pro said the advantage of being a beginner was that he had no bad habits.

"You're awfully tan," Marla said, two weeks later.

"Am I?" He looked at his arms, which were reddish-brown, while his upper arms were still ghostly white. "You know, I changed suntan lotion. I was using a really high SPF, it kept out all the rays."

"When I paid the credit card bill, I noticed you were spending a lot more money at the country club. Are you sneaking in extra games?"

"I'm playing faster," he said, "so I have time to have drinks at the bar, or even a meal. In fact, I might start going out on Sundays, too. Would you mind?"

"Oh, I've been a golf widow all this time," Marla said. "What's another day? As long"—she smiled playfully—"as long as it's really golf and not another woman."

Charlie was stung by Marla's joke. He had always been a faithful husband. That is, he had been a faithful husband for thirty-six years, and then there had been an interruption, one of relatively short duration given the length of their marriage, and now he was faithful again, so it seemed unfair for Marla to tease him this way.

"Well, if you want to come along and take a lesson yourself, you're welcome to. You might enjoy it."

"But you always said golf was a terribly jealous mistress, that you wouldn't advise anyone you know taking it up because it gets such a horrible hold on you."

"Did I? Well, if you can't beat 'em, join 'em."

**Marla came** to the club the next day. She had a surprising aptitude for golf and it gave her extra confidence to see that Charlie was not much better than she, despite his two years of experience. She liked the club, too, although she was puzzled that Charlie didn't seem to know many people. "I kind of keep to myself," he said.

The month passed quickly, so quickly and pleasantly that he found himself surprised when Sylvia called.

"Well?" she asked.

"Well?" he echoed.

"Did you tell her?"

"Her? Oh, Marla. No. No. I just couldn't."

"If you don't tell her, you'll never see me again."

"I guess that's only fair."

"What?" Sylvia's voice, never her best asset, screeched perilously high.

"I accept your conditions. I can't leave Marla, and therefore I can't see you." Really, he thought, when would he have time? He was playing so much golf now, and while Marla seldom came to the club on Thursdays, she accompanied him on Saturdays and Sundays.

"But you love me."

"Yes, but Marla is the mother of my children."

"Who are now grown and living in other cities and barely remember to call you except on your birthday."

"And she's a fifty-seven-year-old woman. It would be rather mean, just throwing her out in the world at this age, never having worked and all. Plus, a divorce would bankrupt me."

"A passion like ours is a once-in-a-lifetime event."

"It is?"

"What?" she screeched again.

"I mean, it *is*. We have known a great passion. But that's precisely because we haven't been married. Marriage is different, Sylvia. You'll just have to take my word on that."

This apparently was the wrong thing to say, as she began to sob in earnest. "But I would be married to *you*. And I love you. I can't live without you."

"Oh, I'm not much of a catch. Really. You'll get over it."

"I'm almost forty! I've sacrificed two crucial years, being with you on your terms."

Charlie thought that was unfair, since the terms had been Sylvia's from the start. But all he said was: "I'm sorry. I didn't mean to lead you on. And I won't anymore."

He thought that would end matters, but Sylvia was a remarkably focused woman. She continued to call— the office, not his home, which indicated to Charlie that she was not yet ready to wreak the havoc she was threatening. So Marla remained oblivious and their golf continued to improve, but his assistant was beginning to suspect what was up and he knew he had to figure out a way to make it end. But given that he wasn't the one who had made it start, he didn't see how he could.

---

**On Thursday,** just as he was getting ready to leave the office for what was now his weekly midday nine, Sylvia called again, crying and threatening to hurt herself.

"I was just on my way out," he said.

"Where do you have to go?"

"Golf," he said.

"Oh, I see." Her laugh was brittle. "So you have someone new already. Your current assistant? I guess your principles have fallen a notch."

"No, I really play golf now."

"Charlie, I'm not your wife. Your stupid lie won't work on me. It's not even your lie, remember?"

"No, no, there's no one else. I've, well, reformed! It's like a penance to me. I've chosen my loveless marriage and golf over the great passion of my life. It's the right thing to do."

He thought she would find this suitably romantic, but it only seemed to enrage her more.

"I'm going to go over to your house and tell Marla that you're cheating."

"Don't do that, Sylvia. It's not even true."

"You cheated with me, didn't you? And a tiger doesn't change his stripes."

Charlie wanted to say that he was not so much a tiger as a house cat who had been captured by a petulant child. True, it had been hard to break with Sylvia once things had started. She was very good at a lot of things that Marla seldom did and never conducted with enthusiasm. But it had not been his idea. And, confronted with an ultimatum, he had honored her condition. He hadn't tried to have it both ways. He was beginning to think Sylvia was unreliable.

"Meet me at my apartment right now, or I'll call Marla."

He did, and it was a dreary time, all tears and screaming and no attentions paid to him whatsoever, not even after he held her and stroked her hair and said he did love her.

"You should be getting back to work," he said at last, hoping to find any excuse to stop holding her.

She shook her head. "My position was eliminated two weeks ago. I'm out of work."

"Is that why you're so desperate to get married?"

She wailed like a banshee, not that he really knew what a banshee sounded like. Something scary and shrill. "No. I love you, Charlie. I want to be your wife for that reason alone. But the last month, with all this going on, I haven't been at my best, and they had a bad quarter, so I was a sitting duck. In a sense, I've lost my job because of you, Charlie. I'm unemployed and I'm alone. I've hit rock bottom."

"You could always come back to the company. You left on good terms and I'd give you a strong reference."

"But then we couldn't be together."

"Yes." He was not so clever that he had thought of this in advance, but now he saw it would solve everything.

"And that's the one thing I could never bear."

Charlie, his hand on her hair, looked out the window. It was such a beautiful day, a little cooler than usual, but still sunny. If he left now—but, no, he would have to go back to the office. He wouldn't get to play golf at all today.

"Who is she, Charlie?"

"Who?"

"The other woman."

"There is no other woman."

"Stop lying, or I really will go to Marla. I'll drive over there right now, while you're at work. After all, I don't have a job to go to."

She was crazy, she was bluffing. She was so crazy that even if she wasn't bluffing, he could probably persuade Marla that she was a lunatic. After all, what proof did she have? He had never allowed the use of any camera, digital or video, although Sylvia had suggested it from time to time. There were no e-mails. He never called her. And he was careful to leave his DNA, as he thought of it, only in the appropriate places, although this included some places that Marla believed inappropriate. He had learned much from the former president and the various television shows on crime scene investigations.

"Look, if it's money you need—"

"I don't want money! I want you!"

And so it began all over again, the crying and the wailing, only this time there was no calming her. She was obsessed with the identity of his new mistress, adamant that he tell her everything, enraged by his insistence that he really did play golf in his spare time. Finally, he thought to take her down to the garage beneath her apartment and show her the clubs in the trunk of his car.

"So what?" she said. "You always carried your clubs."

"But I know what they are now," he said, removing a driver. "See this one, it's—"

"I know what's going on and I'm done, I tell you. The minute you leave here, I'm going to go upstairs and call Marla. It's her or me. Stop fucking with me, Charlie."

"I really wish you wouldn't use that word, Sylvia. It's coarse."

"Oh, you don't like hearing it, but you sure like doing it. Fuck! Fuck, fuck, fuck, fucking!"

She stood in front of him, hands on her hips. Over the course of their two-year affair she had not become particularly more attractive, although she had learned to use a depilatory on her upper lip. What would happen if she went to Marla? She would probably stay with him, but it would be dreary, with counseling and recriminations. And they really were happier than ever, united by their love of golf, comfortable in their routines. He couldn't bear to see it end.

"I can't have that, Sylvia. I just can't."

"Then choose."

"I already have."

No, he didn't hit her with the driver. He wouldn't have risked it for one thing, having learned that it was rare to have a club that felt so right in one's grip and also having absorbed a little superstition about the game. Also, there would have been blood, and it was impossible to clean every trace of blood from one's trunk, according to those television shows. Instead, he pushed her, gently but firmly, and she fell back into the trunk, which he closed and latched. He then drove back to the office, parking in a remote place where Sylvia's thumping, which was growing fainter, would not draw any attention. At home that night, he ate dinner with Marla, marveling over the Greg Norman shiraz that she served with the salmon. "Do you hear something out in the garage?" she asked at one point. "A knocking noise?"

"No," he said.

It was Marla's book club night and after she left, he went out to the garage and circled his car for a few minutes, thinking. Ultimately, he figured out how to attach a garden hose from the exhaust through a cracked window and into the backseat, where he pressed it into the crevice of the seat, which could be released to create a larger carrying space, like a hatchback, but only from within the car proper. Sylvia's voice was weaker, but still edged with fury. He ignored her. Marla was always gone for at least three hours on book club night and he figured that would be long enough.

**It would** be several weeks before Sylvia Nichols's body was found in a patch of wilderness near a state park. While clearly a murder, it was considered a baffling case from the beginning. How had a woman been killed by carbon monoxide poisoning, then dumped at so remote a site? Why had she been killed? Homicide police, noting the large volume of calls from her home phone to Charlie's work number, questioned him, of course, but he was able to say with complete sincerity that she was a former employee who was keen to get a job back since being let go, and he hadn't been able to help her despite her increasing hysteria. DNA evidence indicated she had not had sex of any sort in the hours before her death. Credit card slips bore out the fact that Charlie was a regular at the local country club, and his other hours were accounted for. Even Marla laughed at the idea of her husband having an affair, saying he was far too busy with golf to have time for another woman.

"Although I'm the one who broke ninety first," she said. "Which is funny, given that Charlie has a two-year head start on me."

"It's a terrible mistress, golf," Charlie said.

"I don't play, but they say it's the worst you can have," the homicide detective said.

"Just about," Charlie said.

# PART THREE

# My Baby Walks the Streets of Baltimore

# Easy as A-B-C

Another house collapsed today. It happens more and more, especially with all the wetback crews out there. Don't get me wrong. I use guys from Mexico and Central America, too, and they're great workers, especially when it comes to landscaping. But some other contractors aren't as particular as I am. They hire the cheapest help they can get and the cheapest comes pretty high, especially when you're excavating a basement, which has become one of the hot fixes around here. It's not enough, I guess, to get the three-story row-house with four bedrooms, gut it from top to bottom, creating open, airy kitchens where grandmothers once smoked the wallpaper with bacon grease and sour beef, or carve master bath suites in the tiny middle rooms that the youngest kids always got stuck with. No, these people have to have the full family room, too, which means digging down into the old dirt basements, putting in new floors and walls. But if you miscalculate—boom. Nothing to do but bring the fucker down and start carting away the bricks.

It's odd, going into these houses I knew as a kid, seeing what people have paid for sound structures that they consider mere shells, all because they might get a sliver of water view from a top-floor window or the ubiquitous rooftop deck. Yeah, I know words like ubiquitous. Don't act so surprised. The stuff in books—anyone can learn that. All you need is time and curiosity and a library card, and you can fake your way through a conversation with anyone. The work I do, the crews I supervise, that's what you can't fake, because it could kill people, literally. I feel bad for the men who hire me, soft types who apologize for their feebleness, whining: I wish I had the time. Give those guys a thousand years and they couldn't rewire a single fixture or install a gas dryer. You know the first thing I recommend when I see a place where the "man of the house" has done some work? A carbon monoxide detector. I couldn't close my eyes in my brother-in-law's place until I installed one, especially when my sister kept bragging on how handy he was.

The boom in South Baltimore started in Federal Hill, before my time, flattened out for a while in the nineties, and now it's roaring again, spreading through south Federal Hill, and into Riverside Park and all the way down Fort Avenue into Locust Point, where my family lived until I was ten and my grandparents stayed until the day they died, the two of them, side by side. My grandmother had been ailing for years and my grandfather, as it turned out, had been squirreling away the various painkillers she had been given along the way, preparing himself. She died in her sleep and, technically, he did, too. A self-induced, pharmaceutical sleep, but sleep nonetheless. We found them on their bed, and the pronounced rigor made it almost impossible to separate their entwined hands. He literally couldn't live without her. Hard on my mom, losing them that way, but I couldn't help feeling it was pure and honest. Pop-pop didn't want to live alone and he didn't want to come stay with us in the house out in Linthicum. He didn't really have friends. She was his whole life and he had been content to care for her through all her pain and illness. He would have done that forever. But once that job was done, he was done, too.

My mother sold the house for $75,000. That was a dozen years ago and boy, did we think we had put one over on the buyers. Seventy-five thousand! For a house on Decatur Street in Locust Point. And all cash for my mom, because it had been paid off forever. We went to Hausner's the night of the closing, toasted our good fortune. The old German restaurant was still open then, crammed with all that art and junk. We had veal and strawberry pie and top-shelf liquor and toasted Grandfather for leaving us such a windfall.

So imagine how I felt when I got a referral for a complete redo at my grandparents' old address and the real estate guy tells me: "She got it for only $225,000, so she's willing to put another $100,000 in it and I bet she won't bat an eyelash if the work goes up to $150,000."

"Huh" was all I managed. Money-wise, the job wasn't in my top tier, but then, my grandparents' house was small even by the neighborhood's standards, just two stories. It had a nice-size backyard, though, for a rowhouse. My grandmother had grown tomatoes and herbs and summer squash on that little patch of land.

"The first thing I want to do is get a parking pad back here," my client said, sweeping a hand over what was an overgrown patch of weeds, the chain-link fence sagging around it. "I've been told that will increase the value of the property by $10,000, $20,000."

"You a flipper?" I asked. More and more amateurs were getting into real estate, feeling that the stock market wasn't for them. They were the worst of all possible worlds, panicking at every penny over the original estimate, riding my ass. You want to flip property for profit, you need to be able to do the work yourself. Or buy and hold. This woman didn't look like the patient type.

"No, I plan to live here. In fact, I hope to move in as quickly as possible, so time is more important to me than money. I was told you're fast."

"I don't waste time, but I don't cut corners," I said. "Mainly, I just try to make my customers happy."

She tilted her head up. It was the practiced look of a woman who had been looking at men from under her eyelashes for much of her life, sure they would be charmed. And, okay, I was. Dark hair, cut in one of those casual, disarrayed styles, darker eyes that made me think of kalamata olives, which isn't particularly romantic, I guess. But I really like kalamata olives. With her fair skin, it was a terrific contrast.

"I'm sure you'll make me very happy" was all she said.

**I guess** here is where I should mention that I'm married going on eighteen years, and pretty happily, too. I realize it's a hard concept to grasp, especially for a lot of women, but you can be perfectly happy, still in love with your wife, maybe more in love with your wife than you've ever been, but it's eighteen years and a young, firm-fleshed woman looks up at you through her eyelashes and it's not a crime to think: I like that. Not: *I'd like to hit that,* which I hear the young guys on my crews say. Just: I like that, that's nice, if life were different, I'd make time for that. But I was married, with two kids and a sweet wife, Angeline, who'd only put on a few pounds and still kept her hair blond and long, and was pretty appreciative of the life my work had built for the two of us. So I had no agenda. I was just weak.

But part of Deirdre's allure was how much she professed to love the very things whose destruction she was presiding over, even before I told her that the house had belonged to my grandparents. She exclaimed over the wallpaper in their bedroom, a pattern of yellow roses, even as it was steamed off the walls. She ran a hand lovingly over the banister, worn smooth by my younger hands, not to mention my butt a time or two. The next day it was gone, yanked from its moorings by my workers. She all but composed an ode to the black-and-white tile in the single full bath, but that didn't stop her from meeting with Charles Tile Co. and choosing a Tuscany-themed medley for what was to become the master bath suite. ("Medley" was their word, not mine.)

She had said she wanted it fast, which made me ache a little, because the faster it went, the sooner I would be out of her world. But it turned out she didn't care about speed so much once we got the house to the point where she could live among the ongoing work—and once her end-of-the-day inspections culminated with the two of us in her raw, unfinished bedroom. She was wilder than I had expected, pushing to do things that Angeline would never have tolerated, much less asked for. In some part of my mind, I knew her abandon came from the fact that she never lost sight of the endpoint. The work would be concluded and this would conclude, too. Which was what I wanted as well, I guess. I had no desire to leave Angeline or cause my kids any grief. Deirdre and I were scrupulous about keeping our secret, and not even my longtime guys, the ones who knew me best, guessed anything was up. To them, I bitched about her as much as I did any client, maybe a little more. "Moldings?" my carpenter would ask. "Now she wants moldings?" And I would roll my eyes and shrug, say: "Women."

"Moldings?" Deirdre asked.

"Don't worry," I told her. "No charge. But I saw you look at them."

And so it was with the appliances, the countertops, the triple-pane windows. I bought what she wanted, billed for what she could afford. Somehow, in my mind, it was as if I had sold the house for $225,000, as if all that profit had gone to me, instead of the speculator who had bought the house from my mother and then just left it alone to ripen. Over time, I probably put $10,000 of my own money into those improvements, even accounting for my discounts on material. Some men give women roses and jewelry. I gave Deirdre a marble bathroom and a beautiful old mantel for the living room fireplace, which I restored to the wood-burning hearth it had never been. My grandparents had had one of those old gas-fired logs, but Deirdre said they were tacky and I suppose she was right.

Go figure—I've never had a job with fewer complications. The weather held, there were no surprises buried within the old house. "A deck," I said. "You'll want a rooftop deck to watch the fireworks." And not just any deck, of course. I built it myself, using teak and copper accents, helped her shop for the proper furniture, outdoor hardy but still feminine, with curvy lines and that verdigris patina she loved so much. I showed her how to cultivate herbs and perennials in pots, but not the usual wooden casks. No, these were iron, to match the décor. If I had to put a name to her style, I guess I'd say Nouvelle New Orleans—flowery, but not overly so, with genuine nineteenth-century pieces balanced by contemporary ones. I guess her taste was good. She certainly thought so and told me often enough. "If only I had the pocketbook to keep up with my taste," she would say with a sigh and another one of those sidelong glances, and the next thing I knew I'd be installing some wall sconce she simply had to have.

One twilight—we almost always met at last light, the earliest she could leave work, the latest I could stay away from home—she brought a bottle of wine to bed after we had finished. She was taking a wine-tasting course over at this restaurant in the old foundry. A brick foundry, a place where men like my dad had once earned decent wages, and now it housed this chichi restaurant, a gallery, a health club, and a spa. The old P&G plant became something called Tide Point, which was supposed to be some high-tech mecca, and they're building condos on the grain piers. The only real jobs left in Locust Point are at Domino Sugar and Phillips, where the red neon crab still clambers up and down the smokestack.

"Nice," I said, although in truth I don't care much for white wine and this was too sweet for my taste.

"Viognier," she said. "Twenty-six dollars a bottle."

"You can buy top-shelf bourbon for that and it lasts a lot longer."

"You can't drink bourbon with dinner," she said with a laugh, as if I had told a joke. "Besides, wine can be an investment. And it's cheaper by the case. I'd like to get into that, but if you're going to do it, you have to do it right, have a special kind of refrigerator, keep it climate controlled."

"Your basement would work."

And that's how I came to build her a wine cellar, at cost. It didn't require excavating the basement, luckily, although I was forever bumping my head on the ceiling when I straightened up to my full height. But I'm six-three and she was just a little thing, no more than five-two, barely a hundred pounds. I used to carry her to bed and, well, show her other ways I could manipulate her weight. She liked me to sit her on the marble counter in her master bath, far forward on the edge, so I was supporting most of her weight. Because of the way the mirrors were positioned, we could both watch and it was a dizzying infinity, our eyes locked into our own eyes and into each other's. I know guys who call a sink fuck the old American Standard, but I never thought of it that way. For one thing, there wasn't a single American Standard piece in the bathroom. And the toilet was a Canadian model, smuggled in, so she could have the bigger tank that had been outlawed in the interest of water conservation. Her shower was powerful, too, a stinging force that I came to know well, scrubbing up afterward.

The wine cellar gave me another month—putting down a floor, smoothing and painting the old plaster walls. My grandparents had used the basement for storage and us cousins had played hide-and-seek in the dark, a made-up version that was particularly thrilling, where you moved silently, trying to get close enough to grab the ones in hiding, then rushing back to the stairs, which were the home-free base. As it sometimes happens, the basement seemed larger when it was full of my grandparents' junk. Painted and pared down, it was so small. But it was big enough to hold the requisite refrigeration unit and the custom-made shelves, a beautiful burled walnut, for the wines she bought.

I was done. There was not another improvement I could make to the house, so changed now it was as if my family and its history had been erased. Deirdre and I had been hurtling toward this day for months and now it was here. I had to move on to other projects, ones where I would make money. Besides, people were beginning to wonder. I wasn't around the other jobs as much, but I also wasn't pulling in the kind of money that would help placate Angeline over the crazy hours I was working. Time to end it.

Our last night, I stopped at the foundry, spent almost forty bucks on a bottle of wine that the young girl in the store swore by. Cakebread, the guy's real name. White, too, because I knew Deirdre loved white wines.

"Chardonnay," she said.

"I noticed you liked whites."

"But not chardonnay so much. I'm an ABC girl—anything but chardonnay. Dennis says chardonnay is banal."

"Dennis?"

She didn't answer. And she was supposed to answer, supposed to say: Oh, you know, that faggot from my wine-tasting class, the one who smells like he wears strawberry perfume. Or: That irritating guy in my office. Or even: A neighbor, a creep. He scares me. Would you still come around, from time to time, just to check up on me? She didn't say any of those things.

Instead, she said: "We were never going to be a regular thing, my love."

Right. I knew that. I was the one with the wife and the house and the two kids. I was the one who had everything to lose. I was the one who was glad to be getting out, before it could all catch up with me. I was the one who was careful not to use the word "love," not even in the lighthearted way she had just used it. Sarcastic, almost. It made me think that it wasn't my marital status so much that had closed off that possibility for us, but something even more entrenched. I was no different from the wallpaper, the banister, the garden. I had to be removed for the house to be truly hers.

My grandmother's parents had thought she was too good for my grandfather. They were Irish, shipworkers who had gotten the hell out of Locust Point and moved uptown, to Charles Village, where the houses were much bigger. They looked down on my grandfather just because he was where they once were. It killed them, the idea that their precious youngest daughter might move back to the neighborhood and live with an Italian, to boot. Everybody's got to look down on somebody. If there's not somebody below you, how do you know you've traveled any distance at all in your life? For my dad's generation, it was all about the blacks. I'm not saying it was right, just that it was, and it hung on because it was such a stark, visible difference. And now the rules have changed again, and it's the young people with money and ambition who are buying the houses in Locust Point and the people in places like Linthicum and Catonsville and Arbutus are the ones to be pitied and condescended to. It's hard to keep up.

My hand curled tight around the neck of the wine bottle. But I placed it gently in its berth in the special refrigerator, as if I were putting a newborn back in its bed.

"One last time?" I asked her.

"Of course," she said.

She clearly was thinking it would be the bed, romantic and final, but I opted for the bathroom, wanting to see her from all angles. Wanting her to see, to witness, to remember how broad my shoulders were, how white and small she looked when I was holding her. When I moved my hands from her hips to her head, she thought I was trying to position her mouth on mine. It took her a second to realize that my hands were on her throat, not her head, squeezing, squeezing, squeezing. She fought back, if you could call it that, but all her hands could find was marble, smooth and immutable. Yeah, that's another word I know. Immutable. She may have landed a few scratches, but a man in my line of work gets banged up all the time. No one would notice a beaded scab on the back of my hand, or even on my cheek.

I put her body in a trash bag, covering it with lime left over from a landscaping job. Luckily, she hadn't been so crazed that she wanted a fireplace in the basement, so all I had to do was pull down the fake front I had placed over the old hearth down there, then brick her in, replace the fake front.

Her computer was on, as always, her e-mail account open because she used cable for her Internet, a system I had installed. I read a few of her sent messages, just to make sure I aped her style, then sent one to an office address, explaining the family emergency that would take me out of town for a few days. Then I sent one to "Dennis," angry and hate-filled, accusing him of all kinds of things. Finally, I cleaned the house best I could, especially the bathroom, although I didn't feel I had to be too conscientious. I was the contractor. Of course my fingerprints would be around.

Weeks later, when she was missing and increasingly presumed dead according to the articles I read in the Sunpapers, I sent a bill for the things that I had done at cost, marked it "Third and Final Notice" in large red letters, as if I didn't even know what was going on. She was just an address to me. Her parents paid it, even apologized for their daughter being so irresponsible, buying all this stuff she couldn't afford. I told them I understood, having my own college-age kids and all. I said I was so sorry for what had happened and that I hoped they found her soon. I do feel sorry for them. They can't begin to cover the monthly payments on the place, so it's headed toward foreclosure. The bank will make a nice profit, as long as the agents gloss over the reason for the sale; people don't like a house with even the hint of a sordid history.

And I'm glad now that I put in the wine cellar. Makes it less likely that the new owner will want to dig out the basement, risk its collapse, and the discovery of what will one day be a little bag of bones, nothing more.

# Black-Eyed Susan

The Melville family had Preakness coming and going, as Dontay's Granny M liked to say. From their rowhouse south of Pimlico, the loose assemblage of three generations—sometimes as many as twelve people in the three-bedroom house, never fewer than eight—squeezed every coin they could from the third Saturday in May, and they were always looking for new ways. Revenue streams, as Dontay had learned to call them in Pimlico Middle's stock-picking club. Last year, for example, the Melvilles had tried a barbecue stand, selling racegoers hamburgers and hot dogs, but the city health people had shut them down before noon. So they were going to try bottled water this year, maybe some sodas, although sly-like, because they could bust you for not charging sales tax, too.

They had considered salted nuts, but that was more of a Camden Yards thing. People going to the track didn't seem to want nuts as much, not even pistachios. Candy melted no matter how cool the day, and it was hard to be competitive on chips unless you went off-brand, and Baltimore was an Utz city.

Parking was the big moneymaker, anyway. Over the years, the Melvilles had figured they could make exactly six spaces in their front yard, plus two in the driveway. They charged $30 a spot, which was a fair price, close as they were to the entrance, and that $30 included *true* vigilance, as Uncle Marcus liked to say to the people who tried to negotiate. These days, most of their business was repeat customers, old-timers who had figured out that the houses south of the racetrack were much closer to the entrance than the places on the other side of Northern Parkway. The first-timers, now they were a little nervous about coming south of the track, but once they made that long, long trek back to the Northern Parkway side, they started looking south.

So, eight vehicles times thirty—that was $240. But they weren't done yet. All the young ones ran shopping carts, not just for the Melvilles' own parkers but for the on-the-street ones who couldn't make it the whole way with their coolers and grocery sacks. Dontay and his cousins couldn't charge as much as the north side boys, given the shorter distance, but they made more trips, so it came out about the same. Most of the folks gave you at least ten dollars to haul a cooler, although there was always some woe-is-me motherfucker— that's what Uncle Marcus called them, outside Granny M's hearing—who tried to find a reason to short you at the gate.

The money didn't end just because the race did. On the day after Preakness, the older Melvilles all signed up for cleanup duty in the infield, and there wasn't a year that went by that someone didn't find a winning ticket in the debris. Never anything huge, but often good for twenty bucks or so. People got drunk, threw the wrong tickets down. You just had to keep the Sunpapers in your back pocket, familiarize yourself with the race results. This was going to be Dontay's first year on cleanup, and he couldn't help hoping that he would find a winning ticket. His uncle had lied about his age to get him a spot on the crew, so he'd make the minimum wage up front. But the draw was what you might find—not just tickets, but perfectly good cartons of soda and beer, maybe even jewelry and wallets without ID.

But Preakness itself was the best day, the biggest haul. The night before, Dontay oiled his cart's wheels and polished his pitch. There was a right way to do it, bold but not too much so. People didn't like to feel hustled. He also pondered the downside to Preakness: no one needed the carts to carry stuff away because the coolers were always empty by day's end, light enough for the weakest, most sissified men to heave onto their shoulders or drag on the pavement behind them. Which was a shame, because people were looser by the end of the day, wavy with liquor and their winnings. Dontay was still thinking on how to develop a service that people needed when the race was over. The main thing everyone wanted was a fast getaway, another virtue of the Melvilles' location, which had several ways out of the neighborhood. What would people pay to ride a helicopter, though? There had to be other possibilities. Dontay thought on it. Besides, more and more people were bringing in wheeled coolers, a troubling development.

Dontay was a Melville and all the Melvilles were industrious by nature. True, some had focused their energies on less legal businesses, which is why the number of the people in the house tended to fluctuate. They were at the high end right now, with Uncle Stevie home from Hagerstown and Delia's twins staying with them, while Delia was spending time on the West Side, in that place that Granny M called "thereabouts." When's our mama coming? the twins asked late at night, when they were sleepy and forgetful. Where's our mama? "Thereabouts," Granny M said. "She'll be coming home shortly." Granny M pledged that her house was open to all her children and her children's children and, when the time came, and it was coming, her children's children's children, but she had rules. Church was optional if you were over twelve. Sobriety was not. That's why she had squashed Uncle Marcus's plan to buy some cheap tallboys, layer them beneath the bottled waters and sodas, in case some folks had second thoughts about paying track prices for beer or decided they hadn't brought enough beer of their own.

**The track** didn't open its doors until nine, but the Melvilles' Preakness Day started at 7 A.M., with Uncle Marcus and Ronnie Moe, a shirttail relation, taking the two cars over to the Wabash metro stop, then cabbing back before traffic started peaking. Weather for Preakness was seldom fine—either it fell short of its potential and ended up rainy and cool or it overshot spring altogether, delivering a full-blown Baltimore scorcher with air that felt like feathers. Today was a chilly one, and Dontay was on a roll, ferrying coolers faster than he ever had before, his money piling up in the Tupperware container that Granny M had marked with his name. He would have liked to keep his bills in his pocket, a fat roll to stroke from time to time, but he knew better. Even with the streets crowded as they were today, with uniformed police officers everywhere, the bigger boys, the lazy ones who didn't like to extend themselves, wouldn't hesitate to knock him down and take his money.

In his head, he tried to add up what he had made so far. Granny M took a cut for the collection plate, but he'd still have enough for the new version of *Grand Theft Auto.* Or should he buy some new Nikes? But Granny M would buy him shoes, no matter how much she bitched and moaned and threatened to get him no-brands at the outlets. Beneath her complaints, she knew that shoes mattered. Even when Uncle Marcus was a kid, so long ago that there weren't any Nikes, just Keds and Jack Purcell's, it had been death to come to school in no-brands. Fishheads, they called them then. Granny M wouldn't do that to him, as long as he passed all his classes, which he had more than done. Dontay not only had almost all B's going into the final grading period, his stock-picking club had come in third in the state for all middle schools. And Dontay deserved most of the credit for that because he had said they should buy Apple before Christmas, then drop it quick, all those people buying iPods and shit.

An iPod—now wouldn't that be something to have, although the Melvilles had only one computer and it was hard to get any time on it, even for homework. Plus, the big kids in the neighborhood knew to look for those white wires, and they would smack a man down for them, then kick him harder if it turned out to be some knockoff player. He counted up in his head again, but naw, he was nowhere close. And here it was going on 3 P.M., the meaty part of the day gone. Unless he found a winning ticket at the cleanup, he wasn't going to be buying anything like that. His own CD player, though. That was within reach.

The big race was only ninety minutes away and the neighborhood had pretty much gone quiet when a man and a woman in a huge-ass Escalade inquired about the final space at the Melvilles', which had opened up unexpectedly after some couple had a fight earlier in the afternoon. That was what Dontay thought had happened, at least. He had escorted two people in, a man and a woman, and the woman had shown up not even an hour later, so anxious to get away that she had shot the car right over the curb, no thought to the shocks. The Melvilles were wondering what would happen at day's end, when the man returned for the car that wasn't there. Maybe they could offer to take him home, undercut the local cabbies.

"How much to park here?" asked this latecomer, the woman behind the wheel of the Escalade.

Uncle Marcus hesitated. This late in the day, she might expect a discount. Before he could answer, she jumped in: "Forty dollars?"

"Sure," he said. "Back it in."

"I admit I can't maneuver this thing into such a tight space," she said. "It's new and I'm still not used to it. Would you do it for me?"

She hopped out and let Uncle Marcus take her place, her dude still sitting stone-faced in the passenger seat. Dontay thought that was cold, making a man look weak that way, but the man in the Escalade didn't seem to notice. Uncle Marcus showed off a little, whipping the SUV back into the space and cutting it a lot closer than he should have, but he pulled it off. The woman counted two twenties into his hand, then added a ten.

"For the extra service," she said. Her man didn't say anything.

Oh, how Dontay prayed they would have a cooler, but they didn't look to be cooler people. She looked like a grandstand type—polka-dotted halter dress, big hat and dark glasses, high-heeled shoes in the same yellow as the background of her dress. The man had a blazer and a tie and light-colored pants. Those types usually didn't have coolers. In fact, those types didn't usually park in the yards, but it was late. Maybe the lots at the track were full.

Still, it never hurt to ask.

"You need help? I mean, you got any things you need carried in?" He indicated his parking cart. It had been in the Melville family for years, taken from a Giant Foods that wasn't even in business anymore.

"What's the going rate?" the woman asked. Not the man. She seemed to be in charge.

"Depends on what needs transporting," Dontay said. After seeing how things had worked out with Uncle Marcus, he wanted to see what she would offer to pay before he named a price.

"We have three large coolers." She opened the back of the Escalade, showed them off. They looked brand new, the price tags still on their sides.

"That's a big job," Dontay said. "They'll be piled so high in my cart, I'll have to go real slow so they don't tumble."

"Twenty dollars?"

Twice the going rate. But before he could nod, the woman quickly added.

"Each, I mean. Per cooler."

"Sure." He loaded them up, one on top of the other. "But you know I can only take you up to the gate. You got to get them to your seats by yourselves. How you going to do that?"

"We'll figure it out," she said. The man had yet to say a word.

The three coolers fit into the shopping cart, just, and rose so high that Dontay could not keep a quick pace. What did it matter? Sixty dollars, the equivalent of six trips. They must be rich people, the kind who brought champagne and—well, Dontay wasn't clear on what else rich people ate. Steak, but you wouldn't bring steak to the Preakness. Steak sandwiches, maybe.

"You do this every year?" the woman asked.

Usually, people walked ahead or behind, a little embarrassed by the transaction. But this woman kept abreast of him, her yellow high heels striking the ground with a loud clackety-clack, almost as loud as the wheels on the shopping cart.

"Yes ma'am."

"You ever think about going to the race?"

"No'm. I make too much money working it." He wished he could take that back. It wasn't good manners, much less good business to draw attention to how much a person was paying you. No one wanted to feel like a mark, Uncle Marcus always said.

"Want me to place a bet for you?" she asked. She was white-white, her skin so fair it had a blue tint to it, with red hair like a blaze beneath her black straw hat.

"Naw, that's okay. I wouldn't know what horse to bet for."

"The favorite in the Derby often comes through in the Preakness. That's a safe bet."

Dontay liked talking to the woman, liked the way she treated him, but he couldn't think of anything to say back. He tried nodding, as if he were very smart in the ways of the world, and all he did was hit a pothole, almost upset the whole load.

"But you probably don't like safe bets." The woman laughed. "Me either."

The man, who was walking behind them, still hadn't said anything.

"I'm going to bet a long shot, a horse coming out of the twelfth gate. Know how I picked it?" She didn't wait for Dontay to reply. "Horse bit his rider during a workout this week. Now that's my kind of horse."

He finally had something to contribute. "What's its name?"

"Diablo del Valle. Devil of the Valley. It's a local horse, too. That's also in its favor. A local horse with a great name who bit his jockey. How can I lose?"

"I don't know," Dontay said. "But based on what I see, a lot of people do."

She loved that, laughing long and hard. Dontay hadn't been trying to be funny, but now he wished he might do it again.

"I'll probably be one of them," the woman said. "But you know, I don't gamble to win. The track is interactive entertainment, theater in which I hold a financial stake in the outcome. If I ever found myself too invested, I'd have to stop. Don't you think? It's awful to care too much about something. Anything."

Dontay wasn't sure he followed that, but he nodded as if he did. He was wondering if the woman was cold, her shoulders and back as bare as they were. With her yellow dress with the black dots, yellow heels, and big black hat, she looked like something.

"You're a black-eyed Susan," he said.

She nodded, clearly pleased. "That I am. But they're fake, you know."

"Ma'am?"

"The black-eyed Susans. They're not in season until late August, so they buy these yellow daisies from South America and color the centers with a Magic Marker. Can you imagine?"

"How much that pay?" It hadn't occurred to Dontay that there was a single opportunity in Preakness that his family had missed. Coloring in flowers sounded easy, like something the twins could do.

"Oh, I don't know. Not enough. Nothing is ever enough, is it? Doesn't everyone want more?"

The question seemed like a test. Did she think him ungrateful or greedy?

"I'm fine, ma'am."

"Well, you're a rare one."

They had reached the entrance to the grandstand, but to Dontay's amazement, the woman didn't stop there. "We're in the infield," she said. The infield? She was paying almost as much to bring her stuff as she was paying for the tickets. The infield was mud and trash. The woman would get messed up in the infield, where no one would care that she had taken the time to look like a flower. Dontay looked for the man, but he had disappeared.

"You'll just have to let this young man help me," the woman told the ticket taker, but not in a bossy way. She had the ability to say things directly without sounding mean, as if it was just logical to do what she said.

"Not unless he's going to pay admission, too. And he can't bring that shopping cart in."

She peeled more money from her wallet.

"And ma'am?"

"Yes?"

"We need to inspect them, make sure there's no glass, nothing else that's forbidden." The Preakness ticket had a whole long list of things you couldn't bring in and Dontay stuck close to his clients, in case they needed to send things back with him.

"Why, they're just sandwiches." The woman opened the top cooler, pulled out a paper-wrapped sub. "Muffulettas. Muffies, we call them. We make them every year with that special tapenade from the Central Grocery down in New Orleans, so they're practically authentic."

She unwrapped one. It was an okay sandwich, although a little strong smelling for Dontay. He didn't much care for cheese.

The man quickly looked inside each cooler, saw the array of wrapped subs, and waved her through.

It took Dontay and the woman three trips to carry in all the coolers. It seemed like a math problem to him—how could they protect the unattended coolers at either end?—but the woman found a man at either end to keep watch. She had that way about her. They stacked each one just inside the entrance. The people around looked nasty to Dontay, and he worried about leaving the woman there, in her pretty dress.

"Diablo del Valle," she said, handing him four twenties. "You heard it here first."

"Yes ma'am," he said. "But that's extra—"

"I'll lose more than that today. At least you'll still have the money when all is said and done."

She took off her hat, fanned herself with it, and Dontay realized with a start that one of the shadows on her face was still there—a purplish bruise at the temple.

He pushed the empty cart back quickly, flying along, wondering if he might catch one more trip, then wondering how it mattered. Eighty dollars! Still not enough for an iPod, not even when it was added to all he had already earned today. He wondered briefly if he had the discipline to save it all, but he knew he didn't. The woman was right. Nothing was ever enough.

Back at the house, the Escalade was gone. "Man came back and said he forgot something," Uncle Marcus said. Dontay worried that something was wrong between the man and the woman, that he had abandoned her to the infield. He thought of her again in her yellow dress and high heels, her big black hat— and that bruise, near her eye. He hoped the man was nice to her.

**The day-after** cleanup started at 9 A.M. sharp. Just the sight of the garbage took Dontay's breath away, not to mention the smell. There was a reason this job paid, of course. But it seemed impossible that this patch of ground would ever be clean again. A bandanna around his face, Granny M's kitchen gloves shielding his hands, he picked up cans and wrappers and cigarettes, examining the tickets he found along the way, comparing them to the results page in his back pocket. But he hadn't noticed the three red-and-white coolers stacked in a column near the gates until another worker ran toward them, said, "These mine."

"How you figure?" Uncle Marcus asked.

"Called 'em, didn't I? They're in good shape. Hell, they're so new the price tags are still on them. I can use some coolers like that."

He opened the drain on the side and the water ran out, the ice long melted.

"If there sodas in there, they still be cold," one woman said hopefully. "You'd share those, wouldn't you?"

"Why not?" the man said, happy with his claim. He popped the lid—and started screaming. Well, not screaming, but kind of snorting and gagging, like it smelled real bad.

Uncle Marcus tried to hold Dontay back, but he got pretty close. Overnight, the water had soaked through the paper-wrapped sandwiches, loosening the packaging, so the sandwiches floated free. Only a lot of them weren't sandwiches. There were pieces of a person, cut into sub-size portions, cut so small that it was hard to see what some of them had been. Part of a forearm, he was pretty sure. A piece of leg.

"Well, it's definitely a dude," said one kid who got even closer than Dontay did, and Dontay decided to take his word for it.

Police came, sealed off that part of the infield, and tried to stop the cleanup for a while but saw how useless that would be. There weren't enough officers in all of Baltimore to sift the debris of the infield, looking for clues. Besides, it wasn't as if the crime had been committed there. The coolers were the only evidence. The coolers and the things within them.

Dontay watched the police talking to grown-ups—the man who had claimed the coolers, folks from Pimlico, even Uncle Marcus. No one asked to talk to him, however. No one asked, even generally, if anyone had anything they wanted to volunteer. That didn't play in Northwest Baltimore.

Later, walking home, Uncle Marcus said: "Them coolers look familiar to you?"

"Looked like every other Igloo. Nothing distinctive."

"Just that there were three and they was brand-new. Like—"

"Yeah."

"What you thinking, Dontay?"

He was thinking about the woman's face beneath her hat, her observation that nothing was ever enough. She had a nice car, a wallet thick with money, a man who seemed to do her bidding. She was going to bet on a horse that bit its rider, the Devil of the Valley. She admired its spirit, but admitted it wouldn't win in the end.

"Doesn't seem like any business of ours, does it?"

"No, I s'pose not."

The Melvilles had Preakness coming and going. You could park your car on their lawn, buy a cold drink from them, get help ferrying your supplies into the track, and know that your vehicle would be safe no matter how long you stayed. Thirty dollars bought you *true* vigilance, as Uncle Marcus always said. Over the years, they built up a retinue of regulars, people who came back again and again. The woman in the hat, the woman with the Escalade—she wasn't one of them.

# Ropa Vieja

The best Cuban restaurant in Baltimore is in Greektown. It has not occurred to the city's natives to ponder this, and if an out-of-towner dares to inquire, a shrug is the politest possible reply he or she can expect.

On the fourth day of August, one such native, Tess Monaghan, was a block away from this particular restaurant when she felt that first bead of sweat, the one she thought of as the scout, snaking a path between her breasts and past her sternum. Soon, others would follow, until her T-shirt was speckled with perspiration and the hair at her nape started to frizz. She wasn't looking forward to this interview, but she was hoping it would last long enough for her Toyota's air conditioner to get its charge back.

The Cuban Restaurant. Local lore about the place—and it had all been dredged up again, as of late—held that another name had been stenciled over the door on the night of its grand opening many years ago. The Havana Rum Co.? Plantain Plantation? Something like that. Whatever the name, the *Beacon-Light* had gotten it wrong in the review and the owner had decided it would be easier to change the name than get a correction. It had, after all, been a favorable review, with raves for the food and the novel-for-Baltimore gas station setting. If the local paper said it was The Cuban Restaurant, it was willing to be just that, and the new name was hastily painted over the old.

*Live by publicity, die by publicity.* That's what Tess Monaghan wanted to stencil above her door.

She slid her car into the empty space next to the old-fashioned gas pumps where attendants had so recently juggled a nightly crush of Mercedeses, Cadillacs, and Lincoln Navigators. Inside the cool dining room, a sullen bartender was wiping down a bar that showed no sign of having held a drink that day, and two dark-haired young waitresses stood near the coffeepot, examining their manicures and exchanging intelligence about hair removal. If Tess had been there for a meal, that conversation would have killed her usually unstoppable appetite.

She found the owner, Herb Marquez, in an office behind the bar. The glass in front of him might have held springwater, or it might have been something else. Whatever the substance, the glass was clearly half empty in Marquez's mournful eyes. His round face was as creased as a basset hound's, his gloom as thick as incense. Even his mustache drooped.

"You see that?" He waved a hand at the empty dining room.

"I saw."

"A week ago, maybe—*maybe*—you could have gotten a table here at lunch if you were willing to wait twenty, thirty minutes. At night—two weeks to get a reservation, three on weekends. That may be common in New York, but not in Baltimore. I been in the restaurant business forty years—started as a busboy at O'Brycki's, worked my way up, opened my own place, served the food my mama used to make, only better. And now it's all over because people think I polished the most popular guy in Baltimore."

"*Most* popular?" Tess had a reflexive distaste for hyperbole. "Bandit Gonzales isn't even the most beloved Oriole of all time. He's just the flavor of the month."

An unfortunate choice of words. Herb Marquez winced, no doubt thinking about the flavors he had served Bandit Gonzales, that subtle blend of spices and beef that went into *ropa vieja*. Literally, "old clothes," but these old clothes had been credited with making a new man out of the aging pitcher, having the greatest season of his life.

Until last Sunday, when a sold-out crowd in Camden Yards—not to mention the millions of fans who had tuned into the Fox game of the week—had watched him throw three wobbly pitches to the first batter, fall to his knees, and give new meaning to the term "hurler."

"Well, I'd put him in the top three," Marquez said. "After Cal Ripken and Brooks Robinson."

"No, you gotta put Boog Powell ahead of him, too. And Frank Robinson. Maybe that catcher, the one who led the crowd in 'Thank God I'm a Country Boy.' Then there's Jim Palmer and—"

"Okay, fine, he ain't even in the top five. But he was the only bright spot in the Orioles' piss-poor lineup this season and he thinks, and everyone else thinks, that he spent twenty-four hours puking his guts out because of my goddamn food. It was in all the papers. It was on *Baseball Tonight*. Those late-night guys make jokes about my food. And now the guy's talking lawsuit. I'm gonna be ruined."

He gave the last word its full Baltimore pronunciation, so it had three, maybe four syllables.

"Do you have insurance?"

"Yeah, sure, I'm so careful my liability policies have liability policies."

"So you're covered. Besides, I can't see how Gonzales was damaged, other than by heaving so hard he broke a couple of blood vessels beneath his eyes. Those heal. Trust me."

"Yeah, but he was on the last year of a three-year contract and had an endorsement deal pending. Local, but still good, for some dealership. Now they don't want him. The only endorsement Bandit could get is for Mylanta."

"That's still your insurance company's problem."

"Yeah, they'll take care of their money," Marquez said, "but me and my restaurant will be left for dead. I gotta *prove* this wasn't my fault."

"How can I help you do that? I'm a private investigator, not a health inspector."

Herb Marquez walked over to the door and closed it.

"I don't trust no one, you understand? Not even people who worked for me for years. This is a jealous town and a jealous business. Someone wanted to hurt me, and they did it by pissing in Gonzales's dinner."

Tess decided she was never going to eat out again as long as she lived.

"Not literally," Marquez added. "But someone doctored that dish. Forty people ate from that same pot Saturday night, and only one got sick. It's not like I made him his own private batch."

"You told the press you did."

"Well, it sounded nice. I wanted him to feel special."

Tess had a hunch that a handsome thirty-five-year-old man who made $6 million a year for throwing a baseball 95 mph probably felt a little too special much of the time.

"I pulled your inspections at the health department after you called me. You have had problems."

"Who hasn't? But there's a world of difference between getting caught with a line cook without a hairnet and serving someone rancid meat. If I had any of the original dish left, I could have had it tested, shown it was fine when it left here. But it was gone and the pot was washed long before he took the mound."

"Did he eat here or get takeout?"

"We delivered it special to him, whenever he called. That's why I wanted you. Your uncle says you do missing persons, right?"

She didn't bother to ask which uncle, just nodded. She had nine, all capable of volunteering her for this kind of favor.

"I had a busboy, Armando Rivera. Dominican. He claimed to play baseball there, I don't know, but I do know he was crazy for the game. Plays in Patterson Park every chance he gets. He begged me to let him take the food to Bandit. So I let him."

"Every time?"

Marquez nodded. "Locally. When he was on the road, we shipped it to him. I'm guessin' Armando delivered the food at least six times. You see, the first time he came in, it was coincidental-like, the night before opening day, and he was homesick for the food he grew up with in Miami—"

"I know, I know." Tess wanted to make the rotating wrist movement that a television director uses to get someone to speed up. The story had been repeated a dozen times in the media in the past week alone.

"And he pitched a shutout, so he decided to eat it every night before a start," Marquez continued. "And he told reporters about it, and people started coming because they thought *ropa vieja* was the fuckin' fountain of youth, capable of rebuilding a guy's arm. And now he thinks it ruined him. But it wasn't my food. It was the busboy."

"Armando Rivera. Do you have an address for him? A phone?"

"He didn't have a phone."

"Okay, but he had to provide an address, for the W-2. Right?"

Marquez dropped his head, a dog prepared for a scolding. "He didn't exactly work on the books. The restaurant business has its own version of don't ask, don't tell. Armando said he lost his green card. I paid him in cash, he did his job, he was a good worker. That is, he was a good worker until he walked out of here Saturday night with Bandit's food and disappeared."

"So, no address, no phone, no known associated. How do I find him?"

"Hell, I don't know—that's why I hired you. He lived in East Baltimore, played ball in Patterson Park. Short guy, strong looking, very dark skin."

"Gee, I guess there aren't too many Latinos in Baltimore who fit that description." Tess sighed. It was going to be like looking for a needle in the haystack. No—more like a single grain of cayenne in *ropa vieja*.

**Tess could** walk to Patterson Park from her office, so she leashed her greyhound, Esskay, and headed over there at sunset. It was still uncomfortably muggy, and she couldn't believe anyone would be playing baseball, yet a game was under way, with more than enough men to field two teams.

And they were all Latino. Tess had noticed that Central and South Americans were slowly moving into the neighborhood. The first sign had been the restaurants, Mexican and Guatemalan and Salvadoran, then the combination *tienda-farmacia*-video stores. Spanish could be heard in city streets now, although Tess's high school studies had not equipped her to follow the conversations.

Still, to see twenty, thirty men in one spot, calling to one another in a language and jargon that was not hers, was extraordinary. Stodgy Baltimore was capable of changing, after all, and not always for the worse.

The players wore street clothes and their gloves were as worn as their faces, which ran the gamut from pale beige to black-coffee dark. They were good, too, better than the overcompetitive corporate types that Tess had glimpsed at company softball games. Their lives were hard, but that only increased their capacity for joy. They played because it was fun, because they were adept at it. She watched the softball soar to the outfield again and again, where it was almost always caught. *Muchacho, muchacho, muchacho.* The center fielder had an amazing arm, capable of throwing out a runner who tried to score from third on a long fly ball. And all the players were fast, wiry and quick, drunk as six-year-olds on their own daring.

When the center fielder himself was called out at third trying to stretch a double, the players quarreled furiously, and a fistfight seemed imminent, but the players quickly backed down.

Dusk and the last out came almost simultaneously and the men gathered around a cooler filled with Carling Black Label. It wasn't legal to drink in the park, but Tess couldn't imagine the Southeast cop who would bust them. She sauntered over, suddenly aware that there were no other women here, not even as fans. The men watched her and the greyhound approach, and she decided that she would not have any problem engaging them.

Getting them to speak truthfully, about the subject she wanted to discuss—that was another matter.

"*Habla inglés?*" she asked.

All of them nodded, but only one spoke. "*Sí,*" said the center fielder, a broad-shouldered young man in a striped T-shirt and denim work pants. "I mean—yes, yes, I speak English."

"You play here regularly?"

"Yessssss." His face closed off and Tess realized that a strange woman, asking questions, was not going to inspire confidence.

"I have an uncle who owns a couple of restaurants nearby and he's looking for workers. He's in a hurry to find people. He wanted me to spread the word, then interview people at my office tomorrow. It's only a few blocks from here, and I'll be there nine to five."

"We got jobs," the spokesman said. "And not just in restaurants. I'm a—" He groped for the word in English. "I make cars."

"Well, maybe some of you want better jobs, or different ones. Or maybe you know people who are having trouble finding work—for whatever reason. My uncle's very . . . relaxed about stuff. Here's my card, just in case."

The card was neutral, giving nothing away about her real profession, just a name and number. The center fielder took it noncommittally, holding it by a corner as if he planned to throw it down the moment she left. But Tess saw some bright, interested eyes in the group.

"Hey, lady," the spokesman said as she began to walk away.

"Yes?" She couldn't believe that she was getting results so swiftly.

"If your uncle plans on cooking *tu perro,* your dog, he better put some meat on it first. You—you're fine."

Even the men's laughter sounded foreign to her ears—not mean or cruel, just different.

**The next** day, she kept her office hours as promised, although she wasn't surprised when no one showed up. She filled the time by reading everything she could find about Bandit's bout of *turista*. Herb Marquez thought this was all about him, but wasn't it also possible that someone had targeted Bandit? But she was stunned by the sheer volume of baseball information on the Internet. She wandered from site to site, taking strange detours through stats and newspaper columns, ending up in an area earmarked for "roto," which she thought was short for rotator cuff injuries. It turned out to be one of several sites devoted to rotisserie baseball, a fantasy league. Overwhelmed, she called her father, the biggest baseball fan she knew.

"You're working for Bandit Gonzales?" He couldn't have been happier if she had called to announce that she was going to marry, move to the suburbs, have two children, and buy a minivan.

"Not exactly," Tess said. "But I need to understand why someone might have wanted to make him sick last week."

"Well, a real fan would have made the owner sick, but it's not all bad for the Orioles, Bandit getting the heaves."

"How can that be good for the fans?"

"Because it happened July thirtieth."

His expectant silence told Tess that this should be fraught with meaning. But if a daughter can't be ignorant in front of her father, what's the point of having parents?

"And . . .?"

Mock-patient sigh. "July thirty-first is the trade deadline."

"Let me repeat. *And?*"

"Jesus, don't you read the sports section? July thirty-first is the last day to make trades without putting guys on waivers. A team like the Orioles, who's going nowhere, tends to dump the talent. The Mets—" Her father, as was his habit, appeared to spit after saying that team's name; 1969 had been very hard on him. "The Mets were going to take Bandit to shore up their pitching. I gotta admit, the thought of it just about killed me."

"So is he going to the Mets?"

"Jesus, the least you could do is listen to *Oriole Baseball* on 'BAL. The Mets decided to pick up some kid from the Rangers. Maybe they would have gone that way no matter what. Maybe not."

"Dad, I know you were joking about poisoning Bandit's food"—Tess hoped he was joking—"but could someone have done it? Who benefited? The

Orioles, as you said, wanted to dump him. So who gained when he didn't go?"

"The Atlanta Braves."

"Seriously, Dad."

"I was being serious." He sounded a little hurt.

"What about Bandit?"

"Huh?"

"Is there any reason he might not want to be traded?"

"You're the private detective. Ask him."

"Right, I'll just go over to where Bandit Gonzales lives and say, 'Hey, did you make yourself puke?'"

"Yeah. *Yeah.*" Her father suddenly sounded urgent. "But before you ask him that, would you get him to sign a baseball for me?"

**The problem** with looking for something is that you tend to find it.

Once Tess fixated on the idea that Bandit Gonzales might have doctored his own food, she kept discovering all sorts of reasons why he might have done just that. A property search brought up property in the so-called Valley, not far from where Ripken lived. Gonzales had taken out various permits and a behemoth of a house was under construction. At the state office building, Tess found the paperwork showing that Gonzales had recently incorporated. A check of the newspaper archives pulled up various interviews in which Gonzales mulled his post-baseball future. He had started a charity and seemed knowledgeable about local real estate.

Oh, and he wanted to open a restaurant. He had even registered a name with the state—Bandit's Cuba Café.

**Bandit lived** at Harbor Court, a luxury hotel-condo just a few blocks from Camden Yards. His corner unit had a water view from its main rooms but paid respect to Bandit's employers with a sliver of ball-park visible from the master bath. Tess knew this because she faked a need for the bathroom upon arriving, then quickly scanned Bandit's medicine cabinet for ipecac or anything that could have produced vomiting on demand. She didn't find anything, but that didn't persuade her that she was wrong in her suspicions. She went back to the living room, where a bemused Bandit was waiting. Well, waiting wasn't exactly the right word. He was sliding back and forth on an ergometer, a piece of workout equipment that Tess knew all too well. A sweep rower in college, she still worked out on an erg, and a proper erg workout pushed you to the point where you didn't need bad meat to throw up.

"You said you were from the health department?"
Bandit had no trace of an accent; his family had
escaped to Miami before he was born.

"Not exactly. But I am looking into your . . .
incident."

Bandit didn't look embarrassed. Then again, athletes gave interviews naked, so maybe getting sick in
front of others wasn't such a big deal. He slid back and
forth on the erg, up and back, up and back.

"So who do you work for?" he asked after a few
more slides.

"Do you know," Tess sidestepped, "that Johns
Hopkins is doing all this research in new viruses?
We're talking parasites, microbes, the kind of things
you used to have to travel to get."

He stopped moving on the erg, his complexion
taking on a decidedly greenish cast. "Really?"

"Really."

"How can you know if you have one?"

"Dunno." Tess shrugged.

"But you work for Hopkins."

"I didn't say that." She hadn't.

"Still, you're looking for this thing, this bug. You
think I might have it?"

Another shrug.

"Jesus fucking Joseph and Mary." He bent forward,
his head in his hands. He was a good-looking man

by almost anyone's standards, with bright brown eyes and glossy blue-black hair. His heavily muscled legs and arms were the color of flan. He was a young man by the world's standards, but his sport considered him old, and this fact seemed to be rubbing off on him. His face was lined from years in the sun and his hair was thinning at the crown.

"Did you do it yourself," Tess asked, "or did you have help?"

He lifted his face from his hands. "Why would I give myself a parasite?"

"I don't think you intended to do that. But I think you asked someone to help you last weekend because you didn't want to leave a city where you had finally put down some roots."

"Huh?"

"Or maybe it's as simple as your desire to open a restaurant that will rival the one you helped to make famous. I can see that. Why should someone else get rich because you eat his food? If someone's going to make money off of you, it should be you, right?"

Bandit began to massage his left arm, rubbing it with the unself-conscious gesture that Tess had noticed in athletes and dancers. They lived so far inside their bodies that they saw them as separate entities.

"You don't know much about baseball, do you?"

"I know enough."

"What's enough?"

"I know that the Orioles won the World Series in 1966, 1971, and 1983. I know that the American League has the DH. And I can almost explain the infield fly rule."

Now Bandit was working his knees, rubbing one, then the other. They made disturbing popping sounds, but Bandit didn't seem to notice. He could have been a guy tinkering on a car in his driveway.

"Well, here's the business of baseball. I was going to be sent to New York, in exchange for prospects. But the Mets probably wouldn't have kept me past this season, and my agent let the Orioles know I'd come back for one more season, no hard feelings. It could have been a good deal for everyone. Now I'm tainted as that meat that Herb sent over. Look, I know he didn't do it on purpose, but it happened. He's accountable."

"Could it have been anything else? What else did you eat that day?"

"Nothing but dry cereal because I felt pretty punky when I got up that morning. I shouldn't have tried to start."

It was Tess's practice to give out as little information as possible, but she needed to dish if she was going to prod Bandit into providing anything useful. "Herb thinks the delivery guy did it, on his own."

Bandit rolled his shoulders in a large, looping shrug. "Then he shouldn't have used someone new. Manny was a good guy. I signed a ball for him, chatted with him in Spanish."

"Someone *new*?"

"Yeah, and he was kind of a jerk. His attitude came in the door about three feet in front of him, then he treated it like a social call, as if I should offer him a beer, ask him to sit down and take a load off. He acted like . . . he owned me. I thought he might be a little retarded."

"Retarded."

He mistook her echo for a rebuke. "Oh yeah, you're not supposed to say that anymore. I mean, he was over forty and he was a delivery boy. That's kind of sad, isn't it? And he wouldn't shut up. I just wanted to eat my dinner and go to bed."

"I assume this building has a video system, for security?"

Another Bandit-style shrug, only forward this time.

"I dunno. Why? You think he spit in my meat on the elevator or something?"

Tess was going to be a vegetarian before this was over.

"Do people sign in? Do they have to give their tag numbers, or just their names?"

"The doorman would know, I guess." She started moving toward the door. "Hey, don't you want a photo or something?"

"Maybe for my dad. His name is Pat."

He walked over to the sleek, modern desk, which didn't look as if it got much use, and extracted a glossy photo from a folder. "Nothing for you?"

"No, that's okay."

Bandit gave her a quizzical look. "If I told you I had an ERA under four, would that impress you?"

"No, but I would pretend it did."

**The doorman** proved to be a nosy little gossip. Tess wouldn't want to live next door to him, but she wished every investigation yielded such helpful busybodies. He not only remembered the motormouth delivery "boy," but he remembered his car.

"A dark green Porsche 911, fairly new."

"You gotta be kidding."

"Why would I make that up? Guy got out in a rush, handed me his keys like he thought I was the fuckin' valet. I told him to go up and I'd watch his precious wheels. He even had vanity plates—'ICU.'"

"As in 'Intensive Care Unit'?"

"Could be. Although, in my experience, the doctors drive Jags while the lawyers who sue them pick Porsches. Hey, do you know the difference between a porcupine and a Porsche?"

"Yes," Tess said, refusing to indulge the doorman's lawyer joke, on the grounds that it was too easy.

Everything was too easy. She ran the plates, found they belonged to Dr. Scott Russell, who kept an office in a nearby professional building. Too easy, she repeated when she drove to the address and saw the Porsche parked outside. Too easy, she thought as she sat in the waiting room and pretended to read *People,* watching the white-jacketed doctor come and go, chatting rapidly to his patients. He had a smug arrogance that seemed normal in a doctor, but how would it go over in a delivery boy? A motormouth, the doorman had said. As if he were on a social call, Bandit had said. The doctor may have dressed up like a delivery boy, but he hadn't been prepared to act like one.

The only surprise was that he wasn't a surgeon or a gastroenterologist, but an ophthalmologist specializing in LASIK. ICU—now she got it. And wished she hadn't. But his practice, billed as Visualize Liberation, was clearly thriving. He presided over a half-dozen surgeries while she waited. It was easy to keep count, because each operation was simulcast on a screen in the waiting room, much to Tess's discomfort.

By 2:45 P.M., the last patient had been ushered out. The receptionist glanced curiously at Tess.

"Do you have an appointment?"

"No, but I need to speak to Dr. Russell."

"It's almost three P.M. He doesn't see anyone after three, not on Wednesdays."

"He can see just me now, or meet with me and the Baltimore city police later."

"But it's three P.M. and it's *Wednesday.*"

"So?"

"That's trade deadline. The last girl who interrupted him on a Wednesday afternoon got fired."

"Luckily, I don't work for him."

Tess walked past the receptionist, assuming someone would try to stop her. But the receptionist sat frozen at her desk, face stricken, as if Tess were heading into the lion's den.

Dr. Russell was on the phone, a hands-free headset, his back to her as he leaned back in his chair and propped his feet up on the windowsill.

"—no, no, Delino is healthy, I swear. You always think I got inside information because I'm a doctor, but all I know is eyes, not backs. I want to trade him because I don't need run production as much as I need pitching, so I'm unwilling to give you him for a closer. Look, you're not even in the hunt for one of the top four slots. It's bad sportsmanship to refuse a good trade just because you don't want me to take first place."

"Hey," Tess called out. "ICU. Get it?"

When he turned around, his narrow, foxy features were contorted with rage. "I am BUSY," he said. "I know everyone wants to consult with me, but the other doctors here are quite competent to do the intake interviews."

"I've got twenty-twenty vision," Tess said. "So does the doorman who saw you and your car at Harbor Court when you delivered food to Bandit Gonzales. Here's a tip—the next time you attempt a felony, don't use a Porsche with vanity tags."

"I'll call you back," he said into the headset. "But think about Delino, okay?" Then to Tess: "Felony? He didn't get that sick. I love Bandit Gonzales and would never hurt him. I'm counting on another win from him in his next start."

"You love Bandit Gonzales so much you poisoned him?"

"It's August and I'm in first place by only three points. There's five thousand dollars at stake. But also a principle."

In fact, five thousand dollars was what Visualize Liberation charged for one of its higher-end surgeries, a procedure that took almost fifteen minutes to perform.

"First place?"

"In roto. Rotisserie baseball. I've been in the No Lives League for almost fifteen years and never won. Never even finished in the money. Bandit Gonzales was going to help me change that. I picked him up cheap, in the draft. It was genius on my part, genius. But if he goes to the Mets . . ." He was getting visibly agitated, shaking and sweating, swinging his arms.

"But it's a fantasy league. You'd still have him, right?"

"We're an American League–only roto. When our players go to the National League, they might as well have died or quit baseball." He jumped up, began pacing around his desk. "You see? If they traded him to the Mariners, I'd be fine. But they were talking about the Mets, the Mets, the fuckin' Mets. I've hated the Mets since 1969 and they're still finding ways to screw me."

He was now hopping around the room, Rumpelstiltskin in his final rage, and Tess wondered if he would fly apart. But all he did was bang his knee on his desk, which made him curse more.

"How much did you pay Armando Rivera to let you deliver the food?"

"Two thousand dollars."

"So if you win roto, you'll only be up three thousand."

"It's not about the money," he said. "I've never won. This was supposed to be my year."

"And if you're arrested for a felony—and what you did to Bandit constitutes felonious assault—would you be disqualified?"

Russell looked thoughtful. "I dunno. I think it's all just part of being a good negotiator. That trade I was about to make, when you came in? I was lying my ass off. I do know the team doctor and he told me Delino is headed for the DL. But I had to make the trade by three, so you screwed me out of that."

**A week** later, Tess went back to the baseball diamond in Patterson Park, where the same group of men were playing their nightly game. The weather wasn't any cooler, but it held a promise of fall and the men seemed to have extra energy.

Between innings, she waved to the center fielder she remembered from the last time. He loped over warily.

"What's the score?"

"*Quatro-tres,*" he said. "Four-three. But I plan to make a home run in my next bat. Maybe I will call it, like Babe Ruth."

"I'm looking for a man named Armando Rivera— to tell him some good news, news he'll want to hear. You know him?"

"Maybe."

"Well, if you see him, tell him that Herb Marquez is cool with him, now that the guy has been forced to confess. The thing is, Marquez doesn't know that Rivera got paid to let the other man make the delivery. He thinks it was an honest mistake, that Rivera just wanted to go home early that night. And the guy who did it, he decided that any discussion of money would just make it look even more deliberate. He was keen to make a plea, put this behind him. Plus, despite having twenty-twenty vision, he doesn't really see other people so well. He couldn't pick Armando Rivera out of a lineup."

"It's an interesting story," he said. "But it doesn't mean anything to me."

He walked to the on-deck circle, picked up a bat, and began swinging it.

"By the way," Tess said, "what did you do with the two thousand dollars?"

"I don't know what you're talking about. I am a mechanic."

"Okay, you're a mechanic. But remember, it's only a game."

"At least I play the game," he said. "I don't move men around on paper and call that baseball."

He jogged to home plate with a springy, athletic stride that Tess envied. The days were getting shorter, losing a few minutes of light every day. They would be lucky to get nine innings in tonight.

# The Shoeshine Man's Regrets

Bruno Magli?"

"Uh-uh. Bally."

"How can you be so sure?"

"Some kids get flash cards of farm animals when they're little. I think my mom showed me pictures of footwear cut from magazines. After all, she couldn't have her only daughter bringing home someone who wore white patent loafers, even in the official season between Memorial Day and Labor Day. Speaking of which—there's a full Towson."

"Wow—white shoes and white belt and white tie, and ten miles south of his natural habitat, the Baltimore County courthouse. I thought the full Towson was on the endangered clothing list."

"Bad taste never dies. It just keeps evolving."

Tess Monaghan and Whitney Talbot were standing outside the Brass Elephant on a soft June evening, studying the people ahead of them in the valet parking line. A laundry truck had blocked the driveway to the restaurant's lot, disrupting the usually smooth operation, so the restaurant's patrons were milling about, many agitated. There was muttered talk of symphony tickets and the Oriole game and the Herzog retrospective at the Charles Theater.

But Tess and Whitney, mellowed by martinis, eggplant appetizers, and the perfect weather, had no particular place to go and no great urgency about getting there. They had started cataloging the clothes and accessories of those around them only because Tess had confided to Whitney that she was trying to sharpen her powers of observation. It was a reasonable exercise in self-improvement for a private detective—and a great sport for someone as congenitally catty as Whitney.

The two friends were inventorying another man's loafers—Florsheim, Tess thought, but Whitney said good old-fashioned Weejuns—when they noticed a glop of white on one toe. And then, as if by magic, a shoeshine man materialized at the Weejun wearer's elbow.

"You got something there, mister. Want me to give you a quick shine?"

Tess, still caught up in her game of cataloging, saw that the shoeshine man was old, but then, all shoeshine men seemed old these days. She often wondered where the next generation of shoeshine men would come from, if they were also on the verge of extinction, like the Towson types who sported white belts with white shoes. This man was thin, with a slight stoop to his shoulders and a tremble in his limbs, his salt-and-pepper hair cropped close. He must be on his way home from the train station or the Belvedere Hotel, Tess decided, heading toward a bus stop on one of the major east-west streets farther south, near the city's center.

"What the—?" Mr. Weejun was short and compact, with a yellow polo shirt tucked into lime-green trousers. A golfer, Tess decided, noticing his florid face and sunburned bald spot. She was not happy to see him waiting for a car, given how many drinks he had tossed back in the Brass Elephant's Tusk Lounge. He was one of the people who kept braying about his Oriole tickets.

Now he extended his left foot, pointing his toe in a way that reminded Tess of the dancing hippos in *Fantasia,* and stared at the white smear on his shoe in anger and dismay.

"You bastard," he said to the shoeshine man. "How did you get that shit on my shoe?"

"I didn't do anything, sir. I was just passing by, and I saw that your shoe was dirty. Maybe you tracked in something in the restaurant."

"It's some sort of scam, isn't it?" The man appealed to the restless crowd, glad for any distraction at this point. "Anyone see how this guy got this crap on my shoe?"

"He didn't," Whitney said, her voice cutting the air with her usual conviction. "It was on your shoe when you came out of the restaurant."

It wasn't what Mr. Weejun wanted to hear, so he ignored her.

"Yeah, you can clean my shoe," he told the old man. "Just don't expect a tip."

The shoeshine man sat down his box and went to work quickly. "Mayonnaise," he said, sponging the mass from the shoe with a cloth. "Or salad dressing. Something like that."

"I guess you'd know," Weejun said. "Since you put it there."

"No, sir. I wouldn't do a thing like that."

The shoeshine man was putting the finishing touches on the man's second shoe when the valet pulled up in a Humvee. Taxicab yellow, Tess observed, still playing the game. Save the Bay license plates and a sticker that announced the man as the member of an exclusive downtown health club.

"Five dollars," the shoeshine man said, and Weejun pulled out a five with great ostentation—then handed it to the valet. "No rewards for scammers," he said with great satisfaction. But when he glanced around, apparently expecting some sort of affirmation for his boorishness, all he saw were shocked and disapproving faces.

With the curious logic of the disgraced, Weejun upped the ante, kicking the man's shoeshine kit so its contents spilled across the sidewalk. He then hopped into his Humvee, gunning the motor, although the effect of a quick getaway was somewhat spoiled by the fact that his emergency brake was on. The Humvee bucked, then shot forward with a squeal.

As the shoeshine man's hands reached for the spilled contents of his box, Tess saw him pick up a discarded soda can and throw it at the fender of the Humvee. It bounced off with a hollow, harmless sound, but the car stopped with a great squealing of brakes and Weejun emerged, spoiling for a fight. He threw himself on the shoeshine man.

But the older man was no patsy. He grabbed his empty box, landing it in his attacker's stomach with a solid, satisfying smack. Tess waited for some-one, anyone, to do something, but no one moved. Reluctantly she waded in, tossing her cell phone to Whitney. Longtime friends who had once synched their movements in a women's four on the rowing team at Washington College, the two could still think in synch when necessary. Whitney called 911 while Tess grabbed Weejun by the collar and uttered a piercing scream as close to his ear as possible. "Stop it, asshole. The cops are coming."

The man nodded, seemed to compose himself—then charged the shoeshine man again. Tess tried to hold him back by the belt, and he turned back, swinging out wildly, hitting her in the chin. Sad to say, this physical contact galvanized the crowd in a way that his attack on an elderly black man had not. By the time the blue-and-whites rolled up, the valet parkers were holding Weejun and Whitney was examining the fast-developing bruise on Tess's jaw with great satisfaction.

"You are so going to file charges against this asshole," she said.

"Well, I'm going to file charges against him, then," he brayed, unrepentant. "He started the whole thing."

The patrol cop was in his mid-thirties, a seasoned officer who had broken up his share of fights, although probably not in this neighborhood. "If anyone's adamant about filing a report, it can be done, but it will involve about four hours down at the district."

That dimmed everyone's enthusiasm, even Whitney's.

"Good," the cop said. "I'll just take the bare details and let everyone go."

The laundry truck moved, the valet parking attendants regained their usual efficiency, and the crowd moved on, more anxious about their destinations than this bit of street theater. The shoeshine man started to walk away, but the cop motioned for him to stay, taking names and calling them in, along with DOBs. "Just routine," he told Tess, but his expression soon changed in a way that indicated the matter was anything but routine. He walked away from them, out of earshot, clicking the two-way on his shoulder on and off.

"You can go," he said to Whitney and Tess upon returning. "But I gotta take him in. There's a warrant."

"Him?" Whitney asked hopefully, jerking her chin at Weejun.

"No, him." The cop looked genuinely regretful. "Could be a mix-up, could be someone else using his name and DOB, but I still have take him downtown."

"What's the warrant for?" Tess asked.

"Murder, if you really want to know."

Weejun looked at once gleeful and frightened, as if he were wondering just who he had challenged in this fight. It would make quite a brag around the country club, Tess thought. He'd probably be telling his buddies he had taken on a homicidal maniac and won.

Yet the shoeshine man was utterly composed. He did not protest his innocence or insist that it was all a mistake, things that even a guilty man might have said under the circumstances. He simply sighed, cast his eyes toward the sky as if asking a quick favor from his deity of choice, then said: "I'd like to gather up my things, if I could."

**"It's the** damnedest thing, Tess. He couldn't confess fast enough. Didn't want a lawyer, didn't ask any questions, just sat down and began talking."

Homicide detective Martin Tull, Tess's only real friend in the Baltimore Police Department, had caught the shoeshine man's case simply by answering the phone when the patrol cop called him about the warrant. He should have been thrilled—it was an easy stat, about as easy as they come. No matter how old the case, it counted toward the current year's total of solved homicides.

"It's a little *too* easy," Tull said, sitting with Tess on a bench near one of their favorite coffeehouses, watching the water taxis zip back and forth across the Inner Harbor.

"Everyone gets lucky, even you," Tess said. "It's all too credible that the warrant was lost all these years. What I don't get is how it was found."

"Department got some grant for computer work. Isn't that great? There's not enough money to make sure DNA samples are stored safely, but some think tank gave us money so college students can spend all summer keystroking data. The guy moved about two weeks after the murder, before he was named in the warrant. Moved all of five miles, from West Baltimore to the county, but he wasn't the kind of guy who left a forwarding address. Or the cop on the case was a bonehead. At any rate, he's gone forty years, wanted for murder, and if he hadn't been in that fight night before last, he might've gone another forty."

"Did he even know there was a warrant on him?"

"Oh yeah. He knew exactly why he was there. Story came out of him as if he had been rehearsing it for years. Kept saying, Yep, I did it, no doubt about it. You do what you have to do, officer. So we charged him, the judge put a hundred thousand dollars' bail on him, a bail bondsman put up ten thousand dollars, and he went home."

"I guess someone who's lived at the same address for thirty-nine years isn't considered a flight risk."

"Flight risk? I think if I had left this guy in the room with all our opened files, he would have confessed to every homicide in Baltimore. I have never seen someone so eager to confess to a crime. I almost think he wants to go to jail."

"Maybe he's convinced that a city jury won't lock him up, or that he can get a plea. How did the victim die?"

"Blunt force trauma in a burglary. There's no physical evidence and the warrant was sworn out on the basis of an eyewitness who's been dead for ten years."

"So you probably couldn't get a conviction at all if it went to trial."

"Nope. That's what makes it so odd. Even if the witness were alive, she'd be almost ninety by now, pretty easy to break down on the stand."

"What's the file say?"

"Neighbor lady said she saw William Harrison leave the premises, acting strangely. She knew the guy because he did odd jobs in the neighborhood, even worked for her on occasion, but there was no reason for him to be at the victim's house so late at night."

"Good luck recovering the evidence from Evidence Control."

"Would you believe they still had the weapon? The guy's head was bashed in with an iron. But that's all I got. If the guy hadn't confessed, if he had stone-walled me or gotten with a lawyer, I wouldn't have anything."

"So what do you want me to tell you? I never met this man before we became impromptu tag-team wrestlers. He seemed pretty meek to me, but who knows what he was like forty years ago? Maybe he's just a guy with a conscience who's been waiting all these years to see if someone's going to catch up with him."

Tull shook his head. "One thing. He didn't know what the murder weapon was. Said he forgot."

"Well, forty years. It's possible."

"Maybe." Tull, who had already finished his coffee, reached for Tess's absentmindedly, grimacing when he realized it was a latte. Caffeine was his fuel, his vice of choice, and he didn't like it diluted in any way.

"Take the easy stat, Martin. Guy's named in a warrant and he said he did it. He does have a temper, I saw that much. Last night it was a soda can. Forty years ago, it very well could have been an iron."

"I've got a conscience, too, you know." Tull looked offended.

Tess realized that it wasn't something she knew that had prompted Tull to call her up, but something he wanted her to do. Yet Tull would not ask her directly because then he would be in her debt. He was a man, after all. But if she volunteered to do what he seemed to want, he would honor her next favor, and Tess was frequently in need of favors.

"I'll talk to him. See if he'll open up to his tag-team partner."

Tull didn't even so much as nod to acknowledge the offer. It was as if Tess's acquiescence were a belch, or something else that wouldn't be commented on in polite company.

**The shoeshine man**—William Harrison, Tess reminded herself, she had a name for him now—lived in a neat bungalow just over the line in what was known as the Woodlawn section of Baltimore County. Forty years ago, Mr. Harrison would have been one of its first black residents and he would have been denied entrance to the amusement park only a few blocks from his house. Now the neighborhood was more black than white, but still middle-class.

A tiny woman answered the door to Mr. Harrison's bungalow, her eyes bright and curious.

"Mrs. Harrison?"

"Miss." There was a note of reprimand for Tess's assumption.

"My name is Tess Monaghan. I met your brother two nights ago in the, um, fracas."

"Oh, he felt so bad about that. He said it was shameful, how the only person who wanted to help him was a girl. He found it appalling."

She drew out the syllables of the last word as if it gave her some special pleasure.

"It was so unfair what happened to him. And then this mix-up with the warrant . . ."

The bright catlike eyes narrowed a bit. "What do you mean by 'mix-up'?"

"Mr. Harrison just doesn't seem to me to be the kind of man who could kill someone."

"Well, he says he was." Spoken matter-of-factly, as if the topic were the weather or something else of little consequence. "I knew nothing about it, of course. The warrant or the murder."

"Of course," Tess agreed. This woman did not look like someone who had been burdened with a loved one's secret for four decades. Where her brother was stooped and grave, she had the regal posture of a short woman intent on using every inch given her. But there was something blithe, almost gleeful, beneath her dignity. Did she not like her brother?

"It was silly of William"—she stretched the name out, giving it a grand, growling pronunciation, *Will-yum*—"to tell his story and sign the statement, without even talking to a lawyer. I told him to wait, to see what they said, but he wouldn't."

"But if you knew nothing about it . . ."

"Nothing about it until two nights ago," Miss Harrison clarified. That was the word that popped into Tess's head, "clarified," and she wondered at it. Clarifications were what people made when things weren't quite right.

"And were you shocked?"

"Oh, he had a temper when he was young. Anything was possible."

"Is your brother at home?"

"He's at work. We still have to eat, you know." Now she sounded almost angry. "He didn't think of that, did he, when he decided to be so noble. I told him, this house may be paid off, but we still have to eat and buy gas for my car. Did you know they cut your Social Security off when you go to prison?"

Tess did not. She had relatives who were far from pure, but they had managed to avoid doing time. So far.

"Well," Miss Harrison said, "they do. But Will-yum didn't think of that, did he? Men are funny that way. They're so determined to be gallant"—again, the word was spoken with great pleasure, the tone of a child trying to be grand—"that they don't think things through. He may feel better, but what about me?"

"Do you have no income, then?"

"I worked as a laundress. You don't get a pension for being a laundress. My brother, however, was a custodian for Social Security, right here in Woodlawn."

"I thought he shined shoes."

"Yes, now." Miss Harrison was growing annoyed with Tess. "But not always. William was enterprising, even as a young man. He worked as a custodian at Social Security, which is why he has Social Security. But he took on odd jobs, shined shoes. He hates to be idle. He won't like prison, no matter what he thinks."

"He did odd jobs for the man he killed, right?"

"Some. Not many. Really, hardly any at all. They barely knew each other."

Miss Harrison seemed to think this mitigated the crime somehow, that the superficiality of the relationship excused her brother's deed.

"Police always thought it was a burglary?" Tess hoped her tone would invite a confidence, or at least another clarification.

"Yes," she said. "Yes. That, too. Things were taken. Everyone knew that."

"So you were familiar with the case, but not your brother's connection to it?"

"Well, I knew the man. Maurice Dickman. We lived in the neighborhood, after all. And people talked, of course. It was a big deal, murder, forty years ago. Not the happenstance that it's become. But he was a showy man. He thought awfully well of himself, because he had money and a business. Perhaps he shouldn't have made such a spectacle of himself and then no one would have tried to steal from him. You know what the Bible says, about the rich man and the camel and the eye of the needle? It's true, you know. Not always, but often enough."

"Why did your brother burglarize his home? Was that something else he did to supplement his paycheck? Is that something he still does?"

"My brother," Miss Harrison said, drawing herself up so she gained yet another inch, "is not a thief."

"But—"

"I don't like talking to you," she said abruptly. "I thought you were on our side, but I see now I was foolish. I know what happened. You called the police. You talked about pressing charges. If it weren't for you, none of this would have happened. You're a terrible person. Forty years, and trouble never came for us, and then you undid everything. You have brought us nothing but grief, which we can ill afford."

She stamped her feet, an impressive gesture, small though they were. Stamped her feet and went back inside the house, taking a moment to latch the screen behind her, as if Tess's manners were so suspect that she might try to follow where she clearly wasn't wanted.

**The shoeshine** man did work at Penn Station, after all, stationed in front of the old-fashioned wooden seats that always made Tess cringe a bit. There was something about one man perched above another that didn't sit quite right with her, especially when the other man was bent over the enthroned one's shoes.

Then again, pedicures probably looked pretty demeaning, too, depending on one's perspective.

"I'm really sorry, Mr. Harrison, about the mess I've gotten you into." She had refused to sit in his chair, choosing to lean against the wall instead.

"Got myself into, truth be told. If I hadn't thrown that soda can, none of this would have happened. I could have gone another forty years without anyone bothering me."

"But you could go to prison."

"Looks that way." He was almost cheerful about it.

"You should get a lawyer, get that confession thrown out. Without it, they've got nothing."

"They've got a closed case, that's what they've got. A closed case. And maybe I'll get probation."

"It's not a bad bet, but the stakes are awfully high. Even with a five-year sentence, you might die in prison."

"Might not," he said.

"Still, your sister seems pretty upset."

"Oh, Mattie's always getting upset about something. Our mother thought she was doing right by her, teaching her those Queen of Sheba manners, but all she did was make her perpetually disappointed. Now if Mattie had been born just a decade later, she might have had a different life. But she wasn't, and I wasn't, and that's that."

"She did seem . . . refined," Tess said, thinking of the woman's impeccable appearance and the way she loved to stress big words.

"She was raised to be a lady. Unfortunately, she didn't have a lady's job. No shame in washing clothes, but no honor in it either, not for someone like Mattie. She should have stayed in school, become a teacher. But Mattie thought it would be easy to marry a man on the rise. She just didn't figure that a man on the rise would want a woman on the rise, too, that the manners and the looks wouldn't be enough. A man on the rise doesn't want a woman to get out of his bed and then wash his sheets, not unless she's already his wife. Mattie should never have dropped out of school. It was a shame, what she gave up."

"Being a teacher, you mean."

"Yeah," he said, his tone vague and faraway. "Yeah. She could have gone back, even after she dropped out, but she just stomped her feet and threw back that pretty head of hers. Threw back her pretty head and cried."

"Threw back her pretty head and cried—why does that sound familiar?"

"I couldn't tell you."

"Threw back her pretty head . . . I know that, but I can't place it."

"Couldn't help you." He began whistling a tune, "Begin the Beguine."

"Mr. Harrison—you didn't kill that man, did you?"

"Well, now I say I did, and why would anyone want to argue with me? And I was seen coming from his house that night, sure as anything. That neighbor, Edna Buford, she didn't miss a trick on that block."

"What did you hit him with?"

"An iron," he said triumphantly. "An iron!"

"You didn't know that two days ago."

"I was nervous."

"You were anything but, from what I hear."

"I'm an old man. I don't always remember what I should."

"So it was an iron?"

"Definitely, one of those old-fashioned ones, cast iron. The kind you had to heat."

"The kind," Tess said, "that a man's laundress might use."

"Mebbe. Does it really matter? Does any of this really matter? If it did, would they have taken forty years to find me? I'll tell you this much—if Maurice Dickman had been a white man, I bet I wouldn't have been walking around all this time. He wasn't a nice man, Mr. Dickman, but the police didn't know that. For all they knew, he was a good citizen. A man was killed and nobody cared. Except Edna Buford, peeking through her curtains. They should have found me long ago. Know something else?"

"What?" Tess leaned forward, assuming a confession was about to be made.

"I did put the mayonnaise on that man's shoe. It had been a light day here, and I wanted to pick up a few extra dollars on my way home. I'm usually better about picking my marks, though. I won't make that mistake again."

**A lawyer** of Tess's acquaintance, Tyner Gray, asked that the court throw out the charges against William Harrison on the grounds that his confession was coerced. A plea bargain was offered instead—five years' probation. "I told you so," Mr. Harrison chortled to Tess, gloating a little at his prescience.

"Lifted up her pretty head and cried," Tess said.

"What?"

"That's the line I thought you were quoting. You said 'threw,' but the line was 'lifted.' I had to feed it through Google a few different ways to nail it, but I did. 'Miss Otis Regrets.' It's about a woman who kills her lover and is then hanged on the gallows."

"Computers are interesting," Mr. Harrison said.

"What did you really want? Were you still trying to protect your sister, as you've protected her all these years? Or were you just trying to get away from her for a while?"

"I have no idea what you're talking about. Mattie did no wrong in our mother's eyes. My mother loved that girl and I loved for my mother to be happy."

So Martin Tull got his stat and a more or less clean conscience. Miss Harrison got her protective older brother back, along with his Social Security checks.

And Tess got an offer of free shoeshines for life, whenever she was passing through Penn Station. She politely declined Mr. Harrison's gesture. After all, he had already spent forty years at the feet of a woman who didn't know how to show gratitude.

# The Accidental Detective

*by Laura Lippman*
*Special to the* Beacon-Light

BALTIMORE—Tess Monaghan spends a lot of time thinking about what she calls the relief problem. Not relief to foreign hot spots, although she can become quickly vociferous on almost any political subject you wish to discuss. No, Monaghan, perhaps Baltimore's best-known private investigator, thinks a lot about what we'll call feminine relief.

"If you're a guy on surveillance, you have a lot more options," she says, sitting in her Butchers Hill office on a recent fall morning and flipping through one of the catalogs that cater to the special needs of investigators and private security firms. Much of this high-tech gadgetry holds little interest for Monaghan, who admits to mild Luddite tendencies. That said, she's so paranoid about caller ID that she uses two cell phones—one for outgoing calls, one for incoming.

"Do you know that the tracks in Delaware, the ones with slot machines, find dozens of adult diapers in the trash every day?" she asks suddenly. "Think about it. There are people who are so crazed for slots that they wear Depends, lest they have to give up a 'hot' machine. Do you think Bill Bennett wore Depends?" Monaghan, who assumes that others can follow her often jumpy train of thought, has moved on to the former secretary of education, reported to have an almost pathological addiction to slot machines, even as he made millions advocating family values.

"No, no, no," she decides, not waiting for answers to any of the questions she has posed. "That's why he had the machines brought to him in a private room. Slots—what a pussy way to lose money. Give me the track every time. Horse plus human plus variable track conditions equals a highly satisfying form of interactive entertainment. With gambling, that's the only way to stay sane. You have to think of it as going to a Broadway show in which you have a vested interest in the outcome. Set aside how much you're willing to lose, the way you might decide how much you're willing to pay to go to a sporting event. If you go home with a dollar more than you were willing to lose, you've won."

So now that Monaghan has held forth on compulsive gambling, adult diapers and, by implication, her own relief needs, could she share a few biographical details? The year she was born, for example?

"No," she says, with a breezy grin. "You're a reporter, right? Look it up at the Department of Motor Vehicles. If you can't track down something that basic, you're probably not the right woman for the job."

Rumor has it that Monaghan loathes the press.

"Rumor," Monaghan says, "isn't always wrong."

## BALTIMORE BORN, BRED AND BUTTERED

She has been called Baltimore's best-known private detective, Baltimore's hungriest private detective and, just once, Baltimore's most eligible private detective. (Her father went behind her back and entered her into *Baltimore* magazine's annual feature on the city's "hot" singles.) But although her work and its consequences have often been featured in the news, Monaghan, a former reporter, has been surprisingly successful at keeping information about herself out of the public domain. At least until now. Oh yes, Ms. Monaghan, this reporter knows her way around public documents.

Monaghan was born in St. Agnes Hospital, and while official documents disagree on the year, she's undeniably a member of Generation X or Y, a post-boomer born to an unlikely duo who prove the old adage that opposites attract. Patrick Monaghan, described by his daughter as the world's most taciturn Irishman, was the oldest of seven children. He grew up in a crowded South Baltimore rowhouse and, later, the Charles Village area.

Meanwhile, Judith Weinstein was the youngest of five from a well-to-do Northwest Baltimore family. She was just entering college when her father's eponymous drugstore chain entered a messy and devastating bankruptcy. Monaghan and Weinstein met via local politics, working on Carlton R. Sickle's failed 1966 bid for the Democratic nomination for governor. The couple remains active in politics; Monaghan remembers riding her tricycle around the old Stonewall Democratic Club as a five-year-old. Her father worked for years as a city liquor inspector, then began running his own club, the Point, which has thrived in an unlikely location on Franklintown Road. Her mother works for the National Security Agency and says she cannot divulge what she does.

"I'm pretty sure she's a secretary," Monaghan says, "but for all I know she's a jet-setting spy who manages to get home by five thirty every night and put supper on the table."

The family settled in Ten Hills on the city's west side and Monaghan attended public schools, graduating from Western High School's prestigious

A-course and then attending Washington College in Chestertown, where she majored in English. By her testimony, she discovered two lifelong influences on the Eastern Shore—rowing and Whitney Talbot. A member of a very old, very rich and very connected Valley family, Talbot has a work ethic as fierce as the one instilled in Monaghan by her middle-class parents, and the two have long reveled in their competitive friendship.

Upon graduation, Monaghan joined the *Star* as a general assignments reporter, while Talbot—who had transferred to Yale and majored in Japanese— landed a job on the *Beacon-Light*'s editorial pages. But Monaghan's timing turned out to be less than felicitous—the *Star* folded before she was twenty-six, and the *Beacon-Light* declined to hire her. Cast adrift, she relied on the kindness of family members to help her make ends meet on her meager freelance salary. She lived in a cheap apartment above her aunt's bookstore in Fells Point and relied on her uncle to throw her assignments for various state agencies. It was in Kitty Monaghan's store, Women and Children First, that she met her current boyfriend, Edward "Crow" Ransome. When she was twenty-nine, she fell into PI work and likes to call herself the "accidental detective," a riff on Anne Tyler's *The Accidental Tourist*.

"Does anyone plan to become a private detective?" Monaghan asks. "It's not a rhetorical question. I suppose somewhere there's a little boy or girl dreaming of life as an investigator, but everyone I know seems to have done some other kind of work first. Lawyer, cop. All I know is I did a favor for a friend, botched it royally, and then tried to help his lawyer get him out of the mess I created. When it was over, the lawyer pressed me to work for him as an investigator, then pushed me out of the nest and all but forced me to open my own agency."

That lawyer, Tyner Gray, would end up marrying Tess's aunt Kitty. Monaghan pretends to be horrified by this development but seems to have genuine affection for the man who has mentored her since she was in her late twenties.

Her agency, Keys Investigation Inc., is technically co-owned by Edward Keys, a retired Baltimore police detective who seems to spend most of his time in Fenwick Island, Delaware. (Asked to comment for this story, Keys declined repeatedly and would not respond to rumors that he has, in fact, met Monaghan in the flesh only once.) Monaghan appears to be the sole employee on the premises of the onetime dry cleaner's that serves as her office, although she jokes that there are two part-time workers "who have agreed to accept their compensation in dog biscuits." Those would be Esskay, a retired racing greyhound named for her love of Baltimore's best-known sausage, and Miata, a docile Doberman with infallible instincts about people. "If she had growled at you, I wouldn't have let you over the threshold," Monaghan says. "I've learned the hard way to trust Miata."

The office is filled with Baltimore-bilia—the old "Time for a Haircut" clock from a Woodlawn barbershop and several Esskay tins. "People give them to me," Monaghan says. "I'm not prone to collecting things."

Has anyone ever commented on the irony that Monaghan, who sits beneath that "Time for a Haircut" clock, once had a most untimely haircut, in which a serial killer sliced off her signature braid? Monaghan shot the man in self-defense, but not before he killed a former transportation cop with whom she was working.

"I don't talk about that," she says. "I understand you have to ask about it. I was a reporter, and I'd have asked about it, too. But it's something I never discuss."

Okay, so life and death have been shot down as topics. What would she prefer to talk about?

"Do you think the Orioles are ever going to get it together? One World Series in my lifetime. It's so depressing."

## A DAY IN THE LIFE

Monaghan lives in a renovated cottage on a hidden street alongside Stony Run Park in the prestigious Roland Park neighborhood. That's how she puts it, her voice curlicued with sarcasm: "Welcome to the prestigious Roland Park neighborhood." The house continues the rather whimsical decorating themes of her office, with a large neon sign that reads "Human Hair." What is it with Monaghan and hair?

"You're a little overanalytical," she counters. "One of the liabilities of modern times is that everyone thinks they're fluent in Freudian theory, and they throw the terms around so casually. I don't have much use for psychiatry."

Has she ever been in therapy?

"Once," she admits promptly. "Court-ordered. You know what, though? I'd like to reverse myself. In general, I don't have much use for psychiatry and I thought it was bulls--t when they put me in anger management. But it did help, just not in the way it was intended."

How so?

"It's not important," she says, reaching for her right knee, a strange nervous tic that has popped up before. "Let's just say that it doesn't hurt sometimes to be a little angry."

Monaghan is speaking in low tones, trying not to awaken her boyfriend. Six years her junior, Ransome works for Monaghan's father, scouting the musical acts that appear at the father's bar. Ransome's work-day ended a mere four hours ago, at 4 A.M., while Monaghan's day began at 6 A.M. with a workout at the local boathouse.

Monaghan and Ransom have been a couple, on and off, for more than four years. Do they plan to marry?

"You know what? You and my mom should get together. You'd really hit it off. She asks me that every day. Ready to experience the exciting life of a private detective?" She draws out the syllables in "exciting" with the same sarcasm she used for "prestigious."

What's her destination this morning?

"The most wonderful place on earth—the Clarence Mitchell Jr. Courthouse."

And, truth be told, the courthouse does seem to be a kind of fairyland to Monaghan, who stalks its halls and disappears into various records rooms, greeting many clerks by name. But wouldn't it be more efficient to work from her office? Isn't most of the information online?

"Some," says Monaghan, who also relies on an online network of female investigators from across the country. "Not all. And there's a serendipity to real life that the Internet can't duplicate. Do you use the library? For anything? Well, sometimes you end up picking up the book next to the book you were looking for, and it's that book that changes your life. Google's great, but it's no substitute for getting out and talking to people. Plus, the courthouse is only a block from Cypriana. So whenever I come here, I can reward myself with a celebratory chicken pita with extra feta cheese."

Isn't 11:30 a little early for lunch?

"I've been up since six! Besides, you want to get there before the judges release the various juries for their lunch break."

## A TREE GROWS IN BALTIMORE

Whitney Talbot strides into Cypriana with the authority of a health inspector on a follow-up visit. Her green eyes cut across the small restaurant with laser-like intensity.

"She's the opposite of Browning's duchess," Monaghan whispers. "Her looks go everywhere, but she dislikes whatever she sees."

"I heard that," Talbot says, even as she places her order. "And I like Cypriana just fine. It's the clientele that worries me. I saw the mayor in here just last week. How am I supposed to digest lunch under those circumstances?"

She settles at our table with an enormous Greek salad, which she proceeds to eat leaf by leaf, without dressing. "Whitney's not anorexic," Monaghan assures me. "Her taste buds were simply destroyed by old WASP cooking."

"I prefer to get my calories through gin," Talbot says primly. "Now what do you want to know about Tess? I know everything—EVERYTHING. I know when she lost her virginity. I know the strange ritualistic way she eats Peanut M&M's. I know that she re-reads *Marjorie Morningstar* every year—"

"I do not," Monaghan objects, outraged only by the last assertion.

"—and cries over it, too. I re-read the *Alexandria Quartet* every year."

"Because you're so f---ing pretentious."

" 'Pretentious' suggests pretending, trying to make others believe that you're something that you're not. There's not a pretentious bone in my body."

"There's nothing but bones in your body, you fatless wench."

Perhaps it would be better if Talbot were interviewed separately, out of Monaghan's hearing?

"Why?" Talbot wonders. "It's not as if I could be any more candid. My first name should have been

Cassandra. I'm a truth-teller from way back. It saves so much time, always telling the truth—"

"And never worrying about anyone's feelings," Monaghan mutters.

"Tess is still miffed because I'm the one who called her Baltimore's hungriest detective, back when the *Washington Post* did that travel piece on her favorite haunts. She does like a good meal, but she wears her calories well. So, okay, here's the unvarnished truth about Theresa Esther Weinstein Monaghan, aka Tesser, although Testy suits her better."

Talbot leans forward while Monaghan visibly steels herself.

"She's a good friend, utterly loyal. She lies as if it were her second language, but only when she has to. She's smarter than anyone gives her credit for—including Tess herself. She's brave. You know those tiresome women who don't have any female friends? I'm not one of those. I don't have any friends, period. I don't like people much. But I make an exception for Tess."

"With friends like these . . ." Monaghan shrugs. In the time it has taken Talbot to eat five lettuce leaves, Monaghan has polished off her chicken pita, but still seems hungry. "Vaccaro's?" she suggests hopefully. "Berger cookies? Otterbein cookies? Something? Anything? I rowed this morning and I plan to run this afternoon. I'm almost certainly in caloric deficit."

Does she work out for her job? How much physical stamina is required? (And does she know that she won't be able to eat like that forever?)

"There's actually very little physical activity involved in my work, and when there is—look, I'm five-foot-nine and my body fat is under twenty percent. I can run a mile in seven minutes and I could still compete in head races if I was that masochistic. And for all that, there's not an able-bodied guy on the planet I could beat up. So, no, it's not for work. It's for peace of mind. Rowing clears my head in a way that nothing else does—alcohol, meditation, pot—"

"Not that Tess has ever broken the drug laws of this country," Talbot puts in.

Monaghan sighs. "With every year, I become more law abiding. A business, a mortgage. I have things to lose. I want to be one of those people who lives untethered, with no material possessions."

"She talks a good talk," Talbot says. "But you've seen the house, right? It's filled with stuff. She's put down roots—in Roland Park, of all places. You know what Tess is like? The ailanthus, the tree that grew in Brooklyn. Have you ever tried to get rid of one of those things? It's darn near impossible. No one's ever going to be able to yank Tess out of Baltimore soil."

"Now that's a novel I do read every year," Monaghan says. "An American classic, but not everyone agrees. Because it's about a girl."

Talbot yawns daintily, bored. "I vote for Otterbein cookies. They have them at the Royal Farms over on Key Highway."

## FAMILY TIES

It is late afternoon at the Point and Crow Ransome— "No one calls me Ed or Edgar, ever," he says, and it's the only time he sounds annoyed—agrees to take a break and walk along Franklintown Road, where the trees are just beginning to turn gold and crimson.

"I love Leakin Park," he says of the vast wooded hills around him. The area is beautiful, but best known as the dumping ground of choice for Baltimore killers back in the day, a fact that Ransome seems unaware of. "I'm not a city kid by nature—I grew up in Charlottesville, Virginia—and I like having a few rural-seeming corners in my life."

Will he stay in Baltimore, then?

"It's the only real condition of being with Tess. 'Love me, love my city.' She can't live anywhere else.

Truly, I think she wouldn't be able to stay long any-place that wasn't Baltimore."

What is it about the private eye and her hometown?

Relative to his girlfriend, Ransome is more thought-ful, less impulsive in his comments. "I think it's an ex-tension of her family. You know Tess's family is far from perfect. Her uncle, Donald Weinstein, was involved in a political scandal. Her grandfather Weinstein—well, the less said about him, the better. Her uncle Spike, the Point's original owner, served time, although I've never been clear on what he did. No one ever speaks of it, but it had to be a felony because he wasn't allowed to have the liquor license in his own name. Anyway, she loves them all fiercely. Not in spite of what they've done, but because they are who they are, they're family.

"I think she feels the same way about Baltimore. It's imperfect. Boy, is it imperfect. And there are parts of its past that make you wince. It's not all marble steps and waitresses calling you 'hon,' you know. Racial strife in the sixties, the riots during the Civil War. F. Scott Fitzgerald said it was civilized and gay, rotted and polite. The terms are slightly anachronistic now, but I think he was essentially right.

"The bottom line," Ransome says, turning around to head back to the Point, "is that Tess really can't handle change. When I first knew her, she had been eating the same thing for breakfast at Jimmy's in Fells Point for something like two years straight. Oh, she will change, but it's very abrupt and inexplicable, and the new regimen will simply supplant the old one. When she crosses the threshold to our neighborhood coffeehouse, they start fixing her latte before she gets to the cash register. She's that predictable.

"Truthfully, I keep worrying that I'll wake up one morning and I'll no longer be one of Tess's ruts."

But Ransome's smile belies his words. He clearly feels no anxiety about his relationship with Monaghan, whatever its ups and downs in the past. What about marriage or children?

Unlike Monaghan, he doesn't sidestep the question. "If children, then marriage. But if children—could Tess continue to do what she does, the way she does it? The risks she takes, her impulsiveness. All of that would have to change. I don't want her on surveillance with our baby in the car seat, or taking the child on her Dumpster diving escapades. I'm well suited to be a stay-at-home father, but that doesn't mean I'll give Tess carte blanche to do whatever she wants, professionally."

Is he signaling, ever so subtly, an end to Monaghan's involvement in Keys Investigations?

"Everything comes to an end," he says. "When you've had near-death experiences, as Tess and I both have, that's more than a pat saying or a cliché."

Yes, about those near-death experiences—but here, Ransome proves as guarded as his girlfriend.

"She doesn't talk about it, and I don't talk about it. But I'll tell you this much—when she reaches for her knee? She's thinking about it. She has a scar there, from where she fell on a piece of broken glass the night she was almost killed. Sometimes I think the memory lives in that scar."

## NOT A LONE WOLF

The private detective has been a sturdy arche-type in American pop culture for sixty-plus years, and it's hard not to harbor romantic notions about Monaghan. But she is quick to point out that she has little in common with the characters created by Raymond Chandler and Dashiell Hammett, and not just because Philip Marlowe and Sam Spade are fictional.

"I'm not a loner, far from it. I live with some-one, I have friends. I have so much family it's almost embarrassing at times. My father was one of seven, my mother one of five. I was an only child, but I was never a lonely one. In fact, most of my clients are referrals from people I know." A rueful smile. "That's made for some interesting times."

A favor for her father, in fact, led to Monaghan identifying a Jane Doe homicide victim—and unraveling an unseemly web of favors that showed, once again, Maryland is always in the forefront when it comes to political scandals. Her uncle Donald asked her to find the missing family of furrier Mark Rubin. And it was Talbot who, inadvertently, gave Monaghan the assignment that almost led to her death. Once one pores over Monaghan's casework, it begins to seem as if almost all her jobs are generated by nepotism.

"Whew," she says. "Strong word. A loaded word, very much a pejorative. How did you get your job?" When no answer is forthcoming, she goes on: "How does anyone get anywhere, get anything in this world? I got into Washington College on my own merits, I guess, but otherwise I've needed family and friends. Not to pull me through or cover for me, but to help me here and there. Is that wrong? Does it undercut what I have done?"

Then what's her greatest solo accomplishment? What can she take credit for?

Monaghan waits a long time before answering. We are in the Brass Elephant, her favorite bar, and she is nursing a martini—gin, not vodka, to which she objects on principle. Monaghan is filled with such idiosyncratic principles. She won't drink National

Bohemian since the brewery pulled up stakes in Baltimore. She says Matthew's serves the best pizza in town, but confesses that her favorite is Al Pacino's. She doesn't like women who walk to work in athletic shoes or people who let their dogs run off lead as a sneaky way to avoid cleaning up after them. She hates the Mets even though she wasn't alive for the indignity of 1969 and has a hard time rooting for the Ravens because of "bad karma." (Cleveland Browns owner Art Modell brought the team here in the mid-nineties and, although the NFL made sure Cleveland kept its name and records—a concession not made to Baltimore when the Colts decamped for Indianapolis—it still bothers Monaghan.)

"I've managed, more or less, to live according to what I think is right. Not always—I can be unkind. I've indulged in gossip, which should be one of the seven deadly sins. I'm quick to anger, although seldom on my own behalf. Overall, though, I'm not a bad person. I'm a good friend, a decent daughter, and a not-too-infuriating girlfriend."

She slaps her empty glass on the counter and says: "Look at the time. We have to go."

"Where?"

"Just follow me."

She runs out of the bar, down the Brass Elephant's elegant staircase and into Charles Street, heading south at an impressive clip. In a few blocks, she mounts the steps to the Washington Monument, throwing a few dollars into the honor box at its foot.

"Come on, come on, come on," she exhorts. "It's only two hundred and twenty-eight steps."

So this is the run that Monaghan planned to take this evening. The narrow, winding stairwell is claustrophobically close and smells strongly of ammonia, not the best fragrance on top of a gin martini, but Monaghan's pace and footing seem unaffected by her cocktail hour. She jogs briskly, insistent that everyone keep up.

At the top, the reason for her rush becomes explicable. The sun is just beginning to set and the western sky is a brilliant rose shade that is kind to the city's more ramshackle neighborhoods, while the eastern sky is an equally flattering inky blue. To the north, Penn Station is a bright white beacon dominated by the monstrous man-woman statue with its glowing purple heart. To the south, lights begin to come on along the waterfront. Monaghan points out the Continental Building on Calvert Street.

"Hammett worked there, as a Pinkerton. And the birds that are used as ornamentation, the falcons? They're gold now, but it's said they were black back in Hammett's day, so we might be the birthplace of the Maltese Falcon. Look to the southwest, toward

Hollins Market, and you can also see where Mencken lived, and Russell Baker. Anne Tylerville is out of sight, but you were there this morning, when you visited my home. That church, virtually at our feet? It's where Francis Scott Key worshipped, while his descendant, F. Scott Fitzgerald, liked to drink at the Owl Bar in the Belvedere, only a few blocks to the north."

She inhales deeply, a little raggedly; even Monaghan isn't so fit that the climb has left her unaffected. She seems drunker now than she did at the bottom, giddy with emotion. She throws open her arms as if to embrace the whole city.

"I mean, really," she says. "Why would anyone live anywhere else?"

# PART FOUR

# Scratch a Woman

# Scratch a Woman

## ONE

The third woman in the pickup line at Hamilton Point Elementary School looks, more or less, like every other woman in the line, although a truly discerning eye might notice that she spends just that much more money and time on her appearance. She has chin-length hair, expertly cut and colored. She wears dainty silver-and-sapphire earrings, a crisp blue shirt, and lightweight wool trousers in the latest style—flat front, tapered at the ankles, fitted through the thighs, which means one had better be doing the latest style of exercise, Pilates or yoga or whatever fitness trend has finally drifted down from New York in the past few months. If Pilates, preferably the kind with machines. If yoga, it should be kundalini or Vikram, true Vikram, licensed Vikram. "You can do ashtanga,

I suppose," Connie Katz told Heloise the other day, at the Saturday soccer game, "but, as my kundalini teacher likes to say, ashtanga will work up a sweat, but it won't fix your spine."

"My spine's fine," Heloise said with a smile, but Connie was already moving away from her, ostensibly to follow her son's progress down the field. Other women always seem to be moving away from Heloise, putting distance between them, disturbed by her aloofness, her lack of giddy complaints about the lives they lead, their mutual misery. As one of only two single moms with kids in Mrs. Brennan's fourth-grade class, shouldn't Heloise complain more, not less, than the rest of them? But Heloise doesn't have a husband, and husbands are the fodder for the majority of the stories, the endless anecdotes about how much these women put up with, the heroic tales that tend to end: "And it was in his closet"—or the refrigerator, or the garage, or the front-hall powder room, or even the man's own pockets—"the entire time!"

Heloise could live somewhere else. Self-employed, she can live anywhere she chooses. But Turner's Grove is convenient for work, equidistant to Washington and Baltimore and Annapolis, and the schools are excellent, consistently in the state's ninety-ninth percentile on testing. In fact, she has switched Scott from private school to the public one just this year, deciding that a larger student body was safer for them. It's in small groups that curiosity gets excited, that idiosyncrasies are more readily noticed. No, a change of address wouldn't change anything except the name of the street, the school, the soccer team. The same vigilance would have to be maintained, the same careful balancing act of not drawing attention to herself, and especially not drawing attention to the fact that she doesn't want to draw attention. Heloise is constantly adjusting her life to that end. She used to have a full-time babysitter, for example, but that stirred up too much envy, too much speculation, so she calls the new girl, Audrey, her au pair and keeps her out of the public eye as much as possible. Her au pair is from Wilkes-Barre, but as it happens Audrey has a hearing loss that causes her to speak in a slightly stilted way, so neighbors assume she's from some Eastern European country they should know, but don't. Here in Turner's Grove, Scott has a good life, Heloise has an easy one, and that's all she can ever hope for.

"And your family's here," neighbors observe, and Heloise nods, smiling a tight-lipped Mona Lisa smile. Easy and good natured, she has managed the trick of seeming totally accessible, all the while sharing almost nothing about herself. She wouldn't dream of confiding in anyone, even loyal Audrey, that discovering her half sister lived one development over was far from ideal. Hard to say who was more horrified when they realized they were in the same school district, Heloise or Meghan. Estranged for years and now virtually neighbors.

Checking her makeup in the rearview mirror—is that a bruise? No, her eyeliner just got smeary at her last meeting—she spots her sister several cars back in the line. If she could see her sister's face, it would not be much different than glancing in this mirror. Only smaller, a little sharper and foxier. And frowning, begrudging Heloise her better spot in line, as Meghan begrudges Heloise everything. They are not even six months apart, beyond Irish twins. If they had been boys, the doctor might have thrown in the second circumcision for free. Then again, they probably only do that when Irish twins have the same *mother*. Heloise and Meghan share a father, a not particularly nice one, who left Meghan's mother for Heloise's, then spent the rest of his life making both women miserable.

But while Heloise has their father's long-legged frame, Meghan favors her little sparrow of a mother, growing smaller and tighter with the years, her bones feeding off her skin. She doesn't have an ounce of fat left on her body, and there are unhealthy hollows beneath her eyes. Heloise wonders if her sister still gets her period. Knowing Meghan, she probably willed it to go away after having four children in five years. Her husband refused to get a vasectomy on the grounds that it wasn't *natural*. Heloise tries to figure out the chicken-or-egg implications. Did Meghan become borderline anorexic to punish her husband, to make herself less desirable to him, or did she stay that way because she welcomed the side effects? There has always, always, been a tightness about Meghan, a kind of controlled fury. You can see it even in baby pictures, her long, skinny body propped up on a sofa, her face pinched with resentment. The youngest child by a bit in Hector Lewis's first family, Meghan believes she was short-changed on everything in childhood: allowance money, new clothes, extra helpings, her father's attention. She has been making up for lost time ever since she landed Brian a year out of college. She keeps score by stuff, and her primary anxiety about having Heloise close seems to be that Heloise is in the top-tier development in Turner's Grove, while Meghan is in Phase II. Larger, but with fewer custom details. Meghan lives for custom details.

Come to notice—Meghan is driving a new SUV today, although her previous car couldn't have been more than three years old. She has moved up to a

Lexus, the hybrid. The last time she and Heloise spoke—if one can call their chance encounters conversations—she was torn between the Navigator, by far the largest of the SUVs on the market, and the Range Rover. "The Rover makes a better statement," she told Heloise, "but Brian vetoed it."

"Statement about what?" Heloise was genuinely confused, but Meghan rolled her eyes as if Heloise were trying to provoke her. Disapproving of Heloise makes Meghan feels so good that Heloise almost—almost— doesn't resent it. If Meghan ever comes to resent her too much, it will be bad, very bad indeed.

The final bell rings and the school seems to inhale before expelling the children in one big breath. Scott used to be one of the first out the door, but he's infinitely cooler now that he's nine and it's a minute or two before he saunters out with his two best friends, Luke and Addison. But he is still young enough to light up when he sees Heloise, to remember, at least for a moment, that no one loves him more than his mother. He doesn't let himself run to the car, but he picks up the pace, walking faster and faster until he bursts into the backseat, bringing noise and light and that wonderfully grubby little-boy smell, all dirt and glue and school supplies.

"Good day?" Heloise asks.

"Pretty good. We talked about genes in science."

"Blue jeans?" she asks, setting him up to correct her.

"The genes that make you what you are. Did you know that two brown-eyed people can have a blue-eyed child, but two blue-eyed people can't have a brown-eyed one? Not without mu-mu—" She lets him struggle for it. "Mutation."

"Really?"

"Yes. So my dad must have had brown eyes, right?"

"Right." She waits a second, then prompts: "And?" She doesn't want him to grow up incurious like so many men, programmed only for their own outgoing messages.

"Oh." He stops and thinks about what he's supposed to say. "How was your day?"

"Pretty good." Wednesday is one of her busiest days. She had two lunch appointments back-to-back.

"Washington, Baltimore, or Annapolis?"

"Washington. I had lunch at Red Sage. Tamales."

"Luc-ky."

She worries for a moment that she has trained him too well, that he might have follow-up questions, and then she'll really have to gild the burrito, pile on more details about the lunch she didn't actually eat, because she seldom eats the expensive meals purchased by her clients. Luckily, Scott launches into a complicated story about that day's science class, and she knows she is safe. For now. But it is only a matter of time before Scott thinks to ask one day, "What does a lobbyist do exactly, Mommy?" Only a matter of time before she will have to muster an explanation boring enough to discourage him from asking still more questions. Sometimes, Heloise wishes she had settled for pretending to be, say, an importer-exporter, but then she would have been forced to do even more research to make her lies plausible. She may not be a real lobbyist, but her work has always centered on politicians and the kind of businessmen who court them, and she has absorbed quite a bit—more than she wants to, actually—about various state and federal issues. She has to watch herself sometimes, when a neighbor says something ignorant about Iraq or the Middle East and she's tempted to contradict. Easier to stay silent than explain how she happens to know more about foreign policy than some fat-ass neighbor, that she actually does have sources in the State Department. And the CIA, come to think of it.

Heloise would have been a great CIA agent. Heloise could have been anything she wanted to be, according to the only man who ever really loved her, which is to say, the only man who never raised a hand against her.

"But I am," she tried to convince him. "I am exactly who I want to be." He could never accept that, which is why they're not together. Well, it's one reason they're not together. The unfortunate truth is that Heloise didn't love him back, although she wanted to, and even tried for a while. But a cop, especially an honest one like Brad, couldn't begin to provide for Scott and her as well she does. Economic inequity. It's a problem in relationships.

For someone keen to avoid exposure, Heloise has a strange fantasy: She likes to imagine being invited to Career Day at Scott's school. She sees herself in an elegant black suit. (Which is, in fact, what she wears to work—tailored suits, silk blouses, and beautiful shoes.) She would sit on the teacher's desk, crossing what everyone agrees are a pair of exceptionally well-kept forty-year-old legs, kundalini or no, and make eye contact with the one girl she knows she will find about two thirds back, in the row closest to the windows. A girl like her, hiding behind too-long bangs and a book, pretending she's not interested in anything. A girl who daydreams during Career Day because she has yet to hear anything that sounds remotely plausible, much less interesting.

Heloise would clear her throat, once, twice, then say: "I work for myself, at a company licensed with the state of Maryland as the Women's Full Employment Network. I make $200 to $1,000 an hour, depending on the services I provide. I wear beautiful clothes and set my own hours. I have been in the finest hotels in the Baltimore-Washington metropolitan area, even in New York, eaten sumptuous meals, gone to gorgeous parties and Kennedy Center galas. There is so much demand for my services that I can pick and choose as I desire, taking only the clients I find acceptable. I work perhaps fifteen hours a week and employ four to eight other women, providing them base salaries and health insurance in return for commissions on the jobs I book them.

"I am, of course, a whore and a madam. And I am here to tell you what no one wants you to know—it's one of the best jobs a woman can have, if you can do it the way I do it." Heloise has done it the other way, too, on the street with a pimp and scant money to show for all her work. Talk about economic inequity in relationships . . .

But Scott is suddenly in a panic in the backseat, and Heloise abandons her daydream. It's music lesson day, and he has left his exercise book in his locker at school. Fearfully, anxiously—although Heloise is always gentle with his mistakes—he asks if they can go back.

"Of course," she says, making a smooth U-turn in her car, a Volvo sedan that the other mothers pretend to envy. But their envy is a kind of condescension—*Oh, if only I could get by with a car that small, but there are five of us in our household. You're just the two.* On Old Orchard Road, she passes her sister Meghan, her narrow face so tight that it has lost the heart-shaped curve it once had and become a triangle. Heloise knows that Meghan still has several more trips—dropping one child at swimming practice, another at soccer, then trying to entertain the youngest two at a Starbucks as there's not enough time to go home before it's time to pick up the one at swimming and the one at soccer. Funny—Meghan, so determined to flee her mother's way of life, has ended up replicating it, albeit with a lot more money and a husband who will never abandon her. Of all Brian's traits, his steadfastness is second only to his income potential. Still, Meghan is her mother all over again, endlessly exasperated, chauffeuring four children around, with no help, except part-time housecleaning, because that's the one thing Brian is stingy about, hiring help. Brian, who hates his job, can't stand the idea that all the money he makes might allow Meghan to enjoy herself. At least, that's what Meghan told Heloise one night last December, when she dropped by to get homework that her youngest son needed, then stayed for a glass of wine, then two, then three. "He says, 'You're free all day.' He says, 'We eat macaroni out of a box and Chinese takeout three days out of five. What more help do you need?' And when I point out that you have an au pair, he says: 'Well, Heloise has a job.' As if I don't! As if four kids is as easy as one!"

Heloise had a few glasses of wine that night, too, and her heart went out to her sister, half though she may be. Meghan never got over the loss of her father, although Heloise thinks she should consider it a blessing. Hector Lewis was a violent, brutal man, who so resented the trap he created by knocking up his girlfriend that he spent most of his time at home beating Heloise's mother and, eventually, Heloise. But he always made his child support payments to his old family and even went so far as to pay for Meghan's college education. Her degree led to a good job in D.C., which brought her into Brian's orbit. Still, Meghan seems to regard Heloise the winner in this nongame because Heloise has managed to create a life of ease and serenity, while Meghan has to bully, cajole, and beg for every dollar she gets out of her husband.

So Heloise told her sister how she did it, how she covered costs in Turner's Grove, the kind of suburb that almost no single parent could afford. There had been no husband, no accident, no life insurance, inferences that she had let stand uncorrected in the community since she moved there. She paid for it all on her own, through her own work. "Call me madam," she said, raising her glass, feeling a rare sisterly camaraderie.

Meghan had not been shocked, not at all. She asked several quick questions—*How did you get started, what about diseases, how much do you make? Do you charge more for the really kinky stuff? What's the worst thing you've ever had to do?*—and Heloise deflected all of them, especially those about money, although she was scrupulously honest with the IRS about her earnings, if not their exact source. It was Meghan's very lack of judgment, her matter-of-fact acceptance, that scared Heloise. She realized her sister was filing the information away until it might be useful to her. Meghan had always been a bit of a squirrel, a saver of money and secrets. Since that night, they were uneasy with each other.

"There's Aunt Meghan! And Michael and Mark and Maggie and Melissa!" Scott squeals. Poor Scott, with no siblings and no grandparents, was thrilled with the sudden gift of four cousins, with one, Michael, exactly his age. He waves wildly, but his cousins have their eyes fixed on their laps, probably fiddling with iPods or video games, and Meghan's terrifying gaze doesn't seem to see anything, not even the curving road in front of her, a gorgeously landscaped death trap of a parkway. Heloise remembers a scrap of a childhood story, something in the moldering, fragile books that her father brought with him when he finally divorced Meghan's mother, in which an animal or magical creature had simply torn himself in pieces from his rage. Meghan looks more than capable of doing just that.

**Meghan Duffy** peers at the small print of the insurance policy, squinting. She's only forty, she can't possibly need reading glasses, but sometimes the fine print is truly fine, designed to keep anyone from reading it. "In the case of an accident that results in injury . . ."

"MOM!" Maggie's thin screech echoes from somewhere out in the family room, put-upon and choked with tears. "Mark changed the channel and it's my turn to pick the program."

"It was on a commercial and I changed it back," Mark shouts, and Meghan knows by his tone that he is fudging the facts, as full of shit as his father when trying to avoid her disapproval for some forgotten chore or absentminded error.

"I missed the part where they sing karaoke," Maggie complains bitterly, and Meghan thinks, *Well, thank your lucky stars.* Because seventy, eighty years from now, when you're on your deathbed, you are not going to be thinking about the day your brother changed the channel and you missed twenty seconds of some stupid pop tart singing karaoke. You are instead going to wonder why you spent sixty of those years married to an idiot who had bad breath and a repertoire of sexual moves that basically boil down to thrust-in thrust-in thrust-in and areyouthereyet?

No, wait, that was Meghan's deathbed. Maggie will have to make her own deathbed and then lie in it.

Meghan shoves the papers back into the cherry-wood pigeonholes above her desk, a touch meant to evoke an old-fashioned rolltop. Meghan's work area is really a corridor, a narrow stretch of hallway between the family room and the mudroom that the Realtor insisted on calling "Mom's office." This not-quite-room is just wide enough to accommodate this built-in shelf, which in turn is just wide enough to hold a computer and a drop tray for a keyboard. "A place for all your work," crooned the salesman, Paul Turner. No, Meghan had yearned to correct him, Mom's work area is every square foot of this 6,800-square-foot house. What Mom needs is a soundproof bunker in the basement. Meghan would trade the whirlpool in her en suite bath, the laundry room that is bigger and nicer than her childhood bedroom, and even her Portuguese-blue Lacanche range for such a retreat. Especially her Portuguese-blue Lacanche, which mocks her with its smug French competence, its readiness.

She marches into the family room and an uneasy truce settles as soon as she appears, so she moves past, into the kitchen, checking to see what ready-made dishes she can pass off as homemade. Meghan once liked cooking, but the level of rejection possible when making food for five people is simply too staggering. She doesn't take it as personally when the rejected salmon comes from the Giant, when the mashed potatoes are whipped by the folks at Whole Foods. She still winces at the waste, but at least she's spared mourning her own time. Her mom had been one of the last of the mackerel snappers, insisting on fishy Fridays despite the Vatican's relaxed rules—and despite the fact that the Catholic church wanted no part of her, after the divorce. The Lewis children had not been allowed to turn up their noses at her worst concoctions. If you didn't clean your plate in the Lewis household, it just followed you through the next three meals. Until it spoiled, you didn't eat again, not in Mother's sight. This was her father's rule originally, but her mother enforced it even more strictly after he left.

She remembered asking Heloise, in their wine-coaxed moment of candor, if things had worked the same way in her version of the Lewis household. "Not exactly," Heloise said, refusing to elaborate, infuriating Meghan, for Heloise was clearly implying that her version of the Lewis household was all lovey-dovey, the place where true love triumphed and who cares if the first Lewis family was left in the dirt, with only support checks and occasional visits from Hector. Visits, Meghan knew, where he often banged the first Mrs. Lewis once Meghan was asleep, or so he thought. Her own mother always called the second Mrs. Lewis that-whore-Beth, just one word, said very quickly. Meghan was eleven or so before she realized it wasn't an actual name, Thatwhorebeth, a distant cousin of Terebithia.

She pulls out the plastic boxes of prepared food—salad, a roasted chicken, asparagus—and places them on the broad granite counter where they eat most of their meals. She could put the food on actual serving platters, but why bother to disguise its origins? Brian, who flew to the home office in Atlanta this morning, won't be home until almost ten, and he's the only one who cares if food is homemade, and only because he hates to think she's had a free moment to herself. As if, she thinks, gathering up the pair of Crocs that Maggie has left in the middle of the kitchen floor, then rinsing the glasses and plates left over from the kids' snacks, which almost certainly ruined any appetite they had for dinner. The phone rings. Once, the kids would have vied to grab it, but the two oldest have cell phones and the youngest have IM accounts, so the phone holds no interest for them. She lets it ring, thinking it might be Brian, whining for an airport pickup, which she has no intention of providing, but then notices that the caller ID is displaying her insurance agent's cell number.

"Meghan," Dan Simmons says. "I didn't think I'd catch you."

"Oh, I'll always let you catch me, Dan." More cute than pretty, Meghan has been an outstanding flirt since her early teens. Much better than Heloise, with her ice princess shtick. Does she drop that superior manner when she is with her clients, or is that part of her appeal? Her sister's secret life excites Meghan, a fact she barely admits to herself. On those rare occasions when Brian wants to have sex with her and she manages to muster up the energy, she pretends she is Heloise and he is a client. That she is in charge and he has to leave when they are done, handing her a nice stack of large bills. As if.

"You're working late," she says.

"Yes and no. I'm in my little home office, returning all my calls, but already starting on cocktail hour, as you can see."

The Simmonses are next-door neighbors, their house a mirror image of Meghan's, only Dan has availed himself of "Mommy's office." Sure enough, she looks through the window over her kitchen sink and sees Dan across the way, hoisting a martini. Dan is fun.

"Ah, Daddy's little helper," she says, walking over to her refrigerator and locating a bottle of wine, suspiciously deep on the bottom shelf. The health education segment at Hamilton Point turns children into anti-alcohol Nazis, and Michael keeps hiding her wine behind the milk. "We'll have a drink together. What's up?"

"You called me," he reminds her. "Two days ago. Left a message at the office."

"Sorry. I forgot."

"Hey, it's a pleasure to have a client who calls me," he says. "Most people run when they see me coming, like I'm that guy in *Groundhog Day.*"

She laughs, although she has no idea what he is talking about. Movies, sports—most of men's conversational milestones are lost to her, but she pretends to get them. "Well, with four kids and a husband who's on the road three days every week, I have to make sure we have all the coverage we need."

"Don't worry," Dan says, "if a plane goes down, you're fine."

"I worry that the airlines are so broke these days that we won't recover a cent."

"Well, it's true, if Brian actually died in a plane crash, there probably would be a war of deep pockets, with my company fighting the airlines' carrier over who had to pay out. But it's also true that we're talking about something that has virtually no odds of happening. What you really have to worry about are the kind of mundane accidents that no one thinks about. Slip in the bathtub, a fall down the steps. And cars, don't get me started on those death traps. I think you have adequate coverage for that, but I'll review everything. I know you told me that Brian has a handgun, but it is kept in a safe, right?"

"Yes, of course."

"Okay, because we require that. Meanwhile, I don't think you have enough disability coverage, but almost no one does. And have you thought about some of the financial products I mentioned to you the last time you both were in—"

Screams rise from the family room, providing her a graceful way to end the conversation. "I better run before blood is shed," she says. "It's so hard to get out of leather."

Dan laughs. He probably wishes that his own wife was so chipper and cavalier about household calamities. Lillian Simmons is a big-boned slob who looks ten years older than her age, but she is also absolutely reliable, the go-to mom of Hamilton Point Elementary, the one who can be counted on to bail out any forgetful snack mom. That's the thing about wives. All men want them, they just don't necessarily want the ones they have.

A slip in the bathtub. A fall down the stairs. An accident on the twisty snake that is Old Orchard. A plane falling out of the sky. She should be so lucky. She trips over another pair of Crocs—the things seem to be breeding—and calls the children to dinner, and something in her voice silences the bedlam instantly, bringing them to the table with heads down. *Mom's mad. Walk carefully.* She hates seeing her children like this, controlling them through her anger, but her incipient fury seems to be the only power she has over them, over anyone.

**Brian Duffy** squeezes into the last open spot at the bar, putting his elbows down before he realizes the wood is still damp from the bartender passing a wet dishrag over it. *As if that filthy bit of cloth could make anything cleaner,* he thinks with a shudder. It takes him several minutes to get the bar wench's attention, and in the time he waits, his order somehow mutates from a defensible light beer to a vodka martini, a double. *Sure, add a quesadilla and some chips.* It's not like he's going to get dinner on the plane and there's never anything waiting for him at home.

Airport bars used to be kind of sexy, based on the movies and television shows he had watched as a kid. Sweeping views of planes taking off and landing, well-dressed people sipping cocktails and speaking low, charged encounters between strangers. Now they tend to be like this one, a cramped windowless room in Atlanta Hartsfield, where you have to fight for every inch of space. On the trip down, he read a paperback that began with a man meeting a beautiful blond in an airport bar and he had found that one detail more far-fetched than the high-tech crime caper that had followed. Airport bars are the new saltpeter.

Look at this one. On his left, two honeymooners, post-honeymooners by all appearances, weary beneath their red-tinged tans, barely speaking to each other as they contemplate the rest of their lives together. To his right, one of those corporate women who travels with a roller bag she can barely lift, the kind of woman who won't make eye contact with a man until she drops her suitcase on his head. A bitch, a ballbuster. Just his type. In fact, she looks uncannily like the woman who fired him three hours ago.

He still can't believe he had to fly to Atlanta to be fired. All the signs were there—the lack of a clear agenda for today's meeting, the fact that they wanted him in and out in a day, when they usually brought people in the night before, put them up at the Ritz-Carlton in Buckhead. Funny, he was the company's de facto executioner for seven years, flying into various branches and firing people under the rubric of "reorganization," and yet he didn't see his own death coming. "You know we always do these things face-to-face, Brian," said Colleen Browne, whom he thinks of as Cold-Faced Bitch, a woman he has wanted to bend over a desk since the first time he saw her, and never more so than when she was firing him. He considered it, for a fleeting second, thought about grabbing her, ripping away her little black suit, forcing her facedown onto her BlackBerry so hard that she would end up sending text gibberish to everyone in her address book.

But negotiating a decent severance had seemed more pressing. At least he had the context to do that, to get a good package. Six months' salary, a full year of medical, no small thing with four kids. Still, he thinks of the CEOs who fuck up companies and walk away with ten, twenty million, and he thinks maybe he should have fucked the brunette instead. The country's tiptoeing into a recession; his sector, financial services, is in particularly bad shape. Six months might not be enough, and thanks to Meghan's free-spending ways, they don't begin to have the savings they should. He orders another drink. He can't bear the thought of going home, having to tell Meghan about this. What would happen if he missed his plane? It happens, and he's in Atlanta Hartsfield, so anything is credible.

But then he would be in some dopey airport hotel, with nothing but porn to keep him company. He wants the real thing, but he can't kid himself, he has no game left. The only way for him to have sex tonight is to pay for it, something he's never done. Okay, something he *says* he's never done. There have been a few furtive hand jobs here and there, on the way home from Baltimore, but nothing more because he's worried about catching something.

He pulls out a card given to him by a guy he met three weeks ago, a lobbyist employed by the company, who got a little loose over dinner and started talking about this amazing escort service in the Baltimore-Washington area. The card has nothing but a number and a set of initials: WFEN. Sounds like an AM radio station. His plane gets in at eight, if he's lucky, but he always fudges his arrivals, tells Meghan he's coming in at least two hours later. What if he just went to this place instead, telling Meghan that he was still in Atlanta? Ah, the beauty of cell phones, the liar's best friend.

The woman who answers the phone has an odd voice, a little toneless and loud. "Yes?"

"Is this . . . WFEN?"

"Yes."

"I'd like to make . . . a date."

"And how did you hear about us?"

"How . . ." He provides the name of the guy and there's endless clicking, like at an airline ticket counter.

"Name and birth date, please, along with the credit card you plan to use."

"What?"

"We do not take new customers without a referral and all customers must be subjected to a criminal background check."

"What if I want to pay in cash?" Meghan does the bills, no way he's putting this on a card.

"That's fine, but we still have to have a credit card on file."

Even in his frustration, he admires the setup. Someone has thought this through. Plus, they're not asking for the security code, so he doesn't think they can charge anything, and if they did, it would be easy enough to get the charge off his card. And the lobbyist said the one he had was worth every penny, a real pro. Brian's just drunk enough to give his real name, although he lowers his voice while reading the card number into the phone.

"Wait, please." He's put on hold, very pleasant jazz music to keep him company. The woman comes back on the line faster than most service reps, that's for sure.

"I'm sorry, we cannot take you."

"Hey, that card is good." Shit, has Meghan pushed it beyond the limit again? And he needs this, he has never needed anything more, he decides, than anonymous, nasty sex with someone who has to do whatever he says.

"We cannot take you."

"Look, if you want another card—"

"We cannot take you."

"Did something come up on the background check? It has to be a mistake because I'm clean as a whistle."

"I'm sorry." The woman hangs up, and when he redials, no one answers.

Seven hundred miles to the north, give or take, Heloise and Audrey sit in Heloise's refinished basement, the one where Heloise keeps her office, and look at the number on caller ID. Audrey opened a document on the computer as soon as she picked up the phone, per Heloise's instructions. But there was no criminal background check, no quick peek at credit records. The moment Audrey put the caller on hold, she summoned Heloise to the basement and asked her what to do.

"My brother-in-law," Heloise says. "My fucking brother-in-law. What are the odds?"

"He would have been eliminated geographically even if he weren't a relative," Audrey says. "He's within the ten-mile radius." Heloise won't take any client with a home address in her son's school district.

"I almost wish I could take him on as a client, give him to Staci down in D.C.," Heloise says. "If Brian got rid of all that tension he's carrying, he might be a better husband and Meghan might not look so furious all the time. But I can't risk it. And, frankly, he can't afford it, based on what I know of that household's finances. If he wants sex, he'll have to sleep with his wife or settle for good old-fashioned adultery with someone at work."

Audrey frowns. She has rather strict views on the sanctity of marriage, an interesting position for a woman who oversees the office of a thriving sex business. It is an even more interesting position for a woman whose hearing loss was caused by a vicious beating by her own husband, who also happened to be her pimp. Still, she was faithful to him, within the compartmentalized system that defined their relationship. She had sex with other men for money, but only her husband had her heart, and this remained true right up until the moment she killed him in the middle of another beating. Paroled a year ago, she was referred to Heloise by an old friend.

"Better to use a street-level worker," Audrey says, using the term Heloise prefers. "As long as he wears a condom. Don't you always say adultery is more expensive in the long run?"

"Indeed," Heloise says. "Now who's out tonight?"

"Gwen, in Annapolis. The senator got a bill out of committee, and he wanted to celebrate. But he never goes late. The GPS shows they're already at the hotel and I expect her safety text within the hour."

Audrey's phone buzzes at just that moment and the two women look down to see the message: "Babycakes." Just as bondage freaks have their safe words, Heloise assigns each of her girls a silly, frequently changing term to text when a date ends. Between that and the GPS that each girl wears on the inside of a wide bangle bracelet—Ho-jacks, the girls call them—she hasn't had a problem. Yet. But that's the nightmare that looms largest, the fear that she will be summoned to the morgue one day, asked to identify one of her employees.

"That was fast," Audrey says. "Even for the senator."

"Well, getting a bill out of committee," Heloise says. "It can be pretty exciting."

She goes upstairs to read to Scott. He's getting too old for this, but Heloise argues that it's really for her, that she won't read the Harry Potter books if they don't read them together. She has a date at ten, but Scott will be tucked in by then, safe under Audrey's care.

## TWO

"Why did we let him sign up for travel soccer?" Brian asks, and not for the first time. "It's not like he's going to grow up to be, what's his face, Beckham. And it's such a drag on the household when he has one of these games out in butt-fuck, Maryland."

Meghan, who actually thinks the same thing all the time, fixes Brian with a disapproving stare. "How does it affect you? The Marshalls are driving Michael, both the girls have already left for sleepovers, and I'm taking Mark to that all-day rehearsal for the regional band competition. By the way, his teacher says he's going to need a new trumpet next year, he can't keep using the school instrument."

"Great, how much is that going to cost?"

"Jesus, Brian, who cares? You make plenty of money."

"Actually, I don't."

He stands up, carries his plate to the sink and rinses it, then puts it in the dishwasher, which is full of clean dishes, but never mind, Meghan knows a sign of the apocalypse when she sees one. Brian has occasionally removed his own dishes from the table, but to rinse it and put it in the dishwasher? Things must be very bad indeed.

"What are you saying, exactly?" *Pay cut, pay cut, pay cut,* she prays. *Please be a pay cut.* Or maybe a bonus didn't come through.

"I was fired."

"When?"

"Almost ten days ago."

Yet he has been putting on a suit every morning and driving away. "So where have you been—"

"Starbucks. I thought I would find something so fast that there was no need to trouble you with it. And I did get severance."

"How much?"

"Jesus, Meghan, don't overwhelm me with your sympathy and concern."

"*How much?*"

"Six months."

"You'll find something new." It's a question, a plea.

"Yeah, but—it's bad out there, Meghan. I may not make as much. We may have to move. Who knows?"

Who knows? Meghan knows. She knows what it's like to live in a house where money is tight. She knows what it's like when a family falls back a step, what it feels like to try to get by with less than one is used to, how it's almost impossible to catch up ever again.

"Clean the basement," she says.

"What?"

"You have a Saturday free, you've been sitting in Starbucks for two weeks, doing nothing, while I run myself ragged—the least you could do is clean the fucking basement."

"You know what, Meghan? This is way harsh, even for you. I lost my job, for no good reason. You're supposed to be on my side. What the fuck is wrong with you?"

"I have to take Mark to this thing. Which you knew. So don't blame me because I can't sit at the kitchen table and rub your head, talking about the job you lost two fucking weeks ago. We'll talk later. You promised to clean the basement months ago, so do it. It might feel good, accomplishing something. For a change." She raises her voice, which has been a tight hiss for this entire discussion. "Mark! Time to go." Then back to the hissing register: "There are boxes in the garage and the county dump is open until two P.M. on Saturdays. Don't forget that broken old computers can't go in the landfill."

She stares him down and he drops his head, shuffling off to the basement. She checks her watch. "Mark!" This is her second-warning voice, louder than the first but still not angry. The children know what Brian has just been reminded, that it's Meghan's softest voice that is to be feared. Funny, because she's never gone beyond that voice, so what is it that they fear, what power do they assign to her? Mark comes bounding down the stairs, ready for the battle of the bands. It will be a long day, and once he's with his friends, he won't want anything to do with Meghan. He certainly won't stop to think what the day is like for her, how it feels to sit for hours in the drafty arena in downtown Baltimore, with only a library book, a mystery from the library, to keep her company. And the girls are giggling with friends while Michael is chasing a soccer ball down a muddy field somewhere in Western Maryland, and there are Melissa's fucking Crocs again, or maybe Maggie's, left in the middle of the mudroom floor.

"Mom, why are you shaking?" Mark asks.

"It's cold for March."

**Brian goes** up and down, up and down, up and down. He considered stopping as soon as Meghan left the house. Who does she think she is, talking to him that way? But the chore is a good distraction and, fuck her, she was right: he feels as if he's accomplishing something for the first time in weeks. Months, actually.

But as the morning turns into afternoon, he begins to lose his enthusiasm. How did one family ever acquire so much crap? Why do they have all these broken camp chairs? A box full of board games that are missing key pieces? In the early going, he thought there might be money to be made, that they would have a yard sale or maybe take things to one of those stores that sells your stuff on eBay, does all the grunt work. But it's all junk, worthless. It makes him feel even worse, the fact that he's been living on top of this storehouse of crap, and he doesn't really seem to be making any progress. Up and down, up and down, up and down. Wasn't there some story about a guy in hell who has to do this? He has a beer, checks in on the NCAA tournament. Okay, why not another? He looks for some food, but most of it requires at least minimal preparation, and he doesn't want to go out, so he returns to the job. Really, the stuff seems to be breeding, there's more of it now than when he started. He comes up with a box full of mysterious hardware, screws and those Ikea wrenches and a broken towel rack. He can barely see over the top of the box, but he does hear the garage door opening. Footsteps in the hall.

"Meghan?" he says, assuming that the person he can't see on the steps must be her. Maybe she sneaked home to make up, he thinks. God, when was the last time they had sex in the afternoon? He gets hard just thinking about the possibility of some quick, ordinary sex with his wife. It is the most erotic thing he has considered in ages, better than the porn sites he sometimes checks out on his laptop, always remembering to erase his cache. He doesn't need a stranger or anything extra. He won't need to imagine he's with someone else. All he wants is to get on top of his wife and go at it. Maybe make it nice for her, too, if there's time before she has to go back to the band practice thing.

"Hey, Meghan," he says, "give me a hand with this."

She does, in a sense. She presents him with two hands, thumping them hard on the chest, as if beginning CPR, and sends him flying backward down the steps, screws and towel racks and Swedish wrenches racing him to the bottom. He sprawls like a starfish, looking back at her, amazed, his mind trying to catch up with everything that has happened, and all he can think is, *So I guess we're not going to have sex, after all.*

**Heloise is** making Scott lunch, glad that his one weekend obligation, soccer, is behind them. She encourages him to do everything he wants—soccer, music lessons, art classes at the Baltimore Museum of Art—but she prefers the quiet afternoons, when there is nothing on his schedule and they simply steep in each other's company, watching television, running errands. She tries to make Saturday dinner an event— Around the World with the Lewis Family, she calls it—and tackles new recipes from different countries. She's going to make Thai food tonight, and she won't have to cut back on the spice for Scott's sake. His mouth is as inquisitive and open as his porous little mind, keen to try new things. He is such a satisfying companion in every way. She has to remind herself that he won't be with her very long, that she has only a few years in which he will find it acceptable to spend Saturday night with his mother.

And then? Then she will be alone. She's through with men. Not through with love, as the song has it, but that's because she never really started with love. Oh, she used the word quite a bit when she was young. She loved the boyfriend who encouraged her to leave home, the boy she followed to downtown Baltimore, only to end up dancing in a strip club, then tricking. She said she loved Val because he demanded that; the fealty of the word was almost as important to him as the money she kicked back, and she said it so often that she came to believe it for a while. She looks at the redheaded boy, eyes fixed on a nature show as he waits for his soup and grilled cheese, and wonders again at the capacity that allows her not to be scared when she sees that miniature version of Val, a man she so feared that she made sure he would be locked up forever. Val doesn't know about Scott. She was only three months pregnant when he was arrested and she managed to conceal her growing girth when she visited him in prison, coming up with a cover story for the last few months, claiming she had to go back home to tend to her ailing mother. As if she would be bothered to do anything for that woman. It was one thing for men to disappoint her, but Heloise can never forgive her mother for failing to protect her.

It was Scott, growing inside her, who changed everything. On her own, accountable only for herself, Heloise could not imagine getting free of Val. She understood the fact that her life was destined to be a short one, that her usefulness as a whore and her biological life span would probably run out about the same time. Val was violent, but he didn't like to damage the goods, as he called them, so as long as she was a good earner, he employed a certain restraint. But as her market value decreased, she knew the violence would escalate. And she accepted it. She could not see a way out. She had a high school education, no money in her own name, and a career that lasted about as long as a pro athlete's, but with far less compensation.

She didn't even have official confirmation of her pregnancy when she resolved to change. She was sitting in a diner in the early evening, drinking a cup of coffee with a friend, and she couldn't get beyond the first sip. She asked the waitress to bring her a cup from a fresh pot, but the new one was bitter, too, no matter how much milk and sugar she added. "Maybe you're pregnant," Agnes said, meaning it as a joke. But Heloise knew at that moment that she was and she suddenly understood what it took to make a great change in one's life.

Agnes was dead within the week, killed by a john. They never found the man, although Heloise gave them a detailed description. She and the other girls had known he was trouble, had seen something in his eyes that scared them. Agnes laughed at their fears; Agnes was found in a vacant lot, her throat slit. If Heloise ever spoke of her real life to anyone, if she ever had the luxury of telling people about herself, they would probably reduce this story to simple cause and effect. Heloise was pregnant and needed to start a new life. The death of her friend inspired her to escape Val, get out on her own, and set up a business where women who sold sex could be safe, above all. Safe and well compensated, with health benefits and flexible schedules. But the linear story line was not quite right. Even if Agnes had not died, Heloise would have found a way to do this. No disrespect to Agnes, but a mouthful of coffee, acrid and syrupy, was what changed her life.

The phone rings, making her jump, because it rings so seldom, the home line. She has no friends. It is lonely at times, but friendship is a luxury she can't afford. One day, perhaps when Scott graduates, she hopes to sell the business and retire on the proceeds, or reinvent herself as a real lobbyist. Once Scott is out of college, she can afford the drop in income. The fact is, she has the contacts, and one of the big wheels in Annapolis has all but given her a standing offer to come on board, help him advance the case of alcohol and tobacco in the state legislature. He wants her to go back to school, though, get one of those weekend MBAs, and she can't do that until Scott is older.

"Meet me at Starbucks."

It takes her a second to realize the caller is Meghan, speaking through gritted teeth.

"I'm just getting Scott's lunch—"

"Now. Leave him with Audrey."

"I give Audrey the weekends off. I mean, she's around, but she's not on the clock, and—"

"This is life and death, Heloise. I need you. And if you can't be there for me—well, I can't be responsible for what happens."

Is Meghan threatening her? The thought is almost laughable, except . . . there is something steely in her sister's voice, something cold and resolute that Heloise recognizes. It is a quality she remembers from Val, the willingness to destroy others, even at the risk of destroying oneself. Val killed a boy just for laughing at his name, and the striking thing to Heloise is that he has never expressed any regret about it. He has never said, I can't believe I ruined my life over such a silly thing. Or: What was I thinking? In fact, whenever he spoke of the crime to Heloise it was in the context of the inevitable death-sentence appeal. He mused how, if he had to be in prison for the boy's death, he wished he could go back and inflict more pain on him, not kill him with the relative speed and kindness of a single bullet to the brain. The cliché about bullies is that they back down when confronted. But Heloise has known a different kind of bully, men—and women—who will happily upend your life just because they can. Meghan knows what Heloise does for a living. Meghan has the power to ruin her and she won't stop to think about how it might boomerang on her.

"The Starbucks by the mall?"

"Yes. As soon as possible."

**"I'm a whore**," Heloise says. "I charge men money for sex. That doesn't mean *I know how to* help you cover up a murder."

"Keep your voice down," Meghan says, although she knows it's her voice that's closer to being out of control. Then: "And who said murder? That's the problem. He's still breathing, I think. His chest looked like it was moving."

"And you left him there?"

It's a curious feeling, seeing the horror in Heloise's eyes, being judged by a whore, Heloise's very word.

"Temporary insanity," she says, gauging Heloise's reaction, wanting to see how this theory might play. "No, seriously, I just lost it. I was sitting there at Mark's battle-of-the-bands practice, and I kept getting angrier and angrier, and when they broke for lunch, I couldn't help myself, I drove back home to have it out with Brian. Don't you hate that thing men do, where they drop some huge piece of information on you when they know there's no time to discuss it?"

Heloise, happily manless, looks baffled.

"I just wanted to talk to him. I don't know why I did what I did. But if he's dead, then it's over, there's nothing to be done. But what if he's not?"

"Maybe he has a head injury. Then if he regains consciousness and starts talking about how you shoved him—"

"I really didn't mean to." She's beginning to believe this, the more she says it.

"You can say it's the result of the fall. If he regains consciousness. You could have crippled him for life, Meghan. Your husband could be a paraplegic now."

It takes a second for Meghan to process the horror of this, the idea that she has created an invalid, someone who will require a lifetime of care and provide nothing in return. Dead, Brian is worth a lot to her. Permanently disabled, all he will cough up is a small lump sum, eighteen months of mortgage payments, and then they have to petition to get on the federal system. She knows this thanks to Dan Simmons, insurance agent extraordinaire. He's been trying to tell her that they don't have adequate coverage for disability, and she's been blowing him off.

"Go home, Meghan," Heloise says. "Don't leave him there, whatever you do."

She shakes her head. "I have to go get Mark. The practice ends in less than an hour."

"But . . . then he'll be with you when you go home. Do you want to do that to your son, have him see his father that way? Don't you at least want to spare Mark?"

Meghan wants to snap: What about Scott? How are you going to feel when someone, possibly me, tells him his mother is a whore? But Heloise is here, she has acknowledged Meghan's power over her, and there really is nothing she can do to help. What had Meghan hoped, when she called Heloise? She assumed her half sister had some mysterious, nefarious connections, men who could make problems disappear. Really, Heloise is kind of bourgeois, not at all the libertine that one might expect in a madam. Meghan almost regrets confiding in her.

"I'll call in a favor, con another mom at practice into taking Mark home for dinner," she says, checking her watch, a tenth-anniversary gift from Brian. She had wanted a Patek Philippe, but he had given her a Rolex.

"And then?"

"I'll figure something out. I'll do the right thing," she says, knowing that she and Heloise may not agree on what that is.

Two hours later, Mark safely at the Pizza Hut with the Bonner family, she creeps back into the house. "Brian?" No answer. She stands at the top of the stairs, but it takes her several minutes to tiptoe down, to investigate. Oh, miracle of miracles, he's not breathing. She feels a quick pang, wondering how long he suffered. She decides he died instantly, that the rise and fall of his chest was an illusion, a trick of the dim light. She's a widow. What a glorious thing to be. There will be money enough and nothing but sympathy for her. Except from Heloise, of course, but if Heloise dares to be too open in her disapproval, Meghan knows how to bring her in line. She's a widow, her problems are solved, it's the happiest day of her life.

She's about to bound up the stairs to call 911, begin her new life as a tragic figure, when she sees something she hadn't noticed before, a large tufted pillow, one of the decorative ones from her bed. How has this gotten here? What was Brian thinking? There's a tiny viscous stain. Brian has always been a drooler in his sleep, but this one looks fresh, still slightly damp, and it smells—she inhales—of Brian's shaving lotion, which makes no sense at all.

Unless someone held it over his face while she was gone, finishing what she started.

She races up the stairs and—after putting the pillow back on her bed—discovers that terror makes it that much easier to sound hysterical with grief when she calls 911.

### THREE

Heloise has a strange insight in the church: this is the first funeral she has attended in her adult life.

How could this be? Her mother is still alive and she refused to attend her father's funeral a few years ago, deciding she could never put up the required façade of sorrow. Too bad, she thinks now. If she had attended, perhaps she would have seen Meghan and they could have swapped notes on where they lived, and she would have planted the idea that Turner's Grove was simply not—what was the word they used now to describe those who wanted to move up, up, up—*aspirational* enough. Then Meghan would not have moved here, and Heloise would never have confided in her, and she would not be stuck now in a murder conspiracy. Would Brian still be alive? She doesn't know, and to be unattractively candid, she doesn't really care. Heloise cares about only one person: Scott. Not Audrey, not her other employees, although she likes them well enough and wants to be a good boss to them. Not her clients, god knows. And not even herself, except to the extent that she's the only one who can take care of Scott. To compare her to a mother bear or lioness is inadequate because, for all their ferocity, they are spared the constant worry and anxiety. An animal roars to life when a threat is imminent but can otherwise relax. Heloise lives in a state of eternal vigilance, worrying about every aspect of Scott's life, determined there will be nothing lacking.

And yet, the only thing Scott really desires is the one thing she took away from him before he was born: his father. A father. Any father. Should she have married Brad, the detective who had yearned after her, the man who was more than willing to pretend Scott was his child? But she couldn't see how Scott's desire for a father would manifest itself as he grew. She barely had one, to her way of thinking, and had wished she had less of one. She yearned to see him . . . not dead, but gone. Heloise has made the mistake that so many parents make, assuming her child will want exactly what she wanted, only to be confronted with the fact that her son is a person, too, and he wants what *he* wants.

She thought about sparing him this farce of a funeral, balancing what was best for Scott against what would cause the least gossip. She doesn't want to see Meghan's mother, the other half-siblings, but, of course, Meghan's mother looks through her, still desperate to pretend that Hector didn't have another family, and Meghan's brothers are so much older—Meghan was born after a long, sad string of miscarriages—that they never really knew Heloise. In fact, there's an uncomfortable moment when one of them seems to be cruising her, and she is almost grateful for Michael's quavering "Hello, Aunt Heloise." Yes, she tells the uncle with a look. *We have the same daddy.* Move along.

Still, hearing that note in Michael's voice, she wishes the two families were close, that it would be natural to sweep him up in a hug. But while she and Meghan have allowed Scott and Michael to have a friendship of sorts—Heloise even more reluctant than Meghan, more fearful of the complications—the two families have never really interacted. The polite fiction is that Heloise and Scott have established their own holiday rituals—Deep Creek Lake for Thanksgiving, someplace warm and sunny for the Christmas holidays. Once, just once, Heloise accompanied Scott to Meghan's annual Easter egg party, an exhausting affair that had clearly taken weeks to prepare but was forced indoors by a rainstorm. It was Heloise's only prolonged exposure to Brian. She wasn't impressed; he was self-absorbed and of no help to Meghan, who seemed about one egg shy of a nervous breakdown. But did he deserve to die? Heloise, who deprived Scott's father of his freedom and may yet see his life taken because of her betrayal, can't make that case.

Meghan can, has begun to. She has called three times since their meeting at the Starbucks. The first was a simple call of notification, left on the answering machine: "Brian's dead, Heloise. It's a horrible accident and things are in a state. Is there any chance you could send Audrey over to stay with the kids tomorrow while I tend to arrangements?" It wasn't really a question. Heloise sent Audrey over and ran the office that evening.

The second time, again on the machine. "I can't believe how long the police were here on Saturday. It's almost as if I were a suspect, when it's so clear what happened. In fact, the autopsy came up with some strange findings, and it's possible Brian had a ministroke just before he fell. At least, I think that's what the medical examiner was trying to tell me. It's all so much to take in."

Third time, one A.M., voice slurry with drink. "He was vicious, Heloise." *Visshus, Hell-wheeze.* "I'm not saying he beat me, but you don't have to hit someone to terrorize them." *Tear-ize 'em.*

Heloise picked up.

"Not on the phone, Meghan. If you need to talk, I'll come by tomorrow. I'll come by now. But please, do not call me here at home and talk about this."

She starts to sob. "He was bad. He was, he was."

"Tomorrow."

But when tomorrow came and Heloise called Meghan to ask if she wanted to have lunch—which would mean a bit of shuffling in her schedule, because although the state legislature had ended, it was now cherry blossom time in Washington, and that was always a busy time for her, for reasons she had stopped trying to fathom—Meghan seemed surprised. "There's so much to do," she murmured absently. And then—"You weren't here, were you?"

"Not on the phone, Meghan."

"You're a good big sister. Thank you."

"I'm coming over, right now."

They sat on Meghan's deck, drinking coffee, two sisters enjoying each other's company on a fine spring day.

"There was a pillow . . ."

"That he tripped on?"

"No, although I did throw Melissa's Crocs down the stairs. She was always leaving them everywhere, so it's utterly plausible that he tried to step over them, then fell." Meghan caught Heloise's look, the intent, the judgment, and added: "They really do think he had some kind of brain function episode. He might have died anyway."

*Uh-huh.* "So what's the thing about the pillow?"

"It was from our bed."

"Why was it in the basement?"

"Exactly. Heloise, I think someone came in and . . . made sure to finish what I started. I thought it might be you." A pause. "I *hoped* it was you."

"As I told you that day, I charge money to sleep with men. I don't kill them. I barely do bondage, and then only with customers with whom I have an established history."

"Then someone—"

"Are you sure? Maybe Brian took the pillow down with him, planned to take a little nap or something."

Heloise knew she was groping and Meghan's withering look confirmed it.

"If it wasn't you—"

A large woman came out on the deck of the house next door and gave Meghan a solemn wave. Heloise was impressed by how much compassion the woman seemed to put into that small gesture. She was less impressed by the approximation of sadness on Meghan's face.

"I'm so sorry, Meghan. Let me know if I can do anything."

"Thank you, Lillian, but you've already done so much. I might not have to cook for a month, given all the food you and the other moms have brought me."

The phone rang, and they never finished that conversation. But Heloise remains uneasy with the calculus of it all: If Meghan is right, then someone knows Meghan's secret. And Meghan knows Heloise's secret, so she is drawn into this against her will. Her silence is a crime, and while Heloise's business was built on violating several sections of the Maryland, D.C., and even Virginia penal codes, she is scrupulous about obeying other laws, keeping her nose clean. Here at Brian's funeral, she still feels that grip of anxiety and fear, something she thought she left behind her when she got Val locked up for life.

**In all** of Meghan's fantasies of Brian's funeral—and, to be truthful, there were several over the years—she had never thought to imagine her own children. Here they are, shattered, and she wants to . . . shake them. *I did this for you.* Okay, perhaps not directly. But if her marriage was going to end, it had to be in a way that would shield her children from financial harm, and she has accomplished that much. She has not only Brian's life insurance but a whopping policy from his former company, which is still in force because of his six-month severance package. She has not sorted out all the financial implications—she has decided it would be a little unseemly to be *too* focused on such details, just yet—but it's her impression that she and the children can live extremely well, if she's prudent. She wonders if Heloise is smart about investments. She can't be planning to be a whore forever, right?

Meghan will marry again. The thought surprises her, for she knows that her next marriage will, in fact, have all the frustrations and irritations of her first. She has no illusions about the institution's limits, about what it takes to live with another person. But—big but—she will be the widow of a beloved man. Her next husband will live in the shadow of dead Brian's perfection and her eternal frailty. Her next husband will be permanently on notice, and she won't have to say a thing. No *pick up your socks, why are you late again, please rinse out the basin after you gargle and spit.* She will simply look at her next husband—two years sounds about right—widen her eyes, and he will fold. It's like rock, scissors, paper, and widow trumps everything.

*And what about the pillow?*

The thought is like some horrible corpse that cannot be buried, no matter how she tries to shove it down into its hole. It comes back to life again and again, often at the most inopportune times; Meghan needs enormous self-control not to have a physical reaction when it does. Here, at least, it's not suspect when she begins shaking all over. There has to be a logical reason for the pillow, right? Not Heloise's stupid supposition, but something similar. Still—why was it damp in the middle? Try as she might, she cannot remember if she locked the door on her way out, if she closed the garage behind her, and everyone in the neighborhood knows each other's garage door codes anyway, and the garage door, the one that leads into the mudroom, is never locked. She really can't remember anything about that afternoon. Temporary insanity is not a bullshit excuse in her case but the only plausible explanation. She went to Mark's band practice, fury mounting in her until it was a fever, until the need to express it overwhelmed her. When the kids broke for lunch and Mark headed out with his bandmates, while parents were left with what the e-mailed schedule had called "lunch on your own," it made perfect sense to drive home and confront Brian. But had she planned to push him, as she did? No, she couldn't know that she would find him at just that moment, in that split second when he was lifting his right leg toward the final step, his posture unsteady because of the box. She saw an opportunity that might never have come again, and she took it.

Meghan has never confided this in anyone, but she has long been susceptible to something she thinks of as "anger dreams." She slaps people, she screams at them, she flails and she wails, she beats her fists on their chests like a cartoon femme fatale, and they . . . laugh. No one feels her blows, no one registers the pitch of her screams. The fact is, it has taken enormous self-control never to raise a hand against her children. She wonders if killing Brian will, at least, exorcise this demon, if the anger has been appeased.

Or if it has simply whetted its appetite.

*The pillow*—the thought hits her again, and it's like a nudge from a cattle prod this time, goosing her so hard that she lurches forward and one of her brothers has to steady her. She's going to burn that fucking pillow when she gets home. But that would probably draw attention, earn her some sort of environmental citation from the county. She'll just order new sheets instead. Porthault? No, better not. Too expensive, too impractical, especially given that Michael has been crawling in with her at night and—once, just once—wetting the bed. But something nice, something new, something in a purely feminine color and pattern to signal this new chapter in her life.

*I love you*, thinks a man in the back of the church. *I love you, Meghan. I can't wait to be with you.* And he reaches for his wife's hand.

## FOUR

The clichés about time, like the clichés about almost everything, happen to be true. It passes, it heals, it even flies. Especially, Heloise thinks, when the problem is not one's own. Well, not strictly hers. In a legal sense, she is accountable. Her silence is a crime, a crime that protects her own crimes. She knows enough to realize that police might offer her immunity from prosecution if it ever came to that, but police cannot offer her immunity from the destruction of Scott's life should the details of her business become public. Still, days go by when she doesn't think about the compromising position in which Meghan holds her. Summer is an interesting time in Heloise's line of work: while she loses many of her political regulars, the growing custom of summer shares, in which Daddy stays in the hot city while the family is at the Delaware shore, produces a nice, steady stream of income from nice, steady men. Oh, a few seem to think they should try to be more decadent than they really are, but they are clearly relieved to find out that not that much imagination is required. She puts the girls on a Monday-through-Thursday schedule, which everyone likes, and handles the few weekend kinkmeisters, as she thinks of them, longtime customers with specialized needs.

On this particular Saturday night, for example, she's meeting a seventy-five-year-old man who really could be happy with the services of a good reflexologist, assuming he could find one who agreed to work naked. All he wants is for someone to squeeze his toes in a very particular pattern, almost as if they were bagpipes or a cow's teats. Easy money, and his feet are beautifully kept, especially for a man his age— the toenails freshly cut and only faintly yellow—but tonight he takes longer than usual to complete, and when he pays Heloise, he shakes his head sadly.

"What happened to Veronica?" he asks. "The dark-haired one?" (And, yes, Heloise has a blond named Betty in her employ as well, and they often tag-team a man who insists on being called Archie. Unless he's calling himself Gilligan, and then they're Ginger and Mary Ann.)

"I try to give the girls weekends off in the summer."

"The thing is—you look great, Heloise. Truly. For your age. But for me, it takes a younger girl . . ."

"I understand," she says, patting his hand. He's not the first one to say this to Heloise in the past two years or so. The fact is, another cliché applies: this hurts him more than it hurts her. He only thinks it's youth he wants. It's novelty he craves, and she's been taking care of him for more than five years. Some men like that, actually, love the groove, the pattern, discover a way to be monogamous twice over, with their spouses and their whores. But, obviously, some are going to get bored, even a man such as Leo, who doesn't even open his eyes while he's being serviced and does most of the heavy lifting himself. At forty, Heloise plans to continue taking calls for at least five more years, tops, and she doesn't think she'll lose that many customers along the way. But when she stops, she will have to hire two girls to take her place, and the way she sees it, every employee elevates her exposure to risk. Plus, it's a bitch, managing other people.

Still, she feels a little pang, leaving Leo that evening. For whatever reason, age or novelty, Heloise has been rejected, and she is unused to rejection, given that she eschews recreational sex, with all its irrationality and head games and confusion.

Her cell phone throbs in its dashboard-mounted holster. "Meghan." Speaking of people who are a bitch to manage.

"You're on Bluetooth," she warns.

"Is there someone else in the car?"

"No, but—"

Meghan's voice rushes ahead, heedless. "He's been in touch."

"Who?" Heloise is confused, and her mind rolls to Brian. Is Meghan having some sort of paranormal episode?

"Pillow man."

"Humph," she says. Then: "I'm on the way back. Why don't I swing by?"

"Heloise . . ." Meghan's voice is urgent, needy, whiny.

"I'm twenty minutes away." More like thirty-five, but Meghan will keep talking if she tells her that. "No phones, Meghan."

**Meghan looks** at the plain piece of paper, mailed in the area and postmarked two days ago. She almost didn't open it—the fussy handwriting looked machine generated, junk mail attempting to masquerade—but she saw at the last moment, before pitching it into the recycling container, that it was, in fact, real handwriting, just enormously fussy.

Inside, a plain piece of paper, unsigned of course: "*Remember the golden rule: Do unto others as you would have them do unto you. I did my part. Now it's your turn.*"

She tells herself that it's not related, that it's some sort of freak chain letter. There are some crazy Christians around here, although most of them home-school. It's a coincidence, like that urban legend about the girls who prank-call various numbers—"I saw what you did!"—only to reach someone who's just tidying up after a murder.

Murder: don't go there.

*Do unto others*—what, exactly, has her correspondent done for her? Finished a job? Saved a man from suffering? Murder? Again, she tries to wall off that thought, but it's awfully hard to avoid. She pours another glass of wine. She drinks less since Brian died, more proof that he was bad for her. But wine goes to her head faster as a result, and she worries that she'll be a little tipsy by the time Heloise arrives. A car in the driveway—it's her! A part of her mind detaches as it always does when Meghan sees Heloise, wonders at the sheer perfection of her sister's appearance. Hair, perfect; nails, perfect; clothes, perfect. Heloise takes care of herself because it's part of her livelihood. But might it not become Meghan's livelihood, too, now that she plans to start hunting for a new husband? Can she afford to keep herself as Heloise maintains herself? Meghan has tried to work out the math, but it's too discouraging. Sleeping with the same man, even a mere twice a week, over a couple of decades simply cannot produce as much income as Heloise's thriving business does. Unless she lands a billionaire, and those aren't found in Turner's Grove. Equity millionaires, men with a lot of house under them, but no real money.

Heloise comes to the front door and knocks, then waits to be admitted. Very unlike Meghan's female friends, who push open the door with a cheery "hello," sure of their welcome. Since Brian's death, Meghan has paid special attention to how people enter her home. Was the door unlocked that day? Did she leave the garage door up when she left, shaking with adrenaline? Heloise, of course, is the one person who could not have sneaked back to kill Brian. Or wait—why not? Meghan went back to band practice. Who knows what happened in those intervening hours?

But the fact is, she cannot imagine Heloise doing that for her, which makes her kind of sad. A real big sister would have done it, and Heloise is the older by six months. But then—a real big sister would have owned up to it, too.

"Look," she says, thrusting the note at her sister. "It was in the mail today. I thought—"

Heloise takes her wrist, gently but authoritatively. "Let's go out, to that wine bar on the highway. Talk there. You can leave the kids, can't you? Melinda can look after them, right?"

"Yes, but—isn't it safer to talk here?"

"It's safer not to talk anywhere. But if we have to talk, let's do it in public, where we'll have to make an effort to be circumspect. Drive with me and we'll agree on some code words."

Meghan is torn. She doesn't want to be careful. She wants to let the pent-up words and emotion spill out. There's no risk from the kids. Kids never register their parents' secrets, not unless those secrets affect them directly. At the same time, she likes the idea of a drink, on a Saturday night, in a popular place. The food is good, the wine list varied. There might be men there. And a drink with her sister in public—the normalcy of it has an appealing novelty. Perhaps Heloise even has some tips for how to meet men.

"Just give me five minutes to change."

**The wine** bar is, in fact, called the Wine Barn, and it's in a converted barn. *Infelicitous,* he thinks. Is he using the word correctly? It was on his word-a-day calendar last week and he liked the sound of it, but he's not sure the usage is precise. "Regrettable" may be better. "Cheesy." But it gets away with the hideous name because the interior décor is simple and chic, by the area's standards, and because it is an unrelievedly adult place in a suburb where everything else is kid-centric. The Wine Barn allows children in the dining room, but they have to play by its rules, eat from its menu. No chicken fingers or other kiddie menu concessions. He never gets to eat here because his wife thinks that's a kind of bigotry.

Saturday is date night for the older folks here, cruising night for those in their twenties, the teachers and firefighters and other essential types who live in the townhouses and apartments at the outer ring of the burg. He used to have quite an eye for those teachers. But now, all he sees is Meghan. *I'm your knight,* he wants to sing out. *Your knight in shining armor. I saved your life. You owe me everything.* But it will be so much sweeter for her to realize this on her own, then do what he needs her to do, just as he has done what she required. Unbidden. Selfless. That's true love.

The sister is handsome, too, but a little self-contained and self-sufficient for him. Once, he saw her on the side of the road with a flat tire, and he offered to change it for her. It seemed the least he could do, given that he was the one who had deflated it back in the parking lot, during their sons' soccer game. "I've already called Triple A," she said with a polite but dismissive wave of her hand. "I'll wait until they show up."

Most women wanted the company, and that's all it ever was, company. It seemed a harmless habit, creating situations from which women would need rescue, then extricating them. A quick poke of a tire gauge. A vaguely ominous note left on someone's windshield. Anonymous phone calls, although caller ID had ruined that pastime. "I'll take care of it," he said time and time again to the women in his social set, requiring nothing more than a smile, acknowledgment that he was needed, that he could help, something he never got at home, where he felt superfluous.

But Meghan—he never dared that trick with Meghan. Perhaps that's because she was too needy. If he helped her once, it would be criminal to stop. Criminal! Heh. Seriously, he had a hunch that Meghan would see through him, that she would figure out that her secret admirer, her benevolent benefactor, was also her malefactor, another new word he had learned in the past month. Malefactor. Male factor. He wants to be the male factor in Meghan's life and there's really no reason he can't be. He simply needs her to kill his wife. The problem is how to introduce this in conversation. He has seen Meghan several times since Brian's death, even allowed himself a quick hug at the funeral—those fragile birdlike bones, so frail in his arms; they could definitely have sex standing up, something he hasn't done for years. But there never seems to be a right time to explain that he finished off Brian and now needs her to return the favor. He wants her to figure it out, to volunteer. Hence the note, which must have arrived by now. He watches carefully through the narrow windows on the addition to the barn, a kind of sunroom. What if she shows the note to her sister? Does her sister know? That would be inconvenient. And traitorous. Brian's death is their secret, his and Meghan's.

A threesome with the sisters would be hot, though. No use denying that. He and Meghan would gang up on the other one, and she wouldn't have that cool, contained smile when they were through with her.

## FIVE

The notes continue through the summer. There are Bible verses, snippets of poetry, one CD with a single song burned into it ("If Loving You Is Wrong"). Meghan wants to scream, *I get the hint.* Only she doesn't, and Heloise cautioned her to do nothing as long as possible. "If the person really knew something, he would press you, make demands." Meghan wonders if it's Heloise, playing a game with her, keeping her on her toes. But, more often than not, she believes that these notes are from her . . . helper. But what does he want? Blackmail seems likely. Brian's death left her pretty well fixed. The insurance company was a little hard-ass at first, demanding a tox screening when it was revealed that Brian had lost his job, fishing for something that would allow them to build a case for suicide. A formality, the family lawyer said, and the screen had come back with only moderate amounts of alcohol, consistent with a beer or two at lunch. Meghan was retroactively pissed when she heard that—*I'm out schlepping the kids, per usual, and you can't clean the basement without breaking for a beer, and probably some couch time.* Her hands and jaw clenched, the emotions of that day rushing back. She was never so angry in her life and she hopes never to be that angry again. But then, with Brian dead, how could she be? Brian was the source of all her problems. Look at how smoothly the house runs without him, how well the kids are doing overall. (She prefers to gloss over Melinda's sudden goth phase and Mark's decision to drop out of band. They have to grieve a little. It's healthy.) The fact is, the house always functioned independently of Brian, given his travel for work. His infrequent appearances were what had kept them from establishing rhythms and norms. Really, Brian was like a houseguest, not a father.

The doorbell, a knock, then a "Hello???????," although it's a male voice today, not one of the girlfriends. Who, come to think of it, don't come around as often.

"It's Dan Simmons, Meghan. Some more paperwork came in today and I thought I'd bring it over. It's about those various annuities you wanted."

The annuities. Dan has been a little pushy about shepherding her investments, and although Meghan thinks the financial arm of his insurance business is not particularly impressive, it's been easier to let him handle everything. She says as much now as they settle in at the dining room table: "I'm so grateful to you, Dan, for handling all this."

He pats her hand. "My pleasure." He leaves his hand there a second too long. Then five seconds, then ten.

"Dan . . ." He's not the first husband to flirt with her, although it happened more in the early days, before she was tired and angry all the time. Only then it was at parties, where there had been some alcohol. This is much more wanton. It's a little exciting, although she's not attracted to Dan. But she likes the idea of him being attracted to her.

"Better be careful," she teases lightly. "Lillian could be standing in your kitchen, looking right at us."

"There's no direct sight line into the dining room. I know because I know where to look to find you. And Lillian's in Rehoboth with the kids all month. I rented a house and even arranged a spa visit for her, for our twentieth anniversary."

"You've always been so thoughtful that way." She tries to move her hand away, but Dan won't let her.

"I thought about plastic surgery. She never mentions it, but it couldn't hurt. And women do die that way, don't they? Even if she didn't die, she would be weak afterward, taking lots of pain meds. Anything could happen."

"Dan—"

"Accidents happen every day. No one knows that better than an insurance agent. Car accidents, slipping in the bathtub, falling down stairs. Stairs are so dangerous. If people only knew. But you know, don't you, Meghan? How dangerous stairs can be?"

Meghan has finally extricated her hand, only to have Dan grab her wrist. She decides to stop fighting him, and when he lets go, she flips her hand so the fingers are facing up. She gives his palm a light, tickling touch.

"Money?" she asks.

"You," he says. "And we have to figure out how to take care of Lillian. I can't afford a divorce. But then—you couldn't, either, could you, Meghan?"

"You were watching that day?"

"Actually, I didn't see what happened. The sight lines again. But I saw you come and go so quickly. Then I came over here to ask Brian if he had a level. I was trying to install one of those closets, from the Container Store. At first I thought only of myself. I didn't know I was finishing what you had started. Then I thought, I'll leave the pillow behind, just in case. If it showed up in the police report—and the insurance company would receive all the reports, of course—I would know that Brian fell. If there was no mention of a pillow . . . well, I would have my answer."

"It was an accident," she says.

"Officially, yes." He caresses her palm. "Smart girl."

"No, I mean that I didn't plan it. I came home to have it out with him. He dropped this bomb on me as I was heading out, which was his way of avoiding arguments, and, for once, I wasn't going to be denied the fight. When I saw him coming up the steps with that box of stuff—I didn't think. It was an impulse. He tripped on the Crocs."

"Let me do the thinking for both of us. The important thing is, this is our secret, right? No one else knows?"

Instinct, as swift and certain as the impulse to shove Brian down the stairs, tells her to lie. "I haven't told anyone. You?"

"No."

"And you haven't been reckless enough to write these things down somewhere, to keep a record that someone else might read?"

"No," he says with a laugh, tapping his head. "It's all up here."

She looks around the room, then past it, into the kitchen, at the big windows. She realizes now how often Dan has looked at her through those windows, how her kitchen, a replica of his but in a different color scheme, came to seem better somehow. While Meghan was dreaming of life without a husband, Dan was persuading himself that all he needed was a change of partner, that the thinner, slightly younger woman he saw could make everything right in his life. Okay, then.

"Let's go upstairs," she says, pleased to see how he shakes, just a little. She's in control. For now.

**Heloise is** heading home from the grocery store when she has to pull over for the cop car, then an ambulance, then another cop car, rushing down Old Orchard. Another car accident, she thinks, but then sees the convoy turn onto her sister's small street, which has no more than a dozen houses, and it gives her pause. What are the odds? Mathematically, one in twelve. She thinks about the recent glimpses of her nephews and nieces, how sad they all are since their father died. She thinks about Meghan's mother, who took a halfhearted swipe at her wrists in a desperate attempt to win back Hector Lewis when the birth of Meghan wasn't enough to bring him home.

A police officer stops her when she tries to enter the house, and it takes enormous self-restraint to remember that he is not a street cop, grabbing the young prostitute she once was. She never feels at ease around cops.

"Ma'am, this is a crime scene—"

"But it's my sister's house."

"Is that Heloise?" It's Meghan's voice, croaking from inside the house. "Please, let me see my sister. I want my sister."

Meghan's eye is freshly bruised, her lip split. She is wearing a robe and a pair of socks, and presumably nothing else. A female police officer sits with her at the kitchen counter, pushing a cup of tea toward Meghan, who keeps pushing it away.

"Our neighbor," Meghan tells Heloise. "Dan Simmons. He came over here with some of the paperwork for the trusts I'm putting together for the kids and he raped me. I—all I was trying to do was protect myself. I thought he was going to kill me."

Paramedics trudge down the stairs, shaking their heads, and now the attendants from the medical examiner's office march up, followed by detectives with rubber-gloved hands. Heloise wants to follow, but she knows they will think her morbid, unnatural. Still, she wants to know, wants to survey the scene.

Some unnerving inconsistencies start to surface as the policewoman talks to Meghan in her deceptively conversational way. Why is Dan Simmons naked? How did he manage to take his clothes off while keeping Meghan under his control? Did she really keep a loaded gun, unlocked, in her nightstand drawer? With kids in the house? Was she crazy? Heloise wishes her sister would stop talking. But Meghan points to the marks on her face, admits how frightening it has been, living without her husband, admits her ignorance and negligence with the gun but says she believes it is the only thing that prevented Dan from killing her. He choked her when they had sex, see? There are marks on her neck. She was blacking out, she thought she was dying, there was nothing to do but reach into that nightstand table, grab the gun, and blow his brains out. Look—there is brain matter in her hair, a fine spray of blood on her face. She knows she has to go to the hospital and talk to police at greater length—Heloise puts in here that she wants her sister to have a lawyer, a good one. She won't use her own man, but she'll ask him for a recommendation.

"Can't my sister drive me to the hospital for the rape kit? Do I really need to go in the ambulance or a police car?"

Meghan walks stiffly to Heloise's car, carrying a duffel bag with clothes to change into after the exam.

"So," Heloise says, letting that one word stand for the two dozen questions she wants to ask.

"I told him I like it rough. It took him a while to warm up—I had to beg him to hit me, bully him, even scratch him a little—but he caught on. And then I told him I wanted to do the autoerotic thing."

"With Brian's gun?"

"Oh, no. I had him wait downstairs, told him I wanted to get ready for him. That gave me time to get it out of the lockbox and load it, then put it in the nightstand."

The hospital is only a mile away now. They will never speak of this again, Heloise knows.

"Are you sure?" she asks. "That he was the one?"

"Yes. And he wanted me to kill his wife, Lillian. Isn't that awful?"

"Awful," Heloise agrees.

"I saved her life, if you think about it," Meghan says. "What a terrible, terrible man."

"Yes."

## SIX

Meghan sits in the little dressing room adjacent to the green room at the *Today* show, waiting for the makeup and hair people. She had hoped for something a little loftier—*Oprah,* to be exact—but she supposes *Today* is the best thing to do if you can't get *Oprah*. She did get *Oprah,* though; *Oprah* just didn't get her. She was asked to be one of several women, up to a half dozen, featured under the theme "She Fought Back." Meghan doesn't want to be one in a crowd, her story reduced to a mere trend. Besides, there were some indications that Oprah might ask a lot of questions about the gun—why was it so near to hand, in a house with children—and the publicist who has been advising Meghan found the course of the pre-interview worrisome and recommended pulling-out. *Today* is more interested in Meghan's decision to speak publicly about being a rape victim, her assertion that women have nothing to fear by coming forward. "There's not just one way to be a rape victim" is the line the publicist impresses upon her to use in interviews, something he apparently cribbed from an Internet site.

"And what are you talking about today?" the makeup girl asks, beginning to apply foundation.

"I was raped and I killed my attacker," Meghan says.

"Oh." The makeup girl's eyes slide upward, meeting the gaze of the hairdresser, who's standing behind Meghan, twirling a round brush through her hair. Meghan sees it all in the mirror—the concern, the pity.

"It's okay," she assures them. "That's why I'm here. Because women should talk about these things. It was horrible, what happened to me, what I had to do to survive. But I have no regrets, and certainly no shame."

Again, her lines are rehearsed, but that doesn't mean they're not true. Even when Meghan allows

herself to think about what really happened—
something she does less and less—she can't imagine
taking a different course of action. No regret, no
shame. She was on top of Dan, their second go-round,
riding him and encouraging him to choke her, when
he saw her reach for the drawer. "What are you getting?" he gasped. "Something to make it better. Close
your eyes." He did as he was told and she managed
to grab the gun, hold it behind her back. "Flip me,
you on top." "I'm too big for a little girl like you, I'll
break you." "I'll be fine." Gracelessly, they switched
positions, and she let him have a few more seconds
of pleasure—"Eyes shut, eyes shut," she crooned—
until he finally asked, "Where's the surprise?"

She had never fired a gun and it bucked in her hand,
but it didn't matter, given how closely it was pressed
to the spot behind his left ear. He looked surprised.
Brian had looked surprised, too. Dan flopped a little
and there seemed to be a delay before blood and other
things began leaking out of him. It didn't bother her.
She was the mother of four kids. She had been vomited
on, peed on, shat on, wiped snotty noses. A little blood
and brain matter was nothing to her. Besides, she did
this for her kids, all of it. Killing Brian, killing Dan.

So why not kill Lillian, as Dan wanted? He loved
her, she wanted a second husband. Eventually. Why

not kill Lillian? But that struck Meghan as wrong. She wasn't a cold-blooded killer. She did the things she did only when backed into a corner. She did what any mother would do, given the same proclivity for quick thinking. It's not as if she enjoyed it, not quite. She appreciated the power it bestowed, however briefly, the sense of besting men who were making her miserable. But it wasn't *recreational*.

It's pleasant, being tended to, the feel of the soft brush across her cheekbones, her hair being blown and teased into something larger and grander than it is. She also enjoyed checking into a hotel room last night, being by herself, ordering room service. A single mother, she is at once alone and yet never alone in her daily life, and this pure solitude was something to cherish. The producers had offered to bring the whole family up, make it a vacation, but she had quickly demurred. "Oh no, that's hardly necessary." Her eyes drift upward, to the monitor above the makeup mirror, and she watches Matt Lauer explaining something, his face grave. Utterly relaxed, she closes her eyes at the makeup woman's instruction, thinking: *I could break Matt's neck like a little twig. If I had to, if it came to that.*

## SEVEN

"Why can't I walk home?" Scott asks. It is the first day of school, the first day of fifth grade for him, his last first day ever at Hamilton Point Elementary School. Next year he will be in middle school, which means a bus. A bus will take him away from Heloise every morning and return him in the afternoon. It's the beginning of his leaving her.

"Why?" he repeats. "Billy does."

"Billy doesn't have to cross Old Orchard." The prettily named street, a monument to a place long gone, a place torn down to make room for the houses there, has the distinction of being the suburb's most dangerous. Three high school students died in a head-on crash there the last weekend before school started, a tragedy so enormous that it has eclipsed the gossip about Dan Simmons going nuts, trying to rape his neighbor.

"I'll be good. I'll look both ways. There's a crossing guard."

Heloise begins to repeat her argument, then says: "We'll talk about it. Maybe soon. But you know what? I like driving you."

She glances in the rearview mirror, sees Scott make a face, but also sees a guilty flush of affection beneath it. "Mom." Two syllables, verging on three.

"What did you learn in school today?"

"Nothing, it's the first day. But I think science is going to be neat. We get to do yearlong projects if we want. Not experiments, but reading projects, where we take on a topic and learn everything about it. I think I want to do nature versus nutria."

"Nurture? Nutria's an animal, I think."

"Right, nurture. It's like, we used to think it was all about how you were raised, but now we think it's about what's in your genes." A pause, a heartbreaking pause. "Why don't we have any photographs of my dad?"

"I've never been much of one for taking photos, except of you. Children change. Grown-ups, not so much. Your father lives in my memory." *And in my scars.*

"But he had red hair, like me?"

"Yes."

"And he was a businessman, who ran a com-, com-, com—" Bright as Scott is, as many times as they have gone over this story, he stumbles on this word.

"Commodities exchange." Oh yes, Val traded in commodities. "I never really understood it. Soybeans. And something to do with pork belly futures." *And the bellies and breasts and thighs and cunts of young women.*

"And he was nice."

"So nice." *Especially after he had beaten a girl. He was never nicer.*

"But he had a bad accident."

"Very bad." His gun ran into a young man, and the woman he thought loved him made sure the police got hold of that weapon, and if he ever finds out, he will arrange to have her killed just for spite. Unless he finds out about you. Then he'll instruct his old friends to kill you in front of her and leave her alive, knowing that will be the truest hell he can fashion.

"I wish I had even one memory of him."

"I do too, baby. I do too."

Nature versus nurture. Hector Lewis had two families. Hector Lewis had two daughters. He beat one. She grew up to be a whore. With the other, he spared the rod, blew hot and cold, providing money and love in fitful amounts, and she grew up to be a cold-blooded killer. Just last week, Meghan moved her family to Florida. A fresh start, she said. It was too awkward, she said, living next door to Lillian after all that had happened. Not that Lillian was going to be living there long. Just as the cobbler's children go barefoot, the Simmons heirs turned out to have hardly any insurance. Except for Lillian, on whom Dan had taken out a huge policy earlier this summer. That information, along with the selected correspondence that Meghan showed the police—the CD, the poetry, but never the Bible verses—and the autopsy findings of some odd, calcified spots in Dan's brain, probably months old, took care of everything. Dan had lost his mind. His obsession with Meghan, the rape, his plans for Lillian, the disturbing pornography that he had neglected to clear out of his computer before he died—it didn't exactly add up to anything, but it served the scenario Meghan had created. Unhinged Dan tried to rape Meghan and she killed him. It made as much sense as anything. It certainly made more sense than the truth. And if the police ever looked into the death of Brian Duffy for any reason, Dan would probably take the rap for that, too. Who was going to contradict Meghan? Not Heloise, certainly.

Nature versus nurture. Heloise glances in the rearview mirror, sees her redheaded son looking out at the passing landscape, thinks of the redheaded man who fathered him, of the grandfather he never knew, of the aunt who has killed two men, of the mother who lies as naturally as breathing.

"Mom!" Scott's yell is horrified, embarrassed. "You're *crying.*"

"Sorry, honey. You're just growing up so fast."

# Afterword

Permit me the indulgence of a brief afterword on this piece, which was written for this collection. It was 2001 when I first began noodling away at the idea of a prostitute in the suburbs. But when I spoke of it to editors and friends, no one seemed particularly enthusiastic. For once in my life, I was ahead of the curve—*Desperate Housewives, Weeds,* and *The Real Housewives of Orange County* were all yet to come. But I never forgot that image of Heloise sitting in the pickup line at her son's elementary school. In 2005, Harlan Coben asked me to write a story for the Mystery Writers of America's annual anthology. The result was "One True Love," inspired by a single line from an early draft of this story, about Heloise's chance encounter with a customer at a soccer game.

And now, at last, here is the story of Heloise and her sister, Meghan. I'm glad that I waited almost seven years to write it, because while I always had empathy for Heloise, I didn't really understand Meghan. Now that I have spent more time on the sidelines of soccer fields and basketball courts, I have some insight into her remarkable anger, if not the way she deals with it.

The story is clearly a straight-up homage to James M. Cain—the lethal lovers of *The Postman Always Rings Twice* and *Double Indemnity*, but also *Mildred Pierce*, which showcases maternal devotion beyond reason. However, I'd also like to dedicate it to my late grandfather, Theodore "Sweetheart" Lippman, an extremely conscientious insurance salesman who had several rules for his employees. Here are two: Always wear a hat, and don't listen to the radio on your way to visit a client. Think about how you're going to make the sale instead. Heloise Lewis, with her strict guidelines, is much closer to my grandfather in spirit than Dan Simmons could ever be.